MURDER IN
THE ACADEMY

MURDER
IN THE
ACADEMY

MAGGIE FEELEY

POOLBEG
CRIMSON

Published 2021 by Crimson
an imprint of Poolbeg Press Ltd
123 Grange Hill, Baldoyle
Dublin 13, Ireland
www.poolbeg.com
Email: info@poolbeg.com

A catalogue record for this book is available from the British Library.

ISBN 978178199-443-6

www.poolbeg.com

About the Author

Maggie Feeley is an Irish educator and an activist on issues of gender, sexuality and equality. As a new endeavour, she is exploring how to continue the discussion of equality and social justice through the medium of writing engaging detective fiction.

For Ann

1

Belfast, Northern Ireland

December 2013

Dr Helen Breen sat with her back to the door, silhouetted against the orange glow of the Anglepoise desk lamp. Outside, the lights of the Belfast nightscape were refracted in the gently falling rain on the external wall of glass around her corner office. The face of the new Belfast City College Campus which looked out onto the Harbour Estate and Belfast Lough was an uninterrupted façade of glass that blurred the distinction between inside and out. In Helen Breen's office, all was meticulously ordered. The two internal walls were lined with an impressive collection of legal books, only some of which she'd actually read. A tasteful arrangement of impersonal images was fixed to the curved surface of the central stone pillar that was a feature of her prime corner-office space. The pillar served as a partial room-divider, concealing the occupant of the desk from the view of anyone coming in through the office door.

Helen heard herself emit a short, guttural purr of contentment.

It was the final day of the lecturing term in DePRec – the Department of Peace and Reconciliation in Belfast City College. Tomorrow she planned to complete her exam entries on the system and be heading for home by lunchtime. She was doodling on the sheet of paper in front of her and absent-mindedly contemplating her position. As was often the case, things were moving in the direction she wanted. She had forensically orchestrated most of the pieces in her latest game plan and now it was just a case of letting things take their inevitable course. The sense of success suffused her with satisfaction, and she sighed deeply. In her memory the pleasant smell of cut grass filled her nostrils and connected with some benign childhood recollection. A flash of her father with shirtsleeves rolled back to reveal muscled, tanned arms caught her unawares. She shook herself free of the image. Waiting was not her forte, but she had taught herself to control the tendency towards impatience and to relish the different stages of each new strategy. For now, what she had internally dubbed 'Project Professor' was definitely moving in the right direction.

The sudden hum of student activity out in the corridors roused her from her reverie. In the silence that followed she smoothed her hair in the reflection in front of her and glanced at the clock on her laptop. It was getting joyfully close to nine twenty. Soon she could head for home, having shown herself to be at her desk for an admirably long day. The head of DePRec, Professor Jackson Bell, had been so grateful that she could cover for him at short notice as senior manager on evening duty. She snorted contemptuously. Obviously, he had an urgent prayer meeting to attend or perhaps a more salacious demand on his attention. She smirked at the very idea of it. In any case, she had filled her time well. She had requisitioned a new state-of-the-art laptop from a research budget, done some online clothes shopping, booked a short break in the sun for April and poked around in the email and Facebook accounts of some colleagues. Best of all, she had freed herself up from family expectations by announcing that she would be away over the holidays. Her brother Michael would have to attend to the demands of family Christmas without her. She relished the expanse of two whole weeks that stretched ahead of her without any tedious responsibilities.

As she closed her laptop and reached for her bag, the door pushed open a little too forcefully, banging against the doorstop and rebounding awkwardly against the incomer's shoulder, eliciting a string of expletives. Helen stood and moved towards the door.

"Oh, it's you," she said, genuinely taken aback. "Why so hot under the collar?" She was only mildly interested in the response.

There was no reply. Only her fixed expression of incredulity as her head was taken in hand by a bunch of her smooth black hair and a dull, stupefying thudding as it was pummelled repeatedly against the concrete pillar, quickly silencing her outrage. So long after life was extinguished, the rhythmic beating continued and garish red-and-grey matter dripped unattractively onto the highly polished industrial concrete floor.

Then all was silent. The lights were extinguished and the distant mosquito-like sound of the lift descending from the fifth floor meant that another day, another term in the academy had almost come to a close.

Despite all her carefully manipulated plans, Helen Breen's ambitions had been forever thwarted.

2

Five months earlier

Wellfleet, Massachusetts
August 2013

Alice Fox rolled effortlessly onto her back and allowed the silky-soft waters of the Great Pond in Wellfleet to ease her spirit. The early sun warmed her bones. She had left her mother and sisters still asleep in their summer cabin on the Cape and cycled the few miles here for one last swim before heading off to Ireland later that same day. She tilted her head back and drank in the big cobalt sky. Overhead, chattering tree swallows dipped and skimmed the surface of the pond, catching insects along the way, and Alice momentarily regretted that she would soon be far away from all this easy tranquillity.

Northern Ireland sometimes assumed a dark profile in her mind, and she had mixed feelings about this new venture. In the next few days, she was due to take up a post-doctoral place in Belfast. She didn't like to be in the limelight and she knew that this new academic post would place her under the scrutiny of strangers, at least initially. Then she would do what she was good at and blend unobtrusively into the background. She wasn't shy as such, but she preferred to be a little off-centre in terms of attention. In that way she could watch what was happening without having to be totally socially engaged. That she had found to be her peaceful place.

Since its formation in the early nineties, the Belfast-based college department, widely known as DePRec, had been in a long-term academic relationship with City University New York (CUNY). Alice, who had just completed her doctoral studies in CUNY, would become the latest item in the human traffic back and forth between the two institutions. Her PhD thesis supervisor had suggested that a spell in Northern Ireland would be a good next step in her career trajectory and so the one-year post-doc position had been negotiated. She was due some time out for thinking, it seemed. As well as helping with some local research projects in her field, she hoped to get a book proposal together and maybe even secure some funding for the following year.

Her work in restorative justice was something about which she felt passionately but, from some preliminary enquiries, she feared there might be a bit of a chasm between her research context with young high-school kids in the US and the unresolved post-war issues that remained a daily reality in the wake of the Northern Ireland conflict. Anyway, she would find out about that all too soon.

Alice stretched and turned to resume her steady crawl across the lake with a growing interest in her last US breakfast. Her sister, Sam, had promised to make a pancake stack with bacon and syrup and her appetite was steadily increasing in urgency as she headed for shore. She strode from the water, feeling the sun warm her well-honed body. She didn't do diets but she loved to be in motion and had her best thoughts on the move.

The youngest of the Fox family, Alice had been a detective in Lowell Police Department for fifteen years, having joined up straight from High School. The job had required her to be fast on her feet and she had made it her business to be strong enough to deal with whatever punks came her way. She had trained in martial arts and enjoyed the discipline and balletic movements of Tae Kwon Do. Although killing wasn't in her nature, she had been a fair enough shot with a pistol when she had needed to be. She was easy in her skin and carried her strength with an effortless beauty that many worked hard to emulate. Yes, she was blonde, tall and shapely but never a cliché. If anything defined her, it was her low-key openness and composure, which she had worked very hard to develop.

The Foxes had a long tradition of service as police officers and firefighters and she had preferred to follow the family track than to carry on with school like most of her peers. In the mid-90s, when her much-loved father was killed by the car driven by a drugged-up teenager she had lost her moorings and little by little her faith in traditional policing. The family had been asked to participate in a restorative justice project with the young joyrider who was by then in juvenile detention. It had been agonising and also ultimately transformational. In the end she had quit the police service and gone to college as a mature student, determined to study more effective alternatives to meeting force with force. Now, fifteen years later, she was an experienced community practitioner working to divert young people from a life of anti-social behaviour and recidivism. Often this highlighted how deep-rooted social inequalities made crime and conflict almost inevitable and, in her opinion, this needed to be the real focus of change.

Now in her forties, Alice had a sense that all the pieces of her life fitted together. Her knowledge of police work, her own painful life experience and her growing understanding and affinity with poor communities had all found a useful place in the person she had now become. Academics respected her knowledge of the real world and high-school kids saw her as a rare, trusted adult and a bit of a hero.

As she cycled back to the house, she inhaled the soft, aromatic Cape air and wondered what the coming year would have added to her life story when next she was back in this most relaxing of places. In her wildest imaginings, she didn't even come close.

3

In his cluttered, ill-smelling rooms, Agent Alan contemplated his drab and dwindling caseload. The Palace Barracks, located in Holywood on the outskirts of East Belfast, housed MI5 alongside some Irish Battalions of the British Army and their families. Since the peace process had taken hold in the province his level of community intelligence-gathering had shrunk to a tedious minimum. He was charged with monitoring the intentions of a few uninspiring dissident groups who spent most of their time between internal bickering and trying to cultivate support from a largely disinterested population. His was a world whose moment was past. Often Alan found he had expanses of time on his hands and an ever-smaller number of colleagues with whom to generate a sense of his own importance.

Another dull encounter with one of his sources the

previous evening had offered little promise in terms of future action. Nevertheless, although Professor Jackson Bell was far from cooperative, the research activity of DePRec still had potential to get under the surface of some seditious community elements and he planned to increase the push in that area. Why not? A number of staff changes were mooted in the college department and he hoped to persuade others to help him in this regard.

He had never held with intellectualising dissent and preferred the traditional approach of covert military intervention. In his view, softly, softly persuasive techniques aimed at influencing political trends would never convince diehard republicans or loyalists to stop playing war games. In that regard he could demonstrate a fair degree of fellow feeling, albeit from the establishment point of view. There was always someone corruptible if you looked hard enough. He hoped that the new academic term would allow him the opportunity to put his theories into practice and felt something quite unfamiliar, akin to enthusiasm, about the prospect.

4

The Irish summer rain thrummed relentlessly on the glass roof of the Belfast City College Human Sciences and Library Building. This was an impressive contemporary construction containing vast sheets of glass that constantly reflected the mix of new and old back to the surrounding area. The animated landscape caught on the glass screen was forever changing. The college had a number of campuses in and around the Titanic Quarter which sat alongside remnants of Belfast's historic shipbuilding industry. In contrast to this ultramodern edifice, the College's nearby Centre for Maritime Studies occupied the heritage-listed, former Shipbuilding Offices that dated from the mid-nineteenth century. Belfast was experiencing a renaissance after the thirty long years of what was euphemistically called 'The Troubles'. More slowly than other European cities, it was developing an obsession with all-day takeaway lattes. Wine bars that offered a place to wind down after work were springing up in middle-class areas, whereas the chipper still held its popularity in poorer enclaves. The Ulster Fry sat stubbornly on menus beside the avocado-and-goat's-cheese on sourdough. It was an awkward city still struggling to determine an identity that wasn't shrouded in sectarianism.

In a room on the most northerly corner of the Library Building's fifth floor, a reluctant assembly of faculty members waited and gazed through the vast windows at the now iconic vista of the Belfast Shipyard. On the meeting-room wall, a colourful post-modern image of a steamship sailing safely around an enormous iceberg bore the cryptic caption: *Let's Change the Past in the Future*. In real time, out in Belfast Lough, a mundane car ferry moved steadily towards the open sea and more than a few of those waiting for the first meeting of the new academic year to begin, firmly wished they were safely aboard that departing vessel.

In the distance, the distinctive, high-pitched mechanical sound of the lift ascending informed them that someone else had arrived at the top floor. After a lapse of the minute or two it took to walk around two sides of the quadrangle of corridor that overlooked the central, sky-filled college library, Professor Jackson Bell made his usual blustering entrance and claimed the vacant seat at the head of the table. With a tap of his biro on the boardroom table and a backward nod of his balding head, the Department of Peace and Reconciliation Studies was brought grudgingly to order.

Two hours later the DePRec staff Common Room resounded with sighs and muttered expletives after the tense and lengthy meeting. It had reprised well-worn themes of budgets and university league-tables and the increased need to attract funding *"to ensure sustainability in the university marketplace"*. Students had featured in the discussion only as a very peripheral commodity and there had been little sign of the virtues of mutual respect and recognition that those present made a living from espousing.

"Christ Almighty! Does nothing ever change in this godforsaken institution?" moaned the department's eldest and least deferential member, Ralph Wilson.

Ralph still resented Bell's appointment as Head of School some ten years previously in that it had simultaneously and definitively confirmed his own devalued academic currency. He was trenchantly and authentically old school and resented any moves towards modernisation or a market approach to academic studies. During the morning's seemingly interminable meeting he had treated his colleagues to a lengthy diatribe on the pervasive and destructive ideology of neo-liberalism in higher education. How were they to promote reconciliation when they were constantly goaded to be more competitive and cosmetically appealing to prospective students? The message and the process were at odds, he claimed. He was articulate and entertaining and eloquently undermined the Head with his declarations of injured moral sensitivities.

The atmosphere in the glass room had been laden with layers of discord that amply represented the now somewhat jaded Irish peace process and the wider faltering social and political structures that provided the core matter for their academic livelihood.

"Ironic question really for those involved in the ever-hopeful business of peace-building and societal transformation," quipped Helen Breen, senior lecturer in legal studies.

Her remark amused the group of precarious part-timers sitting near her and prompted a burst of heartless laughter. Their disgruntlement with the system meant that they particularly relished signs of strife within the ranks of privileged permanent staff. Breen was high-profile amongst those who used and abused part-time tutors to do work that she found unpalatable or inconvenient. She had especially irked one young postdoctoral scholar by offering him book tokens in lieu of payment for covering one of her classes at very short notice. He had reportedly met the offer with the incredulous retort, "Do you think I can pay my fucking bills with book tokens?"

Breen had come hastily up through the ranks from

favoured graduate and doctoral research assistant to fulltime staff member and senior lecturer. Jackson Bell was known to be her ardent supporter and frivolous speculation about the exact nature of their relationship was an ongoing item of common-room gossip. They didn't seem like a potential couple on first or even subsequent impressions but it was hard otherwise to understand Bell's uncritical loyalty to her. There could be no belief that her favour was rooted in hard work or even ideological commitment. With an audacity that left her colleagues exasperated, she worked the system to her own advantage whilst somehow seeming to maintain a workload that was less strenuous than most of her peers. Youth and good looks were possibly on her side. She was forever citing energetic gym practices and regularly ran marathons, allegedly for a host of noble causes. Many suspected correctly that she was uncompromisingly her own good cause. No grey was ever visible in her shoulder-length sleek, black mane that she habitually smoothed downwards from the crown with flattened palms. In a signature movement that rivals mimicked with vitriol, she would trace the contour of her head – hands coming to rest on her shoulders for the length of time it took her to inhale deeply and exhale. It was as if she was reaffirming that all was securely under her control. Her make-up was discreet and flawless and her vague references to a carefree social life all added to the youthful image.

Ralph Wilson, a genuine believer in the departmental mission of 'healing through honest, inclusive dialogue', now felt publicly ambushed. He was unsure if her remark had deliberately contained the degree of malice it had delivered and yet the way she kept him in her sights over the rim of her coffee cup suggested his response was being carefully measured.

Others watched as the struggle that had played out in the meeting continued.

He tightened his jaw, produced some sort of ineffectual snorting sound and, lifting his tobacco tin, headed for the outdoor deck space, vigorously shaking his head and muttering something about "pipes of peace".

Breen barely registered a reaction to this, bar the slight lifting of one eyebrow. Nonetheless, she recorded it as a victory from which she garnered some small degree of satisfaction. She was looking forward to the sport this term would provide as she worked through her plan to reap the greatest rewards for the least effort. This was where she would devote her energies and the wearisome business of peace and reconciliation could be the concern of the muppets who were her colleagues. She was her own area of special interest and the likes of Wilson and his emotional outbursts only served to make her look stable and measured by comparison.

She made a mental note to arrange lunch with the new head of the Faculty of Human Sciences. Janet Hartnett had been a few years ahead of her at school and she could certainly make some mileage out of that. She would let the dust settle on the new term and then devote her efforts to 'Project Professor' as she had secretly dubbed her goal for this academic year. She smoothed her hair in her customary manner and sighed contentedly.

5

Next door to the Common Room was the Department Administrative Centre and the preserve of Mairéad Walsh – Department Operations Manager. A feisty woman of mature years with an enduring Dublin accent, she was a custodian of information, official and otherwise, on all aspects of Department staff and business. She was unflagging in her enthusiasm and capacity to gather, store and analyse data from every staff member that passed through her office. Alongside her privileged role as minute-taker in all department meetings, this made her an invaluable source for those with whom she shared her secrets and those few whose interests she had at heart. Favourite amongst these was Ralph Wilson with whom she had long felt an affinity and with whom she often spent a discreet evening of harmless self-indulgence.

The aftermath of the morning's meeting was playing out in her territory with even greater intensity than the verbal scuffle in the common room next door. She had already set one of the juniors to work transcribing the audio recording of the meeting from which, under normal circumstances, a brief minute would later be produced. The transcribed version would be kept for a period of time to allow for verification of accuracy should any disputes arise. Mairéad was adept at covering her back. Her skills in diplomacy had been honed in the community where she had lived for decades with her six children and her husband Phillip. He was often away because of the nature of his work and as a southern Catholic in the Protestant suburbs of Belfast she had worked hard to preserve amicable relations with most neighbours. She was an artist in the use of humour to diffuse or deflect tension and frequently entertained colleagues with her knowledge of Hiberno-English. Under her tutelage, the term *gurrier*, Dublin slang for an ill-mannered loutish person, had become part of common parlance in the department. It was amazing how many it seemed to aptly describe, both academic staff and students.

"Jackson Bell was practically dancing around the office," Mairéad reported later as she sipped on a large gin in the company of Ralph Wilson. She smiled roguishly as she recalled the performance.

Bell had been anxious about the wording of the

minutes of the meeting, which would be the first official representation of the Department to the new Faculty Head. He particularly didn't want Wilson's criticism of his management style to be elaborated nor the constant accusation to take hold that he was not the epitome of conciliation and consensual working practices. The cosmetic version of the morning's events had taken time to construct before they had been dispatched with every appearance of efficiency to Professor Janet Hartnett's new corner office on the south face of the fifth floor.

Hartnett, originally from the North, was recently returned from London where she had been director of a postgraduate college specialising in counselling, psychotherapy and post-trauma rehabilitation approaches. The snide comments about how her therapeutic background would prepare her for her new post had circulated at all levels of the institution. Despite her disciplinary background, she was reputed to be tough and unforgiving of professional weakness, and Bell had no intention of giving her any opportunities to upbraid him. He had already given his backing to Helen Breen's plan to use her old schoolgirl relationship with Hartnett to further DePRec's standing. Breen was the one staff member that he knew unquestioningly shared his vision and was utterly loyal to the Centre and its work. He would be prepared to stake both their lives on that certainty.

As he was leaving her office, Bell had announced to Mairéad that the smaller inner room off the main office was to be prepared for the visiting postdoctoral scholar from City University New York. The partnership with CUNY had been long-lasting and the exchange of staff and postgraduate students was a regular occurrence. Mairéad Walsh had a son in Boston and she saw it as almost a familial duty to make visitors from the United States feel right at home in Belfast.

"This one should fit in well," sniped Bell in a rare display of emotion. "She's a detective by profession with a PhD in restorative justice." In a tone of mock resignation, he continued, "She could maybe do some work with the staff before she thinks about looking at any community groups. After this morning's meeting we are well on the way to setting ourselves up as a conflict-resolution case study, without ever needing to leave the building." That said, he gave an exasperated sigh and marched out of the room.

Mairéad's eyebrows had arched sharply at this display of petulance.

In the subdued lighting of the city-centre Library Bar, she enacted the entire performance for Ralph and enjoyed his obvious delight at her ridicule of his nemesis. He nodded to the barman to bring another couple of gin and tonics and felt his tensions ebb away in eager anticipation of Mairéad's soothing maternal embrace.

6

Over one hundred miles south in the School of Criminology, South Dublin University (SDU), Professor Tara Donnelly reviewed her plans for the forthcoming Social Harm Convention that she organised annually with a few colleagues from other universities in a number of continents. All these colleagues were committed to exposing harms that were continuously done in society but weren't recognised as crimes in the way that theft of property was. No one, aside from disadvantaged communities, was supposedly responsible for poverty or poor housing or educational inequalities. Tara and her colleagues enjoyed getting together to share their ideas and their research, and their discipline was growing in popularity amongst academics on the left. Because Dublin was the venue this year, she had the bulk of the work to do in relation to all the site issues. She had three months before the event but that wasn't as generous a gap as it might seem. There was a lot to do between this and December and she was a devil for the detail.

Her attic office, in one of the oldest buildings on the huge SDU campus, gave a sense of being housed in the upper levels of the trees. The birdlife outside the window was noisy and totally captivating at different points in the year. Nesting could be synonymous with low academic productivity for Tara as the level of distraction reached a peak. Generally, the peacefulness was a cause of constant appreciation for her, and she had passed up several offers to be re-accommodated in one of the many stylish new builds on campus. Her treehouse office and the refuge it afforded from the wider university bustle was a delight and she had no desire to be closer to the daily battles for parking spaces or the lengthy queues for coffee. She was content to slip into her workplace by a side entrance for pedestrians and cyclists and only join in the madness when it was absolutely necessary.

SDU campus measured about 200 acres and the green areas were well maintained by a fleet of grounds staff. They had recently been clearing areas of shrubs to promote greater safety for women students crossing the campus on dark evenings. The degree of thought that had gone into that decision had impressed Tara almost as much as she had been angry about the need to think like that in the first place. Women were certainly more important than shrubs, but it was a shame to be forced to make those choices because of the misogynistic behaviour of a few Neanderthal men.

Rising levels of email traffic recalled her from her internal chatter. She was one of the university's youngest professors and, despite a genuine lack of ambition, had already had a fairly stellar academic career. Her hurried departure from Northern Ireland was ironically when the peace process was well advanced and because Belfast was no longer the place she felt at home. As a founder of DePRec, she still commanded respect from international donors and academics alike but, since moving south, she had taken a step back from the specifics of the North to a wider interest in social harm generally. Her writing was prolific and widely published and she maintained close connections with communities of interest established to challenge accepted views of what constituted social justice. It was in these local projects that she learned most and where she felt more at home than in the academy.

A believer in research that had a strong 'action' element, Donnelly had constructed a working life that involved a lot of community activism, counterbalanced by enough writing and on-campus visibility to keep her colleagues and managers happy. The funding and public profile she secured for the university gave her a great deal of academic freedom, but she wore this mantle modestly. She worked very selectively and collaboratively with a small number of colleagues dotted about the globe and had no urge to grow that number or participate in the frenetic activity through which some colleagues felt obliged to demonstrate their worth. Although she had family and other connections in the North, she never crossed the border, preferring the quiet domestic arrangements she had made for herself in the South.

Today, for some reason, Tara Donnelly was pulled back repeatedly to her days in Belfast. She was leafing through applications from people who wanted to talk about their work at the two-day December event and was struck by the number of northern would-be contributors. Of course, people were more political there and critical of the state and its potential for simultaneous tyranny and subterfuge. They had good reason. Since the creation of the state in 1921 they had been plunged into a recurring bloody context that laid bare the consequences of inept political decisions, and some of its public face. Of course there was a whole world of political machination to which ordinary people were never made privy. Tara knew from her research that people were easily distracted from the truth. They were seduced by the managed media rhetoric and remained unaware of the clandestine forces that were really influencing northern society in order to bolster their own dogma. Agents of the state employed in various wings of the intelligence services had worked constantly behind the scenes to discredit those who disagreed with partition. To British Intelligence these were enemies of the state. Republican resistance was portrayed as fanatical, and poor nationalist and loyalist communities were set against each other rather than being allowed to see their reasons for common cause. She had come close to learning too much about this darker side of the North and had gladly (and hastily) left it all behind when she had moved across the border.

Reading the conference abstracts from applicants now, she could discern familiar threads of northern life drawing her back to her days up there. She was still conscious of coming from that other jurisdiction even if she herself felt no need for the border to preserve or protect anything she held dear, either material or ideological. The 'borders of the mind' was a favourite theme of hers that she had elaborated down the years both academically and creatively. Back in the early days of DePRec she had worked closely on that subject with a feminist artist in Belfast. They had run creative workshops and mounted exhibitions with schools and communities. Through the work, they had explored the cultural divides that were part of every aspect of northern society. The creative approach had covered ground that would have been gained much more slowly if they had been limited to verbal approaches. In terms of generating research data, images had shown they could go where simple dialogue was less effective.

She was glad that Jackson Bell had continued that

focus on visual sociology in DePRec. She had a lot of time for his work and followed most of the DePRec publications and events from the remote sanctuary she had made for herself in Dublin. Her watchfulness was not without ulterior motive. She knew that manipulative interests were still at work in DePRec and her observations were constantly and vigilantly aimed at tracking the direction those influences were taking. For now she only watched but the day might come, she knew, when she would also need to act.

7

January 2014

Post-doc scholar Alice Fox had spent the latter part of December and the New Year south of the Irish border. There had been the Social Harm Convention in South Dublin University and afterwards two weeks in Wicklow exploring the impressive hillwalking trails that area offered. The first week of January 2014 brought chill winds, freezing temperatures and the threat of snow. On Alice's return north, the city Christmas lights no longer offered any relief to the generally grey Belfast cityscape and even the cheery Santa and sleigh on the front of the City Hall had been extinguished. This everyday Belfast was stern and unforgiving in comparison to the gregarious Dublin she had left behind the previous day.

Since her arrival in Ireland at the end of August, Alice had been dividing her time between DePRec and EXIT, a project for at-risk youth in the west of Belfast. She had cemented a strong relationship there with Hugo, the project leader, and a core group of eight young people, seven young men and one woman. They met several times a week and Alice was piloting a new course in self-defence with them that combined two of her own big interests – Tae Kwan Do and effective relationship management. She wanted them to learn that making good relationships was a way of keeping yourself and those around you safe. Poor communication and an inability to read your own and others' emotions just led to trouble and often that spilled over into conflict and violence. The mix of talk and action was working well so far.

Together, and with a view to challenging academic norms, they had recently co-authored a paper for the conference about social harm and Alice had presented it in Dublin in late December. The group's idea had pleased Alice greatly. She loved the wisdom of those that society disregarded and how it ruffled feathers when it was given a public airing. The group's argument was that although as young offenders they were encouraged to make right their wrongs against society in face-to-face meetings with victims, no one felt moved to take responsibility for the impact that poverty and poor education had on their lives.

She recalled with satisfaction the evening that the gaps in the one-sided restorative-justice system had become clear to them.

Rae, the only young woman in the group, had made the initial breakthrough.

"A lot of what we all do here is face up to the hurt we've caused to other people, right? We have to literally face people and explain ourselves … why we robbed their car or killed their cat or whatever. Am I right?" There had been nods and mutterings of assent around the circle. "Well, then, where is the chance for those ones who have harmed us to account for themselves? Nobody has ever said they were sorry I lived in a shit flat with nothing in the fridge most of the time. Do you see where I'm going, anybody? Why are we the ones doing all the apologising?"

"You're right, Rae. You are so right." Jed's face had been triumphant. "Who has ever taken responsibility for the fact that I can hardly read and write. I'm twenty-three years of age and Ra's wee nephew can read more than me and he's only five. Hugo, you have taught us all that we have to make up for what we have done to people. Restore justice. Isn't that the saying? Who's restoring my justice? And Rae's? And everybody else's? We never had any justice to begin with!"

Alice agreed fully with their analysis. She too had made her own very personal relationship with restorative justice. Day on day, she painstakingly and patiently worked with young offenders and those who hadn't yet made the step into what counted as criminal activity. She was constantly patrolling the borders between what was seen as breaking the law and the idea of social harm, much of which was totally accepted as the just desserts of those from poor and minority communities. The system clearly identified theft as a punishable crime against society but poverty as entirely a matter of individual failure. The preventative approach to creating a less harmful community with those at risk of becoming caught into the criminal system, now occupied the bulk of her time. With the young people already labelled as offenders, Alice carefully facilitated dialogue between those who were viewed as being wronged, and the wrongdoer. She liked the logic of taking the hurts out of the shadows and helping all parties to look for mutually agreeable ways to heal the damage.

In her own experience, she had been forced to confront the life realities of the young man who had caused her father's death. She had moved from rage at the consequences of his anger and disaffection to a realisation that unequal structures were the root of the problem and that if we are not actively against injustice, we are contributing to its persistence. Not all of her family agreed and dealing with their collective hurt was an ongoing story. Her sister Sam got it, but her mother and older brother Red were unsympathetic, albeit for very different reasons.

Now, back in DePRec after her Christmas vacation, she had no inkling just how relevant her life experience was about to become.

8

Mairéad Walsh greeted Alice on her return with a warm embrace and good wishes for the New Year. She was embarked on a fully dramatised version of her own holidays when departmental head, Professor Jackson Bell, appeared. He seemed agitated and, without any niceties, he brusquely demanded if there had been any phone call from Helen Breen to explain her absence from an important meeting he had scheduled for first thing that morning. Mairéad said there had been no call and phoned across to the other office to check that nothing had been received there. It was now nearly nine thirty.

"I have checked her office," he blustered, "but the door is firmly locked. This is not at all like her … she was the one I was sure could always be relied upon."

His level of distress in response to a missed meeting seemed a little extreme, Alice thought, but she put this down to the pressures of the return to work after quite a long break. He had a plan and it was being thwarted and Bell did not appear to her to be one who coped well with losing control.

He instructed Mairéad to try Dr Breen's mobile phone and her home number and to let him know what the outcome was and then he swept out of the room. A vision of a diva in a black-and-white silent movie crossed Alice's mind.

Mairéad rolled her eyes, puckered her brow and her mouth in an expression of exaggerated concentration and assumed her position behind her desk. Alice withdrew to her own inside office space and left her to it.

On loudspeaker, Breen's phone could be heard going directly to the answering service and Mairéad left a terse message asking her to contact DePRec immediately. While Alice made a list of the day's tasks, she heard Mairéad speaking to someone and then placing a call to Jackson Bell.

Alice couldn't help but listen.

"Professor Bell, there is no response from the mobile phone and her mother's Filipino carer says that they haven't seen her since before Christmas. Apparently she told them she was going away on holiday for the entire break so they had no expectation of her being there." Mairéad paused to listen to Bell's reply. "Well, perhaps she mistook the first day of term or had a delayed return flight," she offered without conviction. "I'm afraid I can't be of any more help really ... unless you want me to get the caretaker to open her office – although I'm not sure what use that might be." Bell was obviously making some further suggestions as Mairéad uttered the occasional, "*Hmm*" and "OK" and finally "Well, yes, Professor, I will check what happens to her class at eleven. She may just have been held up this morning and for some reason been unable to get in touch."

The call ended and Mairéad could be heard loudly addressing her computer timetable and noting the location of Breen's mid-morning lecture.

Helen Breen did not appear in DePRec that day nor was any message received to explain her absence. Her class was given unexpected library time and a promise from Bell that the time would be made up for them in the future.

The caretaker came with a passkey to open the corner office and reported back to Mairéad that the room was empty. College security were able to establish that Helen Breen had not been in the building since the penultimate day of term when she had scanned out at nine thirty-six, after she had covered Jackson Bell's evening duty. A replacement law tutor was called in to cover Helen Breen's remaining classes until the mystery of her whereabouts could be solved. As the situation became more widely known about within the department, speculation grew as to the possible explanation but despite numerous fanciful theories there was no definitive answer. By the end of the day the mystery remained unresolved.

On that evening in early January there was a storm of unforeseen proportions. Strong winds and high tides in coastal areas caused substantial structural damage. In the dockland area of Belfast there were power outages that lasted over two days in some cases and these caused considerable disruption to those without a secondary energy source. Restaurants and supermarkets lost frozen produce and those dependent on electrical heating systems had a few very chilly nights. The morning after the storm struck, radio broadcasts told those who were not working in essential services to stay at home and allow emergency crews time to get power lines repaired unimpeded. This was later extended to two days when the extent of the damage became apparent and the storm lingered and delayed repairs getting under way.

Alice had settled in the bohemian Botanic area of Belfast and had discovered the nearby Lagan Towpath not too far from her new home. This was an eleven-mile continuous pathway along river and canal banks and passing through meadows, wetlands and wooded areas. It was almost completely flat and not too busy if you chose the time carefully. Alice did the round trip most days in just under two hours and liked best to start when dawn was breaking and running companions were scarce. After the worst of the storm, on her riverside run she encountered two fallen trees and several places where the river was unusually high. She had received a very early text telling her that DePRec would remain closed for two days and was glad to be heading back to her cosy rooms for the rest of the day and the one that followed.

Only a small number of staff appeared for work in Belfast City College and they had been called in to repair minor problems caused by water and wind damage. As instructed, the entire DePRec staff remained at home.

Then, on the Wednesday evening, Jackson Bell received a call at home from the College President asking him to come in to help with a matter of some urgency. By this stage it was after nine o'clock and the aftermath of the storm was mostly cleared away. The return to work was scheduled for Thursday and it was baffling why he might be needed in the college this evening. He responded rapidly to the most unusual request with a heavy sense of foreboding.

9

A short distance from DePRec, in the Marine Biology section of the Centre for Maritime Studies, a substantial number of specimens of small and larger sea plants and animals were stored in a series of large chest freezers. These were placed like squat sentinels along one side of a first-floor corridor. Unsightly and antiquated, they jarred with the carefully refurbished surroundings of the listed building. Nonetheless they were priceless to the marine biologists who had been amassing them for decades and had yet to find the funding source that would allow them to create a more eye-pleasing form of storage and display. In their previous college accommodation there had been a generator system that automatically kicked in when there was a power failure that placed their treasured collection at any risk. The stylishly regenerated Shipbuilding Offices had not as yet installed such an emergency back-up system.

On the night of the storm a power interruption had caused some defrosting to occur and some leakage to take place from the ageing freezers onto the highly polished wooden floors. Subsequently, on the two days that followed, those charged with the salvage operation were initially concerned only with avoiding water damage and were under orders to keep the fridges closed so as not to accelerate the defrosting process. This seemed to be effective except in the case of one container where, although the power was restored on the afternoon of the second day of exceptional closure, the contents appeared to have become too voluminous to fit. The lid refused to close tightly and seepage of some rather putrid water continued. It was as if through the melting process the contents of this particular freezer had swollen and a call was made to a staff member from Marine Biology to come into the College and advise on how best to cope with this anomaly.

Dr Sam Carter finally arrived late on the Wednesday afternoon and was puzzled by what she found. The inventory for that freezer suggested that the contents should not have altered so radically in the time that the power was off with the freezer unopened. A closer inspection revealed that the specimens in the freezer had been disturbed and beneath the legitimate marine-life samples something entirely out of place had been secreted. Without investigating too closely, Sam Carter had been so alarmed by what she saw that she had phoned the College President directly. He in turn had placed a call to the local police. From there, events had taken on a shocking momentum all of their own in which Jackson Bell now found himself embroiled.

10

Arriving in the lift from the basement car park to the ground floor, Jackson Bell greeted the night porter who was already installed at his station to the side of the reception area. It was clear that he was expected and Bell headed to the seating area outside the President's office and waited to be admitted. There was a hum of serious voices from within that made it abundantly clear that something very grave had occurred. He felt profoundly uneasy about how he might be found to be implicated. Driving towards the Titanic Quarter, Bell had racked his brain for what might be the "matter of some urgency" that required his presence at such a late hour. The President was not known for creating unnecessary dramas. In fact, he was more inclined to let things sort themselves out without his becoming directly involved.

Bell had become overwhelmed by that familiar

anxiety related to secrets being discovered, long hidden shames being finally pulled irrevocably out into the open. As he parked in the underground car park he reassured himself that he had broken no law. His covert identity was entirely because of his personal circumstances and a legacy of past times when attitudes and laws were less liberal. This call, despite its unusual timing could only be a professional matter. More than likely something relating to a member of the DePRec staff. Maybe a complaint about a tutor or some allegation related to the recent exams. He would wait until the real reason was disclosed before jumping to conclusions. His reputation was flawless, he reflected. There was no need to get into a state ... and yet what was so serious that it couldn't wait until after two days of exceptional closure?

While he scanned the possible reasons for this unusual summons, the door to the President's office opened and Lorna, Professor Thompson's PA, emerged. "They are ready for you now, Jackson," she said and the gravity of her voice and demeanour did nothing to calm Bell's sense of dread.

She led the way into the President's spacious office and took her place at the large table used for monthly senior staff meetings. It was clear from the array of paper in front of her that Lorna had been making a record of the discussion that preceded his admittance.

The large office was brightly lit and in addition to the

President there were three other people around the table – one middle-aged woman and two men, one of whom was considerably younger than the other. They were all focused on Jackson as he entered the room and the younger man was also evidently taking notes on the proceedings. Although they were not in uniform, Jackson was sure these were police officers and his level of tension rose a notch.

Unsmiling, Giles Thompson signalled to Bell to take a free seat at the table and thanked him for coming in at short notice and at an unusual hour.

"Let me introduce you to our visitors, Jackson," he intoned. "This is Detective Inspector Caroline Paton and her associates, Detective Sergeant William Burrows and Detective Constable Ian McVeigh."

Jackson nodded to all three in turn as he settled himself in the vacant seat that Thompson had indicated to him.

"Professor Bell is the Head of the Department of Peace and Reconciliation Studies here in the College. He has been in that position for the past ten or eleven years and is a valued member of my senior management team."

These words reassured Jackson. They were not the precursor of any difficult situation where he was to be found culpable and he felt himself regain his confidence and turn his attention to hearing what was really at the root of this gathering.

At a signal from the senior detective, Thompson was

given the go-ahead to outline the situation that had brought these representatives of the Police Service of Northern Ireland (PSNI) to the college on a grim January night.

"So, Jackson, let me begin by giving you the short version of this dreadful story. I am aware it is late and there is potentially a long night ahead." Thompson's voice was care-laden and it suggested that he had already decided that this matter, whatever it was, would have dire consequences. He sighed and continued. "As you are well aware we are just finishing two days of exceptional closure brought about by the recent storm. Our concern these past two days was to secure the building and not bring staff or students out in a potentially dangerous situation. In any case," he reassured himself, "we were following guidance issued by local authorities."

The tendency to affirm that the college was above reproach was ingrained in the President. Maybe it was an integral part of the job, Jackson mused.

"Anyway," Thompson continued, "that all worked out well and the small amounts of storm damage we suffered were easily dealt with by our own caretaking and maintenance staff. That is except for an incident that materialised in the Centre for Maritime Studies – the Marine Biology Department to be precise." He paused as if deeply disturbed by consideration of this mysterious event.

"Are you familiar with the Marine Biology Department, Professor Bell?" the Detective Inspector asked.

43

Her gaze was penetrating and Jackson immediately revised his feeling of being out of the woods. He coughed in a manner that he was sure indicated he was anxious and probably a deserving subject of suspicion.

"There is not a great deal of overlap between our disciplines, but we have had some collaboration on the subject of joint fishing interests across the different regions of the British Isles ..." he hesitated and added, "or as some might prefer, Britain and Ireland." There was never a time, he had learned, when it was a good idea to ignore the local sensitivities about the naming of things. Some in the North took great exception to the twenty-six counties of the Irish Republic being referred to as British and so it was best to use terminology that included everyone's preferences. To be inclusive in Northern Ireland often meant naming places or political agreements several times over to suit all tastes.

"Do you often have occasion to visit the Shipbuilding Offices building, Professor?"

Jackson realised that her question had related to the place rather than the academic area and he felt he had judged his response badly.

"I rarely have occasion to go there but I have attended functions there in my senior-management capacity. The building is a fine example of regeneration done well, in my opinion. DePRec would have had an interest in advising about how to ensure that the remaking of the old building was as cross-community as possible." He was floundering in his attempts to answer her query and conscious of the hollow, evasive sound of his response.

Detective Inspector Paton did not look altogether satisfied but nodded to Thompson to continue his narrative.

"So anyway, this afternoon, while maintenance were dealing with some water leakage from the freezers in Marine Biology, they had difficulty with securing the contents of one container and called a member of Marine Biology staff to come into college to advise them. They were rightly cautious about damage occurring to the specimens." He paused, perhaps so that the efficiency of the staff might be properly recognised and his listeners would have time to reflect the praise back to his own excellent management. "Dr Carter arrived on the scene and in her attempt to refit the freezer contents back into place she discovered that it had been tampered with and something had been added that made it impossible to close properly."

Aware that his every response was being carefully observed, Jackson tried to show that he was following assiduously without having any idea what he was about to be told.

"There is no easy way to say this, Jackson," Thompson said with total gravity. "Dr Carter's exploration revealed that a body had been secreted in the freezer beneath the marine biology specimens. The head was tightly wrapped in black plastic bags and Dr Carter rightly did not interfere with the remains in any way."

Jackson had now all but petrified in his seat. He was refusing to move forward in his mind with the possible direction this account was taking yet he was not totally successful in this regard. Thompson was explaining that he had immediately cautioned the maintenance staff and Dr Carter to keep any speculation about their discovery to themselves until the PSNI had begun their inquiry. He had no desire to have wild rumours being announced on the airwaves before it became clear what had happened.

"No," Jackson heard himself say plaintively, as if in slow motion. He sensed that the attention of everyone present was firmly fixed on him and placed a limp hand over his mouth as if to push his remark back inside, to unsay it.

"Do you have any idea who the unfortunate occupant of that freezer might be, Professor Bell?" This time it was the older man, the sergeant, who posed the question.

Jackson noted his slight stressing of the word "you" and struggled to remain calm. His logical mind reviewed the facts from the first day of term and ran ahead with an outrageous and yet plausible conclusion. "I think I may do," he said very softly before feeling himself overcome with nausea and retching silently into his carefully ironed white linen handkerchief.

The others around the table observed silently and the

Detective Constable wrote continuous notes. This alone was unnerving in the midst of a host of disturbing circumstances. Jackson flashed a look around the group. He saw that Lorna was frozen with her pen in mid-air and a look of abject, open-mouthed horror on her face. He tried to pull himself together.

"Helen Breen," he said a little too loudly. "I think it may be my colleague, Dr Helen Breen. She was unaccountably missing from DePRec on Monday and her family hasn't seen her since before Christmas. We were unable to contact her."

He paused and looked at the President who was almost imperceptibly shaking his head from side to side as if to reject the emerging reality.

"Is it Helen?" Jackson asked with a look of desperation.

Without any pause, Caroline Paton took over control of the conversation and addressed Jackson directly. "We are not in a position to confirm anything at this stage. There was a DePRec identity badge with the remains that we found and so that is why we wanted to speak to you initially. We have removed the entire freezer to police headquarters for closer inspection and will need to ask you to accompany us there, Professor Bell. We require some background information about DePRec and will possibly ask for your help with identification of the victim."

Without further ceremony she stood up and shook hands with Professor Thompson.

"Detective Constable McVeigh will wait and travel with Professor Bell." She looked directly at Jackson. "I imagine you will need a few minutes to inform your family and make preparations for speaking to your staff tomorrow." She turned again to Thompson. "Until we have a definite ID we will need Helen Breen's office to remain locked for close inspection. I imagine you will want classes to continue as normal so we will work alongside the college staff to ensure that our investigation causes as little disruption as possible. We will hold off on a media announcement until the morning and think about an initial press gathering late tomorrow afternoon or Friday morning. It won't be possible to stop the news leaking out, but we can delay giving any detail until we have a little more to say."

The phrase 'leaking out' filled Bell's mind with revolting garish images and he just managed to control an urge to gag a second time.

"We will prepare a room for your use in the college," the President said whilst nodding at Lorna to make sure that this happened. "I imagine it will be the boardroom and some smaller rooms on the fifth floor of the Human Sciences Building."

"Perhaps we can start with the maintenance personnel who were on the scene when the remains were discovered and then Dr Carter," said Detective Paton. "We will be in the reception of the Shipbuilding Offices for eight forty-five tomorrow morning. Can that be arranged?"

The President nodded. Lorna scribbled on her pad and wondered when they might get home and at what time she would need to come in the next day to make sure all these plans could be implemented. She had planned to do her ironing tonight and God only knew when she would catch up on all that. She felt overwhelmed by time pressures but on the surface her demeanour declared unquestioning compliance and unwavering efficiency.

When the senior detectives had left and the constable had withdrawn with Lorna to wait for Jackson outside, Professor Thompson put his hand kindly on his colleague's shoulder. "You will need to talk to staff tomorrow, Jackson. I would suggest at the mid-morning break so as not to disrupt the daily routine." He began to move towards his desk with a sense of purpose. "I will need to prepare some statements, I expect, so that when your identification is definite, I am ready to respond on behalf of the college. You can text me any update on my mobile number, irrespective of the time tonight."

He was demonstrating his usual calm and Jackson wondered what would really ruffle his superior's seemingly imperturbable exterior.

"We are in for an interesting few weeks, I predict," Thompson added.

Jackson had a sense that he had somehow come out of this drama with the most unpleasant role to play, but it was clear there was no way of escaping what lay ahead.

"Hopefully you will get a little sleep, Jackson, before you need to come back tomorrow morning and manage all this." With that, Thompson opened the lid of his MacBook Pro and set to work on his PR preparations.

For his part, Jackson used Lorna's phone to tell Hanna that he would be later than expected due to unforeseen circumstances at work. Then he turned reluctantly to Detective Constable Ian McVeigh and said, "My car is in the underground car park."

As they headed off in silence towards the lift, Jackson Bell began slowly to absorb the dreadful reality of this situation in which he now found himself.

11

Earlier that evening, Jackson Bell had sat sedately across the table from his wife and, as if by premonition, had felt his spirits descend into the gathering gloom. Normally the theatrics of work filled his days with meaning, and often his nights too. Being Director of DePRec was what preoccupied him in a way that his marriage had never done. He and Hanna had struggled to produce one child, a daughter they had named Esther. He was neither an enthusiastic father nor an ardent husband and covertly sought his bodily satisfactions in furtive visits to saunas and anonymous encounters with strangers when away at conferences. If those in work had any idea of his fractured identity, it had never become a focus of discussion. Only Helen Breen had shrewdly spotted something in his demeanour early in their acquaintance and, when she had audaciously confronted him, there had been no point in denying it. There had been some relief in that. They had reached an unspoken understanding that he would look after her academic interests in exchange for her silence. This collusion had evolved, on her initiative, into allowing vague insinuations of a liaison between them to provide a cloak for his true leanings. They had slipped easily into a mutually rewarding situation that neither had any interest in bringing to an end. Her unexplained disappearance led him now to consider the complicated deception that framed his whole way of being in the world.

Home was a lonely, quiet place for all three members of the Bell family. They did not have television or radio or any form of media intrusion that might bring corrupting messages with it. Hanna, his wife of some eighteen years, was from a Brethren family. She had never once cut her hair and her father did not believe that women should attend higher education. Hanna had become accustomed to spending her days at home and socialising only with family and other Brethren. They were not from the 'exclusive' branch of that religious grouping and so, aged twenty-five, she was permitted to marry Jackson who was a Quaker and so seen as religiously compatible. Brethren belonged to the group of Christian peace churches, along with Quakers and others of a similar pacifist faith. Both Brethren and Quakers were against war and violence of all kinds and Hanna's and Jackson's male ancestors had all been conscientious objectors in their time. Their belief was focused solely on the bible, in non-hierarchical but gendered gatherings where male believers shared responsibility for direction and discipline of their group. Homosexuality had traditionally been a particularly heinous aberration for Brethren and a cause of exclusion from the family group. A wave of change was slowly creeping in from the US Brethren, but Northern Ireland would be slow to countenance such modernism.

As a young scholar in his early thirties, Jackson had met Hanna's family when researching the experience of members of a cultural group that rejected all forms of iconography and visual imagery. Thereby he hoped to better understand the diversity of visual expression in political murals in the North, which was then becoming his specialist area of research. The family had liked his seemingly serious demeanour, his prospects and his commitment to an academic study of peace in DePRec. He, forever struggling with his own demons, had seen a safe haven with this unworldly, undemanding young woman whose manner did not unnerve him, as did other female peers.

Their relationship had evolved falteringly, kept distant by his long working days and her continued preoccupation with daily religious and family activities. It was not thought unusual in that strictly patriarchal grouping that he was immersed in his scholarly life on which she could make no meaningful comment. For his part, he had little involvement in the day-to-day Brethren business of scripture readings and kept his attendance at prayers to an acceptable minimum. A companionable distance characterised their union save for the infrequent and unfulfilling silent intercourse that was dutifully endured by both of them under cover of darkness.

When Esther was conceived, Jackson experienced a degree of recognition from family and peers that brought with it a certain release. He felt that he had finally become the character he had been playing for some five long years and the role, like in all successful long-running soaps, was now unquestioningly his for life. Both he and Hanna had relaxed a little and, although the void between them did not diminish in any real way, Esther became both a mutual interest and a way of remaining even further apart. Now aged thirteen, she shared her mother's unadorned beauty and her maternal family's resolute religious extremism. Although he had encouraged her attendance at mainstream secondary school, years of Brethren childcare, home-schooling and all-consuming community immersion meant that, for now, she remained an uncompromising zealot.

Tonight, as ever, they had eaten their evening meal in relative silence before Jackson was called to attend the meeting in the President's office. Now all that comfortable fiction was being shaken by a wholly unexpected turn of events. As he headed for the college car park with the young detective constable, he shuddered inwardly at the possible tumultuous consequences that might result from this evening's events, in every part of his life.

12

The police station was just ten minutes' drive across the city and Bell and DC McVeigh took the M2, then the West Link and came off at the Grosvenor Road exit. Police stations in Belfast had been a major target for attacks during the Troubles and still remained heavily fortified. When they arrived at Grosvenor Road barracks, McVeigh got them through the outer security barrier and then through the inner reinforced metal fence and gates that were at least as high as the two-story building inside. A slanting, fine-mesh grille filled the gap between the inner fencing and the building. This too was a legacy of former days and meant that any missile thrown over the fencing would roll back immediately onto the ground outside.

McVeigh told Bell where to park and led the way into the building. He signed them both in at the desk and the duty officer told him to go to Interview Room 6.

They went down a flight of stairs and found DI Paton and Burrows sitting at a table waiting for them.

Caroline Paton thanked Bell for coming and said they would remain conscious of the demands on him tomorrow and try not to keep him longer than necessary. "You will realise, Professor Bell, that we are at the beginning of a murder inquiry and time is important for us. We realise that it may be that over the holiday period we have already lost valuable momentum." She tapped her pen impatiently as she spoke. "If we can positively ID the remains this evening and gather some background data from you about your department, that will give us something to be getting on with. We will, of course, study your website and all the college information already provided by Professor Thompson."

Bell nodded and muttered that he would help in whatever way he could. He was still struggling to grasp how he had moved so rapidly from the relative gloom of an evening at home to the unthinkable horror he now confronted.

"This is new territory for me, Detective Inspector. I am ill at ease but I understand my responsibilities and will do the best I can to help in whatever way possible." He had a strong sense of duty and it helped him to find a role he could understand and act upon.

"Murder is not an easy situation, Professor Bell. The deceased has undergone a particularly brutal attack but our forensic pathologist has done her best with what we've got. I think that identification should be fairly straightforward. From the photos in your college prospectus, we have a fairly good idea of things but your input will be most useful. Let's get that part done first."

She stood up and motioned to her colleagues to wait where they were. She walked ahead of Jackson to the end of the corridor, pushed through some double doors and entered a brightly lit area where the air was thick with the smell of bleach and other chemicals. Jackson held his breath. Several trolleys loaded with gleaming steel instruments were set against the far wall, ready to be mobilised whenever necessary. Overhead tracks of lighting indicated the location of a number of potential work areas but for the moment they were all vacant.

A young woman in a brightly patterned sweater and jeans greeted Caroline Paton cheerily. "I've done what I could for you, DI Paton. We are out the back on the right here." She pointed to a small room off the larger space where glass panels revealed dimmed lighting behind a partially closed blind. "Go ahead in your own time – I'll be lurking in my lair if you need me." She withdrew to her office, which was to the left across from the room to which Caroline Paton now led the way.

The detective turned to Jackson before they crossed the threshold and spoke quietly and in a not unkindly matter-of-fact tone. "Take your time, Professor. I expect this will be shocking for you but my concern is to do justice by this victim. The first step is to know her identity so that we can begin our investigation in earnest. I will pull back the cover when you tell me you are ready and I will stay beside you throughout." She moved to the top of the trolley where it was clear that a body rested beneath a thick green hospital cover.

Jackson became strangely lost in the study of the visual. He examined the mound and saw no hint that he knew the person. Nothing in the outline reminded him of anyone in particular and yet he spent some time observing the shape of the body and the rise and fall of the material that covered it. After what may have been only moments, he became aware of Caroline Paton's observation of him and felt the need to proceed. He nodded slightly to say he was ready.

She carefully folded back the cloth and stepped back a little to give him more room.

Jackson had seen the corpses of several of his family members in the past. As a young teenager he had seen the dead body of his sole remaining grandparent, his father's mother. At the time, her peacefulness was what had been stressed to him and he had viewed her with curiosity. She had been laid out in a coffin and her skin had been surprisingly cold and waxen. Decades later, he held the memory of that coldness in his fingers. When his father had died suddenly of a heart attack his mother had called him at work to come home immediately. He had not been long married and Hanna had met him at his parents' house and they had sat silently beside the body until the undertaker had come to take it away for embalming. He had not been close to his father and the undemanding nature of the Quaker funeral rite had been a refuge for him from an expectation of outward displays of grief.

In this small room now with DI Caroline Paton, Jackson felt the shock of a life ended in a more intimate way than he had with his own family members. As the cloth was folded back he recognised the black hair and high cheekbones that he associated with his most trusted colleague. Her skin was unlike his memory of her perfect complexion and he could see the trauma wrought by the weeks that might have elapsed since her death. He had to stop looking as the efforts to disguise the harm to the back of her head began to become obvious and he turned away as he spoke.

"These are indeed the remains of Helen Breen. I am certain of it."

The cloth was replaced and Jackson preceded DI Paton from the room. Outside he paused to convey the identity of the cadaver to the College President in the promised text message.

He could see the pathologist sitting behind a cluttered desk and she called through the open door as they emerged. "I am off home now but I'll get to the autopsy first thing in the morning. I'll get my report to you before close of play tomorrow, Caroline."

Jackson walked silently alongside the Inspector until they reached the interview room where they had left Burrows and McVeigh. They took their places around the table and Paton confirmed that they had a positive ID for Dr Helen Breen, Senior Lecturer in Legal Studies in DePRec.

"Until we have notified the family, we'll be keeping the details of this case private. We will make that a priority first thing tomorrow morning and for that reason also your meeting with staff, Professor Bell, would best be delayed until mid-morning."

The background detail that the team of detectives wanted was superficial and mainly administrative. He talked them through the staff list and answered queries about the departmental structure. They asked for minutes of meetings and he said they would be provided the following day. He had a momentary flash of thankfulness for his own attention to sanitising the detail of minutes, aware now that conflictual discussions might be viewed in an entirely different light. At the same time he was aware that the PSNI interviews with staff were beyond his control. His mind was rushing ahead now to organisational detail. Mairéad Walsh would need to be briefed first thing so that staff could be informed about the morning meeting and so that she would be able to guide the team of detectives in navigating the DePRec and wider college system. Jackson confirmed to the detectives that Mairéad was experienced and trustworthy.

He would speak to her before the day's business began.

Much earlier than he had anticipated, he was free to go and he made his way home through the Belfast night with a frozen heart and an immovable image of Helen Breen's ravaged face in his mind's eye. He realised before too long that all his colleagues, and indeed he himself, were now suspects in this matter and that he would have a monumental task in terms of managing what was to come. The prospect was profoundly daunting.

13

In Grosvenor Road Police Barracks, Interview Room 6, the night was just beginning. Since the Northern Ireland troubles had ended, sectarian killings had diminished and other issues like drug-dealing, theft, racist attacks and sexual assaults were demanding more police attention. Homicide was a reasonably infrequent occurrence and quickly focused the attention of the detectives involved.

When occasion demanded, Caroline Paton was used to her evenings being hijacked at short notice by her job as head of the Murder Squad. That was probably a large contributory factor to her solitary lifestyle. She had a reputation for being a Rottweiler who when pushed too far had a bite that was even more vicious than her bark. Burrows and McVeigh found her a fair taskmaster and worked tirelessly under her direction, which was just as well as she could be more exacting than most. As a trio, they had a name for getting the job done and had notched up several high-profile wins in difficult cases. This murder of a college lecturer had many challenging features that had already engaged their interest. In many ways, they relished the task ahead.

Both of the men had families and it made it easier that Paton recognised the knock-on effect of the demands she made on them. She didn't always make life any easier for them but at least she appreciated their work and the costs involved. McVeigh was in his early thirties, well-built and a sharp dresser. He had just recently had a new baby son and showed all the signs of not getting enough sleep. Sergeant Burrows was in his mid-fifties, married and had three grown-up children who had all flown the nest, and the country. The older man had been in the force for decades and, like Caroline, had survived the transformation from the RUC – the Royal Ulster Constabulary to the PSNIs – the reformed and more inclusive Police Service of Northern Ireland. He was thoughtful and methodical and had excellent detection skills born from experience and from being a good learner. For his part, McVeigh had discovered that coming to the role of detective through the graduate route didn't always mean that you were smarter than those who had gained their skills and knowledge on the job. The two men rubbed along well together with Burrows adopting a paternalistic position with McVeigh, but not in an irritating or intrusive way.

Caroline Paton was in her early forties and known as a physical dynamo with an incisive mind and an uncompromising sense of justice. She had joined the police force after college in the early 90s when bombs and sectarian killings in Northern Ireland were a daily occurrence. As such, as a young woman she had seen the bloody results of the war all too often and had been filled with hope when some years later the peace process began to show signs of progress. Up until that point, the Troubles had been a backdrop to her whole life and she was well aware of the many ways in which the population of Northern Ireland continued to exhibit war-related PTSD. School and college friends had left the North never to return but she was too stubborn to give up and had decided that, come what may, she would make her life there. Her parents were now in their 70s and, although she lived alone, she was close to them. Her two siblings had gone to university in England and Scotland and like the majority of that generation of young people, they had never returned.

Paton wrestled with her weight but kept herself fit. She went to the gym as often as possible and tried to counterbalance a dreadful diet and too much chocolate with enough exercise to allow her to run fast whenever needed. She communicated a busy efficiency in her way of dealing with things.

This evening, she emptied a selection of snack bars from her bag onto the table to keep their energy levels up for a few more hours. McVeigh produced a pot of coffee and three mugs, and they settled in to review what information they had amassed in the first few hours of this case.

"OK, so what have we got?" Paton said. "Let's go through your notes, Ian, and take it from there. We'll give it an hour or so and then get a bit of sleep under our belts before we start into the serious interviews in the Shipbuilding Offices and in DePRec tomorrow morning." She paused and then added, "I've asked the Family Liaison Officer to call on the elderly mother tomorrow morning ... not too early so that she is properly awake. The good news is it will be Sandra so we may even get some useful info from her."

Sandra Woods was an experienced uniformed officer who had been an FLO for long enough to have developed considerable skill. She wasn't just good at delivering difficult messages but had a way of getting family members to open up as she unobtrusively made tea and set them at their ease. Paton was sure she was a definite bonus in any investigation.

McVeigh had his notebook at the ready. "Well, we know that the remains are those of Dr Helen Breen, a legal scholar who was one of the senior staff in the DePRec. She was clearly well-liked by the Head of Department, Professor Jackson Bell whose upset when the penny dropped as to the contents of the freezer would have been hard to fake. Don't you think?" He looked to his colleagues for affirmation but found none forthcoming.

Burrows dunked a chocolate biscuit in his coffee and merely said, "No assumptions, Ian. Let's just go with the facts for now."

McVeigh took this remark on board without any rancour, nodded and continued. "Right you are. We know that Helen Breen was registered on the passkey system, leaving the building at nine thirty-six on the last evening class of term, which was Thursday the 19th of December. Her family were reportedly of the opinion that she was away over the holiday period and so didn't miss her. That is according to Jackson Bell who made inquiries, or rather his departmental manager did, when Breen did not show up for work on Monday the 6th of January. We'll remind Sandra to check that out when she is there tomorrow. Today, that is, on Wednesday afternoon of the 8th of January, as part of a routine clear-up after the storm, the remains of Helen Breen were discovered in a chest freezer, secreted under some specimens belonging to the Marine Biology Centre. This was in the Titanic Quarter, in a different college building to DePRec, about a five-minute walk away. We have no information yet as to how the remains came to be in that place or how long she may have been there. What we do know is that a lot of effort went into covering her face and head. The College President, Professor Thompson, alerted the PSNI to the situation. A staff member, Dr Sam Carter, had informed him of an irregularity when she had been called to advise on how to secure the contents of the freezer. These contents had defrosted and increased in volume when the power was cut for a period of around thirty hours. Exact times need to be established when we interview the staff. Maintenance staff could not close the freezer and called for support from the academics. The call to the police by the President was made at four thirty today and we responded immediately. When an ID was located with the body the President contacted the relevant Head of Department, Professor Jackson Bell, who was brought into the picture later this evening. The entire freezer was promptly moved here to Grosvenor Road Barracks for thorough examination. The remains of Helen Breen have been given to the forensic pathologist for autopsy tomorrow morning. Professor Jackson Bell subsequently identified the body as that of his colleague Dr Helen Breen."

"OK," said Paton, folding and unfolding the silver-foil wrapper from the chocolate bar she had just eaten. "Let's see what we need to do straight away. We have FLO going over to Breen's mother as early as possible tomorrow morning. Bill, can you talk to Sandra in the morning about any items we want her to be alert to? Get her to gather whatever background she can. Where did Breen usually live? Was it with the mother or elsewhere and, if so, where? Were there any partners, close associates and so on. We will need to have a good look at her home for anything we can find about her work or private relationships. Who was she close to? We can collect her work and personal computers and any phone records that are available. Again, Bill, you get started on all that. Ian, you and I will go straight to the Shipbuilding Offices and then to DePRec. We will get the lie of the land there and draw up a schedule of interviews that fits around the teaching schedule as much as possible. I expect Bell may get a head-start on that in the morning. I will draft a statement for the Super to release to the press later in the morning and then we will try to keep them away from the college until we get a fuller picture. I am guessing Professor Thompson will be only too happy to help us with that so maybe their security will look after that task. Bill, you can have the pleasure of the autopsy in the morning and then join us in DePRec. Have an initial look at Breen's office first for any interesting stuff. We know she checked out of the system so I am not expecting that to be the murder scene but see what you can dig up. If there is anything suspect, we can get forensics in straight away. In that case I want a total sweep and a full report to me ASAP."

She rattled off the tasks as if she was reviewing a mental list prepared earlier but they knew she was carefully establishing the foundations of a thorough inquiry on the spot, and because that was the way she thought things through.

"What am I forgetting? Oh yes! Did Breen have a vehicle and where is it now?"

They decided that the precise location of Helen Breen's body would remain secret for the immediate future. The other freezers in the Marine Biology Centre were to be checked this afternoon to ensure that there were no other surprises. That entire floor was sealed until it could be thoroughly searched, and any evidence recorded. Staff and students were to be encouraged to believe that this was necessary because of storm damage that would take an additional day to repair. A forensics team would be deployed early next morning.

The team spent another hour or so making a detailed plan for the opening stages of their investigation and then made their way to their various homes to gather as much sleep as they could in the time available. They needed to be as sharp as could be for the hunt that was beginning.

14

Most of those returning to work in DePRec after the two days of exceptional closure were surprised at the unusual security presence on the front doors of their building. The business of swiping in and out was generally treated fairly casually and left very much to individuals to remember. Today, two uniformed security personnel were present and checking ID cards. For DePRec staff there was a printed memo from Professor Bell requesting the presence of all staff at a meeting in the Staff Common Room during the mid-morning break. People looked puzzled but were mostly too pressed for time to linger on the possible reason behind this unusual demand. Those without an early morning lecture engaged in some speculation over their coffee in the staff common room and then proceeded with their daily tasks without giving it any further thought.

In the administration office adjoining the Common Room, Mairéad Walsh was wearing her most serious expression. She had received a very early text from Jackson Bell to ask her to be at her desk as near to eight o'clock as possible "to deal with some extremely serious and urgent departmental business". She had arrived at seven forty-five and found the departmental head already there and waiting for her. He was never one that would be associated with a healthy complexion but his pallor this morning was ghostlike. Mairéad's instinctual sense of dread at these unusual signals deepened as he silently motioned to her to sit down.

"I am afraid that I have some extremely disturbing news to tell you, Mrs Walsh. We have a lot to do before the staff and students arrive so I will have to be more abrupt than I would like in telling this information to you."

Mairéad held her breath as he paused and braced himself as if for delivery of an awkward, prepared announcement.

"The mystery of Dr Helen Breen's non-appearance for work on Monday was resolved last night when I identified her body in the morgue of Grosvenor Road police station."

Mairéad's eyes widened and she inhaled deeply. "My good God! But how? What happened to her? Was she in an accident?"

"No, Mrs Walsh – there was no accident. Helen Breen has been murdered and this morning we will all unavoidably become embroiled in a full-scale murder inquiry." He paused as if to allow this reality to become better absorbed, then reconnected with the moment. "We have a lot to organise here so that the minimum of disruption to everyday college life occurs. I know that sounds heartless, but we will have to delay our grieving for the time being and facilitate the PSNI Murder Squad in their inquiry."

He looked at her almost imploringly, as if at a loss as to how to proceed. Then he seemed to find some of his characteristic sense of occasion and she watched the blood return to his cheeks as he faced the challenge ahead.

"Do you think that you will be able to help me, Mrs Walsh, in this most unusual circumstance where we have no precedent to follow?"

Mairéad's organisational instinct was called immediately into action and she breathed deeply and held her notepad and pencil at the ready. She exuded a comforting aura of competence that enabled him to assume his role with greater assurance.

"What needs to be done, Professor Bell?"

As Bell dictated a memo to be given to all staff on arrival at work, he felt the cold reality of the situation creep in on him. His initial response had been shock and a foggy sense of the horror of violent death. Of course, violence had been part of the Northern Ireland psyche for decades but for the most part it had remained at some distance from him. This was too close to find any comfort in even the small degrees of separation afforded to many people during the three decades of violence. The image of Breen's bloated and misshapen features was burnt into his mind's eye. He had been advised by Caroline Paton the previous evening to avoid going into detail about the circumstances of the location of the body when speaking to colleagues. The unusual conditions of Breen's death would remain undisclosed until more evidence was available. They were all suspects, he supposed, and the detectives would be hoping to catch someone out in their interviewing of department members. For a whole host of reasons, he dreaded the inevitable close scrutiny of his personal movements. Nevertheless, now the focus was on ensuring that departmental work carried on as normally as possible. The gossip machine would be well cranked up as soon as he had given the initial news at breaktime, but students must be as untainted by all of this as possible and that was his responsibility.

While Mairéad typed and printed out copies of memos to be distributed, Bell worked down the list he had made earlier. He called maintenance to set up the boardroom as an onsite incident room for Paton and her team. The detectives would need a list of all staff and their details and the schedule of lectures for the remainder of the week. Mairéad set to work drafting a timetable of interviews that would begin after break and continue until the following afternoon. She organised refreshments to be delivered at regular intervals and connected a PC and printer and two telephones with direct access to outside lines. Of course, they would have their own mobile phones but she wanted all possible bases to be covered.

It was still only twenty past eight and there would be a few further moments of calm before the day got into full swing.

"Call Liam Doyle, please, Mrs Walsh, and ask him to come to my office as soon as he is in college," said the professor. "As their representative, he will be useful as a link to students and any issues that arise for them because of this dreadful event."

Mairéad Walsh wondered what sort of impact news of Helen Breen's death would have on the young student rep. She liked Doyle well enough and knew that his childhood had been rocky. She had sons of her own and was sympathetic to their struggles to become reasonable men in a demanding world. At the Christmas drinks party in Professor Hartnett's house, she had noticed that Doyle and Helen Breen had been very much caught up in each other's company. There had been a lot of whispering and what some might have construed as inappropriate touching. They had been close by when she had been trying to talk to Hartnett's young son who obviously had learning difficulties. She had been sorry for the young lad trying to be sociable with a room full of strangers and not really managing too well, so she had spent some time with him. Doyle and Breen's antics had been a distraction and she had noted that others in the company had been watching them too.

Paused on the threshold, Bell seemed to have thought of something perplexing. "I am conscious that as soon as word of this is announced publicly that we will all be inundated with requests for information from the local papers and other media and probably just nosy busybodies who want to pry into something that doesn't concern them. I can't forbid people from speaking to them but I will need to advise against casual speculation and the type of rumour-spreading that does nobody any favours. Helen Breen has a family who will be directly impacted by what staff and students here say and we must make everyone aware of their ethical duty in that regard." He looked again at his list and back at Mairéad. "I am going to my office to make some serious notes for our meeting at breaktime. I trust you to deal diplomatically with all enquiries here. I will call on Professor Hartnett to make sure she has been brought up to date by Professor Thompson. She and Helen Breen knew each other at school and I expect this will be quite a blow for her. If anyone is asking for me, try to delay them until I speak to the whole staff team at coffee break. Otherwise, in cases of real need you know where to direct them." He turned to leave and then came back. "Thank you, Mrs Walsh, for making this nightmare seem a little bit more manageable. It will be a difficult few days and may even get worse after that but we will do our duty by the staff and students and let the PSNI get on with doing theirs. Who knows where this will all end?" He paused for a moment as if hoping that Mairéad Walsh might be able to offer some solace about the days to come but she remained wisely silent.

Alone in the office, Mairéad paused in dealing with the list before her to consider the bigger picture. Helen Breen was dead. Someone had actually killed her and it appeared from the imminent police presence that it might be a work-related issue. It wasn't a private affair but one that would bring the PSNI into DePRec in search of answers. She didn't like the picture that developed in her mind in response to these considerations. Who would have an interest in having Helen Breen out of the picture? Who might she have angered to the point of these extremes of violence? Might it have been an accident or a prank that went badly wrong? For all the times that she and Ralph had discussed Breen with extremes of vitriol, actually committing an act of brutality and bloodshed was another matter altogether. Ralph Wilson had a fiery character and Mairéad liked that spark in him immensely, but she couldn't believe that he could be a killer. She could, however, see all too clearly that Ralph might well be an object of some suspicion in all this and she instantly felt a desire to protect him from any unpleasantness.

15

Lost in consideration of the enormity of such a murderous act, Mairéad was taken by surprise when the office door opened and Alice Fox came in, slightly flushed from her run up five flights of stairs. She was exuding her customary energy and good humour which clashed tangibly with the atmosphere in the room.

She quickly picked up on Mairéad's perturbed expression and stopped in her tracks. "Everything OK with you, ma'am? The building has survived the flood anyway."

Mairéad motioned for her to close the office door and placed a finger on her pursed lips to communicate that she was about to impart a secret. Alice's attention was fully captured.

"You're going to hear this at breaktime in any case," Mairéad said, excusing her indiscretion in advance.

Alice waved the memo she had just collected at the

front door to show she was following. She sensed a familiar prelude to something of grave significance and the chill that accompanied it. Mairéad confirmed this immediately.

"*Something dreadful has happened*," she stage-whispered.

Alice immediately realised that this was indeed more than the usual daily dramatic performance. She remained still and fixed on Mairéad's perplexed gaze.

"Helen Breen has been murdered. Her body is in the morgue at the police station and Jackson had to identify it last night."

Alice was truly taken aback by the announcement. She had not expected anything from the memo beyond a New Year lecture about student numbers and some fallout from the previous days' storm closure.

"The detectives will be arriving in the Shipbuilding Offices at any minute to begin an inquiry. I don't know why they are going there but the murder seems to be something to do with work. That's all I know. It's all going to be announced at the meeting at breaktime but I know you won't betray the confidence. You understand these things. Just get on about your business as if you never heard a word I said. I just needed to let it out to somebody." And without allowing for any response Alice might make, she turned purposefully back to her schedule for staff interviews as if the lapse in discretion had never happened.

Alice went into her own office and closed the door. She sat at her desk and closed her eyes. This was surely a turn-up for the books. Her old life was encroaching on the new in a most unexpected way. Despite her new identity, she instantly moved into detective mode. Motive, means and opportunity – who might have had all three and acted upon them? Helen Breen had not been a likeable person. In fact, she was quite the opposite but that kind of workplace animosity didn't usually lead to a killing spree in a third-level educational institution. In her experience, people treated the hypocrisy and unpleasantness of colleagues as a reason to whinge and complain but not as an incitement to violence. This wasn't a falling-out in an inner-city housing project in Lowell, Massachusetts, where someone's drug patch was being poached and daggers were swiftly drawn, literally and metaphorically. Northern Ireland may have had a violent profile in the past but, as far as she knew, it was never a means of sorting out differences of opinion in higher education colleges.

From her office framed in glass Alice gazed out over the Titanic Quarter at the iconic vista of the Belfast Shipyard where, somewhat ironically, an ill-fated vessel had become a focus of a successful regeneration drive. The towering yellow gantries, biblically named Samson and Goliath, had come to symbolise much that was anachronistic and intransigent in the northern psyche. Despite the demise of the shipbuilding industry that meant the huge yellow cranes remained largely unused, they were beloved by locals as an iconic image of home for those who had made their lives elsewhere. Holding on to things that had outlived their sell-by date was not unique to Northern Ireland, Alice mused. It was a bad habit for individuals and social groups the world over but perhaps more common in places with a disputed identity and a divided culture. Giving up something did not come easy, and the logic of the attachment was rarely questioned as the entrenched position was taken and then became solidified.

Over the years Alice had thought long and hard about what actually provoked a person to knowingly and wilfully take a life. It was one thing when someone was high on drugs and driving recklessly. Accidental death was no less dreadful but more understandable than the premeditated act designed to permanently remove another human being from the planet. Feuds between criminal gangs were a frequent cause of death in her experience. Punishments were allotted with shocking alacrity by those who operated outside the law as a way of life. In the lives of most of the population, the degrees of anger or fear, or hatred, or jealousy that provoked such acts were not so easily arrived at. Helen Breen had somehow provoked just such an extreme reaction in someone she knew or had moved a stranger to inflict a death sentence on her. The idea was chilling to contemplate and Alice resigned herself to the fact that today she would not be very productive in addressing her own New Year list of resolutions. Her mind was already gripped by the violent death to which she found herself inescapably close.

In the course of her first semester in DePRec, little by little Alice had been acquiring the measure of her colleagues. This information was filtered through Mairéad Walsh whose interaction with them Alice overheard through the thin wall that divided their offices. There was a raft of part-timers who dropped by to discuss administrative matters with Mairéad. She could be overheard smoothing over difficulties, gleaning snippets of departmental gossip and generally holding court. Occasionally one of her admin assistants would leave the office across the corridor and call in person with a query but mostly these conversations took place by phone. The assistants were rarely seen and their work was controlled entirely by Mairéad. They were photocopy drones and behind-the-scenes copy typists with a high production record but little direct contact with staff.

The Professor called fairly frequently, by phone and in person, and Mairéad managed these visits with the utmost diplomacy. Alice noted that Jackson Bell had, in some respects, earned Mairéad's cautious respect and she made sure that DePRec was run in a way that caused him little recrimination from students, temporary teaching staff and other tenured colleagues. She spared him her more flamboyant performances and remained the essence of demure efficiency in his presence. Their relationship was not without warmth but the theatrics that Alice had heard bestowed on Ralph Wilson and a very small chosen few amongst the other college senior admin staff were not performed for the Head of Department. For his part, Bell remained entirely task-focused and rarely engaged in any discussion or revelation about his private life. What Alice did know was that Jackson Bell and Helen Breen had a relationship that surfaced frequently in staffroom gossip. Bell's unshakeable admiration for Breen was a puzzle to many who saw her as self-serving and disinterested in the matters of peace and reconciliation or student welfare. Only a few days previously she had witnessed his extreme distress at Helen Breen's failure to attend a meeting with him on the first day of term. It was unthinkable to him that she would neglect such a commitment and the depth of his reaction had given Alice cause for rumination at the time.

For Professor Janet Hartnett, Faculty Head of Human Sciences, Mairéad's level of delivery was raised to resemble the tone and pitch of a BBC Radio announcer. This involved much pursing and flexing of her upper lip and crisp articulation of every utterance.

Alice had discovered that the diverse range of radio stations she could access from her Belfast flat was a wonderful source of cultural information. Comparing media coverage of the same event locally on Radio Ulster, from the south on Radio Telifis Éireann (RTÉ) and from the UK mainland on BBC Radio 4 was a revealing study for an outsider to complete. The different cultural perspectives, and versions of spoken English, were quite fascinating. Mairéad Walsh's life experience made her fluent in a range of these accents. Her natural Dublin brogue was interspersed with northernisms that she had acquired through decades spent on that side of the border. For her grandest delivery she went full throttle for 'Anglo' landed gentry that was not too far off the textbook BBC delivery. All this she managed to do instinctively and without compromising her own status. She never became fawning or ingratiating and for that she won the admiration of Alice Fox for whom courage was a prized characteristic. Alice had had little or no dealings with Janet Hartnett except to have learned through Mairéad that Hartnett and Helen Breen had known each other at school and that Breen was capitalising on that connection to place herself favourably for an upcoming promotion. Alice had been in Dublin when Hartnett had hosted the departmental Christmas drinks party and so she had missed even the insight that such events afforded of a colleague's homelife.

From her listening post in the inside office, Alice soon learned that Mairéad and Dr Wilson shared more than a sense of humour. Wilson was a frequent telephone caller and Alice could distinguish the tone of voice that Mairéad reserved for these moments. The older woman's voice would deepen and her gurgling laughter often suggested that some salacious innuendo had been uttered at the other end of the line. When Wilson came by in person there was loud whispering and a conversation might end abruptly if someone else came in. It appeared that Mairéad kept a range of snacks in her top drawer with which she rewarded Wilson for his visit. Their conversations were peppered with the rustling of wrappings and munching sounds. Alice was already familiar with Mairéad's devotion to the rice cracker, which she called 'ceiling tiles' for their resemblance to polystyrene wall insulation from the 80s. She worked her way through packets of them and was keen that others should join in her habit. "Sure it's like eating fresh air for all the calorie content in them," she would coax. "Come to think of it, you need something more substantial than this. We need to fatten you up a bit," she would banter playfully with Alice. "You will need a bit of surplus to get through the Irish winter," and she would push the packet a little closer by way of encouragement. The sense of eating slightly salty Styrofoam was not altogether unpleasant and Alice frequently gave way to temptation.

The liaison between Mairéad and Wilson amused Alice, as did the fact that she was not being excluded from knowing about it. By dint of Mairéad's quasi-adoption of her, Alice's inclusion in this inner family unit meant that she quickly gained some insights about

DePRec personnel that otherwise might not have been so readily accessible.

Alice reflected now that Mairéad and Wilson had not guarded too much against what Alice overheard about their shared dislike of Helen Breen. The older woman had displayed a particular clamped-mouth pattern, accompanied by an exaggerated frown when Dr Breen passed by the office. Her response to Breen's request for information or her instruction about an admin task had been noticeably colder than towards other colleagues. This negativity had exceeded simple indifference or the careless observations she exchanged with most people. For her part, Breen had showed no sign of being aware of this and treated Mairéad almost mechanistically. Her indifference was scathing and had often provoked a barely concealed, frosty disdain in Mairéad.

Wilson had been more outspoken in his dislike of his colleague, wasting no opportunity to point out her shortcomings and his perception of her as inexplicably favoured by Jackson Bell. Alice recalled one typical outpouring from Wilson.

"I just can't fathom how an intelligent man is so utterly hoodwinked by her. She rarely delivers on the demands that Bell makes around contributions to publications and stuff like that. Yet she is complimented on every minor utterance no matter how facile. It's as if she has cast a spell on him that clouds his critical faculties." This outburst had been accompanied by a deal of spluttering, desk-thumping and laboured breathing.

"Don't give yourself a coronary over it, Ralphie," Mairéad had soothed. "That would hand her the professorship much too easily altogether."

"You're right, of course." Wilson had sounded downtrodden. "I am far too easily read to be in competition with that sly vixen and that's for sure. It just exasperates me the way she plays people and hoodwinks them. I can see absolutely clearly that she is feckless and egocentric, and I really can't fathom how others are oblivious." He had fallen into a silent reverie about the incomprehensible level of respect Bell held for Breen, then took up his subject again with renewed vigour. "One thing is certain anyway: the influence she has on Jackson allows her to carry on coasting with impunity. I've tried hinting at how flimsy her devotion is to the cause of peace and reconciliation, but it ends up sounding like sour grapes on my part while inevitably Jackson rushes straight to her defence. I was standing next to him the other day when I went in to discuss the trade union postgraduate bursary. His emails were open on his screen and there were at least ten messages from her in his recent mail. Everyone knows it's hard to get her to respond to anything and yet she is on to him about every small issue that arises. No wonder he thinks she is the most loyal, hardworking member of staff. She has him totally groomed."

On that occasion, Mairéad had gently coaxed him

with the exaggerated calm one might use with a petulant child. "Well, maybe you need to think about a change of tactics. If she is gaining all the ground with Bell and Hartnett, you will need to come up with some way of disrupting those advances."

Alice had thought that Mairéad suggested this a little half-heartedly.

"Ralph, you need to focus less on attacking Bell and Breen and more on establishing your own strengths as an international postgraduate programme coordinator. For the new post they want someone who will attract foreign, fee-paying people and inspire confidence about our support networks and academic excellence. Your constant critique of everyone and everything overshadows your many skills. It needs to be 'eyes on the prize', Ralphie! You need to demonstrate you have what it takes and not let her romp away with something that is yours on merit if not by right."

This had been sound advice and, without thinking, at her desk in the next room Alice had found herself nodding in agreement. Now, in the light of today's revelations she really hoped that Wilson had heeded Mairéad's advice and cooled his fury against Helen Breen. Alice had to admit to herself that in her cursory review of staff relations with the murder victim, Ralph Wilson did not emerge covered in roses by any means. She was sure that Mairéad Walsh and others would quickly arrive at the same conclusion.

16

In a leafy suburb of south Belfast, Lisa, the Filipino residential care worker of Agatha Breen, was finishing clearing away the breakfast things when the doorbell sounded. It was early for callers but Frank, eldest child of the Breen family, often sent small packages in the post from Australia to his mother. Sometimes it was a collection of drawings done by her grandchildren and a small treat like a headscarf or some indigenous printed cloth. He was the best of the bunch and, in Lisa's secret opinion, it was a shame he had settled so far away. The two adult children who lived closer to home were infrequent callers unless it was in their own interest. Lisa observed much but said nothing as old Mrs Breen was entitled to her dignity and she remained stubbornly loyal to her son and daughter, Michael and Helen. Michael had a tile-importing business and Helen was an academic. Neither was close to their mother although she held firmly to any details she had about their lives for the rare occasion when she could boast about their achievements to some of her dwindling number of friends.

Lisa opened the door to a uniformed woman police officer of mature years – in her mid-fifties, estimated Lisa, who was in and around that age herself.

"Is Mrs Breen at home?" the policewoman asked. "I have an urgent matter to discuss with her."

It was immediately clear that this was not a casual matter and Lisa nodded and smiled courteously and secretly hoped that documentation was not at issue.

Lisa glanced at the pile of post on a table inside the door and the envelope on top was franked at Belfast City College and addressed to Dr Helen Breen. "Her post," she said, as if considering what should be done with it.

Sandra Woods noted that Helen Breen evidently received her mail at the family home, which explained why this had been provided as her home address by the college.

"Please come in. Mrs Breen is in the living room, reading the morning paper," said Lisa, in the noticeable Belfast accent that suggested she had been there for a good many years.

She directed the constable into a large, comfortably furnished room off the hall which was bright, impeccably tidy and with just a hint of furniture polish hanging in the air.

An elderly woman sat in a winged armchair near French windows that opened onto a well-tended garden. A mobility aid sat to the right of her chair, ready to be deployed if need be. She was reading the local daily paper with glasses that sat halfway down her nose and peered over the top of them as her carer entered.

"Mrs Breen, you have a caller," announced Lisa and turned to the policewoman. "Would you like some tea?"

Before the woman could answer, Mrs Breen said, "Yes, Lisa. A pot of tea and some biscuits, please." Then, as Lisa withdrew, she turned her attention to the policewoman who stood facing her. "I suppose it's about the parking, is it?"

There had been issues on the road between neighbours in dispute about parking access and the local police had been involved in mediating. Mrs Breen enjoyed the chance to gain a little local gossip. She was almost entirely housebound now but relished the fact that others were in a conflict that had required police intervention on several occasions in the past.

"I am Constable Sandra Woods, Mrs Breen, and I am a Family Liaison Officer from Grosvenor Road Barracks." She extended her hand to Agatha Breen who was clearly welcoming the distraction her visit provided. Sandra sat at the end of the sofa nearest to Mrs Breen's armchair and decided to wait until the carer was back in the room before she delivered her difficult news.

"Are you living alone here, Mrs Breen?" she asked,

beginning the process of gathering as much background as she could for the investigation team.

The elderly woman did not seem opposed to entering into what she saw as a friendly chat. Nor did she show any sign that she feared any possible unpleasant purpose behind the policewoman's presence.

"Well, my husband died over twenty-five years ago," she began. "He ran a large refrigeration company and had a major heart attack one day. It was after completing a very substantial business deal that would have further increased the size of the company's dealings. Sadly none of the three children were interested in taking over and it was sold." This was articulated without any significant feeling as if the events were of no particular emotional consequence to the speaker. It was not unusual for elderly people to become very upset when recounting difficult events in the past, but Mrs Breen remained matter-of-fact in her tone.

Sandra noted the irony of the nature of the family business and the location of Dr Helen Breen's remains. She wondered if there might be some connection to a past family issue or if it were just a bizarre coincidence.

"I have three adult children," Agatha continued her dispassionate account. "Frank has been in Australia for a long time now. Michael is in the import and retail business here in Belfast and my daughter, Helen, is a legal academic who works in the Belfast City College. They are all quite successful in their chosen careers but that keeps them busy and I don't see too much of them." She paused as if considering this reality but again there was neither criticism nor recrimination in her voice.

Sandra wondered if Mrs Breen's apparent coldness was a personality feature or if her disassociation from her family members was a form of protection developed because of their absence from her life.

Lisa reappeared, carrying a tray, and proceeded to arrange the contents on a coffee table. When the tea was served and biscuits distributed, Lisa made as if to leave the room.

"Actually I'd prefer if your carer stayed with us, Mrs Breen." Sandra motioned for Lisa to sit beside her and made eye contact with Mrs Breen. "I'm afraid I have some difficult news to tell you." She paused to let the message sink in.

The elderly woman returned her gaze and for the first time showed a flash of alarm. The Filipino woman inhaled sharply.

"Mrs Breen, I am sorry to have to tell you that we have found the remains of a body in suspicious circumstances in the Belfast City College. Professor Bell, from your daughter's place of work, last night identified the remains as those of Dr Helen Breen, your daughter."

The woman's hand went to her chest and her carer went to her side. Both women looked bewildered as if they had accidentally stumbled into unfamiliar surroundings without knowing how they had got there.

Lisa took her employer's hand and stroked it. It was clear from Mrs Breen's surprised expression that this degree of intimacy was unusual in their relationship but she did not reject the act of kindness. She dropped her carefully honed dispassionate exterior and allowed the horror to register on her lined face.

Sandra allowed some time to elapse before adding, "I recognise that this is shocking news for you to receive, Mrs Breen, and I want you to know that I will stay with you and help you cope with this dreadful situation as best I can."

"I did wonder if something was wrong when she didn't call for her post before the start of the new term." Mrs Breen's voice was barely audible, as if she was speaking to herself alone. "Lisa, you must phone Michael. Sometimes I need my family even if they no longer need me."

Lisa looked questioningly at Sandra as if the locus of power in the room had altered suddenly. Sandra nodded assent and turned her attention to Mrs Breen.

Lisa left to make the phonecall from the landline in the hallway.

"Would you like to have a visit from your doctor, ma'am? He may prescribe something to help you deal with this most awful shock."

"Thank you, Constable, but I will self-prescribe a stiff brandy if need be. I am more resilient than I look."

There was a moment's silence, which Sandra was

happy to leave uninterrupted. She found that people opened up more when not put under pressure to do so.

Eventually Mrs Breen let out a lengthy sigh. "Poor Helen," she said quietly. "She was a teenager when her father died and she never really ever forgave him for abandoning her. She and I were never close and she just used the house here as a poste restante really. Lisa took occasional telephone messages for her from work and she called on Sundays to collect any mail that was here." She was silent again for a while. "I never really understood why her own address was a secret from those at work but I didn't ask either."

Sandra was making mental notes of all these revelations and would take the chance to write them down as soon as there was a moment.

Lisa returned and said that Michael was on his way. Mrs Breen made a disgruntled noise but said nothing.

Sandra waited and observed.

17

In the basement of Grosvenor Road Barracks, DS William Burrows waited patiently for the autopsy scheduled for nine to begin. It was already nine thirty but Cynthia Boylan was known for being a little flexible about time schedules. Just as Burrows was thinking he'd be better making his way to join the others at the Titanic Quarter she breezed in, whistling melodically.

"I know I'm a tad later than we planned, Bill, but I promise I'll be speedy with my slicing and dicing and you'll be away before you know it."

Burrow's experience of pathologists was that they were pretty callous in their manner of describing the nature of their work at the same time as being respectful of their subjects and meticulously objective in the quality of what they did. Maybe the cavalier talk was part of how they managed to do a job that was unthinkable for most people, without becoming emotionally drawn into the minutiae of each case. The police used similar defence mechanisms at times but they did not connote any lack of care about the work. He knew there was no offence intended by Cynthia Boylan's culinary references.

Within five minutes the pathologist was in her disposable paper jumpsuit and matching hairnet. She was equipped with a headset linked to a recording system that would ensure the entire process was captured in all its detail. Her young assistant pushed in a trolley bearing the remains of Dr Helen Breen and steered it into position beneath the tracks of strong lights that delineated a workspace. Then he applied the locking system. Since the identification of the remains the previous evening, the assistant had done the preliminary work of photographing, weighing and measuring the body. Clothing, jewellery and other personal effects had been removed, logged and packaged for safe storage. All the data would be centrally stored and available to the detectives online with the appropriate access codes.

DS Burrows was well used to being present at autopsies and had hardened himself to the whole procedure. With older remains like these, he wore a facemask imbued with lavender essential oils and positioned himself off to the side of the workstation where his view was sufficiently interrupted to spare him the most graphic details. Cynthia's commentary was enough to keep him abreast of all the salient facts and his presence allowed him to ask questions that the DI would expect answers to when he returned.

"We are looking at the remains of a white female in her late thirties, early forties. The hair is black and shoulder-length, showing minimal greying and evidence of traumatic disturbance and forced removal of several patches of hair at the roots. This is congruent with brutal handling of the hair and the head both prior to and probably after death. The eyes are green and there are no significant birthmarks, tattoos or other markings." Cynthia had become totally immersed in her task and her concentration was absolute.

Burrows found from experience that her voice took on a kind of chanting quality as she systematically worked through her fairly fixed agenda. Of course she assiduously followed new tangents as they occurred, but her process was routinely guided by the task of examining, dissecting and reconstructing the body of someone whose death poses questions that demand answers.

"Let's look at external evidence first. We know, without here delineating the pathological evidence, that the body has been frozen for a period of time and then defrosted as a result of the protracted power failure occasioned by the recent storm. We can see, and smell too, that the flesh had already begun to decompose prior to freezing."

"Can we gauge a time of death at all?"

"Sorry, no miracles available this time, Bill. We can

set down a number of facts that may eventually allow you to make educated guesses. For example, we can say that before freezing, bodily fluids had released as would be expected and the immediate signs suggest that death occurred between twenty-four and forty-eight hours before decomposition was arrested due to freezing. It takes a body considerable time to freeze so that needs to be taken into account. I will include all those hard sums in my written report."

"That's helpful, thank you." He made hurried notes as the process continued.

"Again prior to freezing, but some time after decomposition had already begun, the head was enveloped in a number of layers of plastic sheeting, secured with sellotape. This was certainly due to the extreme, and rather messy damage caused to the back of the head through substantial penetrating trauma. Moving the body from the place of death would have required quite some clean-up. Cause of death was the penetrating trauma that led to cerebral oedema, which in turn led to catastrophic brain impairment and loss of life. When we get to the internal exam, the brain will reveal more of the detail of that sad story." She broke off from her perusal of the body and looked at Burrows for the first time since the postmortem examination had begun. "There is no evidence of resistance or struggle on the part of the victim. Let's put it this way, Bill. This was a surprise attack but not an accident. The force needed to cause the death of this woman was far exceeded. In fact, we can say that the trauma-inducing actions were continued well after death had already occurred. There are conclusions to be drawn from that fact."

"Any chance of anything useful surviving the period of freezing? Like might we get prints from the tape or the bags used on the head?" Bill Burrows was ever hopeful.

"Some latent prints can survive freezing or being submerged in water over a period of time but I wouldn't hold out any hope here, Bill. In his preliminaries, George has already established that the perp or perps were equipped with gloves, at least by the time the head wrapping was being done. The materials used were standard issue in most institutions so nothing particular there but, of course, we will be ever watchful. We know that black plastic bin bags have identifiable individual markings but they will only allow you to pinpoint the supplier and that won't be of much use to you. One company probably supplies every educational establishment in the country. Now, where was I?"

She returned to her task with the usual total focus. Every so often she asked George to photograph something for inclusion in the file that might help the investigation. There was no sign of sexual assault or indeed any interference with the body other than the ravages visited to the back of the head. The body was turned over, this back view revealing the extent of the fatal damage to the skull, the brain and the spinal column.

Cynthia intoned onwards: "The skull is fractured in multiple places and all of the internal protective sub-cranial layers have been breached. Shattered fragments of the skull bone have ruptured all three meninges, that is the cushioning layers between the skull and the brain itself. There will have been bleeding and grey and white matter at the scene and probably on the clothing of the person inflicting the injury. In order to muster the pressure to cause such injuries they must of necessity have been in close proximity to the body. Close enough for it to get very unpleasant."

Burrows inquired as to the possible means of inflicting these injuries.

Cynthia puckered her mouth, inhaled and exhaled deeply through her nose. "The level and concentration of damage to the bone suggests that the head was repeatedly brought into contact with a smooth, hard surface. There was extreme focus and control exercised to repeatedly target the same point on the skull with such precision. These are not randomly positioned injuries that would result from aiming a weapon at the skull. It would be unlikely to have such a precise intensity of damage in the one area. I will know better when I have the brain extracted and can see the exact nature and shape of the damage. For now I am thinking that the head has been the moving part in this attack.

The head has been smashed against a hard, fixed surface and with relentless brutality. The pattern of shattering of the bone indicates a smooth rather than a sharp façade."

After the external examination was complete and the remains returned to a supine position, Boylan slipped a headrest under the mid-shoulder area of Helen Breen's waxy, discoloured body. This caused the upper part of the corpse to tip backwards with the chest area slightly elevated. From this position, she made a Y-shaped incision beginning from each shoulder to the sternum and from the apex of that point vertically to the pubic bone. In this way the body could be opened to reveal any evidence inside. In fact, in this case, there was little to be gleaned from the study of the internal organs. It was when the body was once again turned over and the brain was the focus of attention that things became really interesting. The rear and top of the skull had suffered the brunt of the attack with other aspects of the autopsy only seeming relevant when it came to trying to establish time of death.

When the brain was removed Cynthia held it aloft on the palm of her hand. "Look at this pattern of impact, Bill! Here's one favour the freezing process has done you!"

The marking on the brain itself had been preserved through the freezing process and confirmed that the repeated and frenzied contact was with an unyielding, curved surface.

"If, as I suspect," continued Cynthia, "the head was controlled by the assailant and battered repeatedly against the solid surface, then that required a certain amount of strength and stamina. Mind you, the adrenalin that rage pumped through the system would have fuelled both. I can't make any assertions about gender because, frankly, it could have been anyone with some knowledge of head injuries and a reasonable amount of energy and muscle development."

With the promise of Cynthia's completed report by the end of the day, Burrows left the pathology section and headed straight to the College to join in the process of interviewing the staff there.

On the way, he called Sandra Woods from the car and arranged to contact her later when she was free to talk. She indicated that she had already made some progress that would be useful to them. Burrows relished the sense of momentum at the outset of an enquiry when all systems were on go and he was at the heart of it.

18

Those listening to the mid-morning news would have heard a short item that announced that the PSNI were beginning an investigation into the circumstances surrounding the discovery of some human remains in suspicious circumstances in the Titanic Quarter. In the maintenance section of the Belfast City College and the Marine Biology Department, where Caroline Paton and Ian McVeigh had already begun their questioning, this caused less surprise than in other quarters.

On the fifth floor of the Human Science's Campus of Belfast City College, the staff of DePRec gathered as instructed in the Staff Common Room at eleven o'clock. Alice had gone in a little ahead of time and taken an empty seat in the corner with a wide view of the room. She was interested in seeing the impact of Bell's announcement on all those present and on some in particular. Most had armed themselves with a cup of tea or coffee and were already seated, chatting vigorously, when Jackson Bell entered the room. His demeanor was even more serious than usual. The Head of Faculty, Janet Hartnett, took up a position slightly behind the departmental leader. With her advance indication of the purpose of the gathering, Alice remarked that Hartnett's face was set in a perfect blend of concern and composure. She was skilled at presenting the appropriate public demeanour and her background in working with those in the caring professions clearly had contributed to this. At the last moment, Mairéad Walsh's admin team and the IT technicians slipped through the door and stood somewhat timidly just inside. Mairéad Walsh herself was not present but, as Alice had observed, she was covering the administrative office next door where Caroline Paton and Ian McVeigh were waiting for Professor Bell's signal to join the meeting. This unusually comprehensive staff attendance caused those waiting to speculate even more widely about what was to come. Without being asked, they came naturally to order as soon as the Common Room Door was closed. All eyes were fixed on the DePRec head.

Jackson Bell politely acknowledged the presence of his superior. "Professor Hartnett has asked to attend this meeting to demonstrate her solidarity with DePRec staff at this time." Eyebrows raised, brows furrowed and questioning expressions settled on the faces of those gathered. Bell carried on with apparent reluctance. "I will not beat about the bush. I have asked you all here to share some shocking news with you."

By now, a total hush filled the room as all eyes fixed even more firmly on Bell.

"The remains of our colleague Dr Helen Breen were discovered by a member of the Marine Biology staff yesterday in another campus of the college."

There was a sharp, collective intake of breath.

"I had the unhappy duty last night of identifying her remains."

At this point he paused and Alice watched as he summoned sufficient self-possession to continue.

"The police were called and a murder investigation is already under way. I have very little detail other than this and am advised that it would be inappropriate anyway to share what I know with you at this moment. When you have had time to think about this you will understand why that is the case." He quelled a potential outburst of comments with a raised hand and a particularly stern look. "I will shortly ask the senior Murder Squad detective and one of her team to join us here when she will outline what we need to do to help this inquiry. But, first of all, I must say that despite this unspeakable reality, we must endeavour to continue business as usual. Classes must continue and students too must be supported at this time. There will be those in the media who will want to talk about Helen Breen with a view to sensationalising what for her family and friends and we, her colleagues, is an out and out tragedy. I hope that no one present here will choose to be part of that circus."

He paused at this point and looked meaningfully around the room. He sighed deeply and continued.

"We must support one another in dealing with this. I will prepare an announcement that can be shared with students and others who need to know what has happened. Mr Doyle, our student representative, will undoubtedly contribute to dealing with any issues that arise in the student body. Otherwise, we must somehow learn to come to terms with this most heinous truth and in whatever way possible assist the police with their investigation. There will be time in the days and weeks to come to pay fitting tribute to Helen Breen but for the moment we must do what the authorities require of us. Both Professor Hartnett and myself will be available to you if needed and will try our best to answer questions or find someone who can. I imagine," he faltered here a little, "that to some of those questions there may be no answer at this time."

At this point he signalled to one of the admin staff who left the room and returned with Mairéad Walsh and the two police officers.

Alice had a better chance now to observe DI Caroline Paton than when she had passed by her in the office next door on her way to the meeting. She was of medium height and looked as if she kept herself physically fit. Alice knew this could be a challenge in the life of a busy detective and she admired those who resisted the temptation to give way to sloth. In her experience they were the minority. Paton exuded confidence and while Bell did the introductions she scanned the room carefully much as Alice Fox herself was doing. In her easy composure she managed to convey the impression of competence and determination and Alice decided on the spot that Caroline Paton was probably excellent at her job.

"This is Detective Inspector Caroline Paton of the PSNI Murder Squad and Detective Constable Ian McVeigh. Detective Sergeant William Burrows will join them later today. Please now give your full attention to DI Paton."

Bell stood aside for the detectives and took his place beside Janet Hartnett. She nodded encouragingly to him and allowed her hand to rest gently on his arm for a moment.

Caroline Paton surveyed the room which held about twenty-five people who had clearly absorbed something of a shock on hearing the news of Helen Breen's death. For her, the idea that potentially one person present was less shocked than the others was to the forefront of her thoughts.

"Good morning, staff of DePRec. I would like to begin by sympathising with you on the loss of your colleague and to assure you that we will do everything we can to solve this crime as rapidly as possible."

Alice saw that Mairéad Walsh was looking towards Ralph Wilson with obvious concern.

"I will be brief and to the point as I know some of you must shortly return to your classes. My fellow detectives and I have established an incident room in the boardroom on this floor. In the next few days we will be interviewing all department staff and gathering evidence that we hope will lead to the discovery of those responsible for the violent murder of your colleague, Helen Breen. A schedule of interviews has been drawn up with the kind assistance of Mrs Walsh and has already been emailed to all of you. A copy has also been posted on the noticeboard in the office next door. We have taken your lecturing commitments into account and want to disrupt the departmental business as little as possible. However," she paused and looked gravely around the room, "our concern is entirely focused on solving a murder and that takes precedence, for us, over other matters. Someone has committed a brutal and fatal attack and our task is to find that person before further harm is done. I put it to you, that it is absolutely in everyone's interest to help us in that task."

The sudden implication that there might be further killing tangibly chilled the room and those within it. Paton had succeeded in getting her audience on track.

DI Paton nodded to McVeigh who looked at his watch and said, "It is now eleven twenty. The first interview will begin at eleven thirty. When our colleague, Sergeant Burrows, joins us later we will be able to have two interviews happening simultaneously. You will see this is reflected in the schedule. Thank you all for your ongoing cooperation."

There followed a short exchange between Bell, Hartnett and the detectives after which they all left the room.

The admin staff and technicians left immediately and those remaining moved from stunned silence to whispered expletives and then noisier processing of the most unexpected of events. People consulted their phones and laptops for the email of the interview schedule and those at the top of the list experienced a flurry of nerves at the unknown situation into which they faced. While some moved reluctantly toward their eleven-thirty lecture, others sat semi-stupefied and tried to process what they had just heard. DePRec had all of a sudden taken on the characteristics of a film set in which they were all now actors.

Alice had watched with close interest the reaction to Jackson Bell's announcement. With the benefit of forewarning she had not experienced the same thunderbolt as the others present. Ralph Wilson had been standing, pipe in hand, beside the door to the outside deck area, as if ready for a quick getaway. He had blanched as Jackson had uttered the words, "the remains of our colleague Helen Breen". Wilson had initially looked incredulous and then, perhaps conscious of his well-known acrimonious relationship with Breen, he had appeared anxious and begun shaking his head from side to side as if rejecting the message altogether. By the time the DI had taken the floor he had assumed the blank expression of one who cannot locate any suitable response and affects an unconvincing concerned expression. He quickly became visibly anxious and Alice could see that the days ahead could get tough for him.

As soon as the meeting broke up, Wilson headed out immediately for a smoke and Alice observed carefully that others were watching his reaction and commenting under their breaths and behind hands. She really hoped he was able to account for himself over the period when the killing had taken place. Despite her interest in her colleagues' response to the news of Helen Breen's killing she too left the room as quickly as possible, almost colliding with Liam Doyle on the threshold. His shoulder-length Titian-red hair contrasted sharply with his uncharacteristic pallor. Alice was used to the easy, capable approach he took to his daily lot of looking after student interests and his distressed appearance startled her. Doyle had met her and acted as guide the first time she had visited the EXIT project which was located near his home in the west of the city. He told her that he had done some of his Master's research project there and knew the youth leader, Hugo. However, she was happy that he had not interfered in her meeting, leaving her at the door and heading off about his own business. Alice was aware that Liam Doyle was close to Helen Breen and had overheard him speak up on her behalf in staff-room conversations. That had surprised her a little and she had briefly wondered if there was something between them beyond the demands of work and student welfare.

"Terrible news," he gasped.

But Alice wasn't feeling like having that discussion just at that moment. In her view, there were definitely times when it was best to say nothing and, with a nod, she continued on towards her office next door.

"Will I bring you a cup of tea?" she asked Mairéad who was looking deeply shell-shocked behind her desk.

"No thanks, lovey," she replied. "I've just eaten a whole packet of ceiling tiles and I'm feeling a bit bloated." She had a pile of handwritten papers beside her and was clearly embroiled in preparing Jackson Bell's announcement to students and organising the many additional things that having a murder inquiry on the premises brought with it.

Alice retired to her own room and consulted her emails to see when she would be meeting the detectives face to face. She was scheduled for three o'clock that afternoon so she wouldn't have long to wait. She was in an interesting position in relation to this new turn-up for the books. It felt as if all her worlds were colliding here in this most interesting of places.

19

The interviewing process was under way and Bill Burrows reported, as planned, to the fifth floor of the college. He collected keys from Mairéad Walsh in the admin office and went first of all to Breen's office. He put on a pair of latex gloves from his jacket pocket and carefully opened the door. The office was at the end of a small, ill-lit corridor off the main quadrangle but as the door opened inwards the light from the glass corner space flooded the room. The panoramic view was of the Belfast cityscape with the Cave Hill in the background and an ice-blue winter sky that was breathtaking. Bill paused and passed his enquiring eyes over the office that had been the workplace of Dr Helen Breen. At first glance, everything appeared ordered. The desk facing a glass wall was empty except for a telephone, a blank pad of paper and a pen. Maybe the desk is too empty, Bill mused, and inhaling deeply was struck by the distinct odour of cleaning products. The polished wooden floor was gleaming and there was the faint outline of pictures that had been removed from the central concrete pillar. A still shot of images splattered with brain matter flashed through Burrow's mind and he grimaced. He relocked the office and returned to the admin office, apologising for disturbing Mrs Walsh a second time.

"Can I ask you, Mrs Walsh, if these offices have been industrially cleaned over the holiday period?"

"They have not, Detective Sergeant Burrows," she responded without hesitation. "Dr Breen was inclined towards a minimalist décor and was always reasonably tidy, and there has been no special cleaning over the break. Of that I am certain."

"In that case I would like now to seal that office until such time as we can do a deep forensic examination. I will hold on to the keys and see if I can get forensics in after close of business this evening. They will cause less fuss if they come after hours." He was heading out of the room when he turned back. "Did Dr Breen work on a laptop and would she normally have carried a briefcase or a handbag?"

"Oh, Detective Sergeant, Helen Breen was a statement-bag carrier. Something large and very expensive. That and her mobile phone were permanently in her presence."

Burrows thanked her and he headed off towards the

boardroom to make a call into Forensics at HQ and report this new development to DI Paton.

In her inside space Alice Fox was processing all she had overheard and concluding that DS Burrows had just identified the possible place of death of Helen Breen. Through the thin dividing wall between herself and Mairéad Walsh she could sense the impact of this latest development on the older woman.

For now, they both decided to keep their responses to themselves.

Caroline Paton and McVeigh were doing a double act and between interviews Bill Burrows briefly let them know what had emerged from the postmortem and from his examination of Breen's office. He knew they would have a lengthy meeting at the end of the day to pool their findings and plan the next stages so he kept the detail for then. Today would be a long day, as DI Paton liked to cover as much ground as possible at the outset of an inquiry. They knew now that they had lost valuable time over the holiday period when the college buildings had been closed for two weeks and this added to the urgency to make rapid advances now.

After a short interlude they regrouped and Burrows and McVeigh took one list and Paton began on a second group of names in a small vacant office space beside the boardroom. By close of play tomorrow they planned that they would have done an initial trawl of all DePRec staff.

20

At two-fifty Alice Fox headed towards the boardroom for her scheduled interview with Caroline Paton. The door of the small adjoining office was open. Alice knocked and looked around the door. Caroline, engrossed in her notes, beckoned to her to come in and sit down. Alice admired the moss-green shade of the other woman's eyes and internally scolded herself for mixing business and pleasure.

"I'm Alice Fox," she said quietly and extended her hand to the DI. "I am a visiting scholar from the City University New York. Prior to becoming an academic I was a detective in the Lowell Police Department in Massachusetts. I am saying that to explain that I understand what is happening here. This is unfortunately a familiar scenario for me."

Paton's stern expression softened and she smiled

tiredly. "We have a lot of ground to cover, Dr Fox, so there will not be much time for the friendly personal exchange that we would both enjoy now, I think." The senior detective paused momentarily here and then brought herself back to the purpose of the meeting. "I am interested to hear your views on the current situation, Alice." She smiled to acknowledge her relaxation of the formalities. "It is valuable for us to have another professional in situ. Perhaps we can call on you for context clarification if need be?"

Alice nodded. "For sure, Detective Inspector. Anything I can do, although I am still something of a rookie here in Belfast." She had already thoroughly evaluated Paton and decided that she could like and respect her. The woman was direct and did not prevaricate or play games in her search for information. Her ego was definitely not blocking out the important aspects of the situation as could be the case with those who were near the top of the police career structure. Paton's sharp focus was something that Alice identified with and she could see that she and Caroline Paton would have much in common were they ever to meet outside of the workplace.

In response to Paton's inquiry about her involvement in end-of-term activities, Alice was happy to recount that she had been at a conference in Dublin, after which she had spent the holidays hillwalking in Wicklow. She had not been present for the end-of-term drinks in Janet

Hartnett's Crawfordsburn home and indeed she had heard little or nothing about how that event had gone.

She explained that her return had been very much affected by the storm and the days of exceptional closure. She recounted in some detail the puzzle posed for Bell and others when Helen Breen did not appear for work as planned on the first day of term. Paton asked her how she would interpret Professor Bell's reactions on that first day. Was he surprised or annoyed? Was his reaction excessive in any way? Alice replied honestly that she had judged his response to be a little disproportionate at the time. At the same time she had rationalised it by acknowledging that the first day of a term could be stressful for people. Often people had made resolutions for the New Year and had unrealistic expectations of what they could achieve. At that point she had smiled and beat her breast saying, "Mea culpa!" and they had both laughed.

The interview held no surprises for Alice and she found Paton to be as able and astute in her work as she had initially judged. She shared all she could about her limited contact with Helen Breen and was honest about what she had observed about the level of contempt with which some of her colleagues had regarded Dr Breen. The expected battle for the new professorship did not appear to be news to the DI. The acrimony between Ralph Wilson and Breen was publicly known in DePRec and Alice had no doubt that information would have been passed on to the detectives by some if not all of her colleagues. Alice was cautious in not disclosing details of conversations overheard between Mairéad Walsh and Wilson. Paton was good at her job and she would glean those items for herself without Alice betraying the camaraderie Mairéad Walsh had shared with her. Paton asked her about Breen's life outside of work and Alice realised she knew nothing whatsoever about the woman.

As the exchange drew to a finishing point, Caroline Paton held Alice in her steady gaze. She was clearly judging whether to trust her and take their conversation to a deeper level.

"I'm going to share some stuff here that is just between us – colleague to colleague," she said. "We are undoubtedly dealing with extremes of rage in the case of the killing of Helen Breen. This was not a simple bit of competition over a promoted post but rather a deep-rooted enmity that unleashed a level of brutality I would not like to see repeated. We want to catch this perpetrator quickly before someone else gets hurt."

"She definitely was not well liked by all her colleagues," Alice said thoughtfully, "but I agree with you, peer rivalry and disputes in the workplace are not why people commit murder. If it were the case, then murder would be a much more commonplace occurrence." She paused to reflect on what her instincts were telling her. "I come from an environment where murder is much more a daily occurrence than in Northern Ireland, despite your reputation for violent conflict. I would be very surprised if this is a simple case of workplace ill feeling driving someone over the edge. That just doesn't seem likely to me but I will be watchful and I promise to come back to you if something leads me to change that view."

Paton seemed satisfied with that pledge. She gave Alice a card from the pile in front of her. "I will be happy to hear from you any time, Alice Fox, however seemingly small the catalyst for that contact may be."

She nodded several times to reinforce the sincerity of her statement and Alice had that rare feeling of having met someone for whom constant explanations of one's position were superfluous. She mused that her list of potential friends in Ireland would soon fill the fingers of one hand.

Alice smiled and extended her hand to Paton and returned to her office to contemplate the updated scenario.

Later, she replayed the interview with DI Paton and the perspective she had shared on her now deceased colleague. From the very beginning Alice hadn't warmed to Breen and had a growing impression that under the surface DePRec was really quite far from being aptly named. Towards the end of her first week in the college, Breen had emailed to ask Alice to call and see her. What ensued had not been an unusual exchange between a senior lecturer and a visiting post-doc and yet Alice had found it gave her cause for some dislike of the more senior woman. Helen Breen demonstrated that she had informed herself about Alice's academic interests and enquired if she would be interested in giving a guest lecture to Breen's postgraduate law module students. Not one to be easily played, Alice was surprised about how flattered she felt to be asked. On reflection, she had probably agreed too readily and Breen had looked quietly victorious. Alice realised a little too late that she had just given Breen a free night off when she would take her class for her whilst supposedly feeling grateful for being given the opportunity. There was no question of payment, as this would be seen as part of her post-doc position. When the offer of some student tutorial work was added to the available options Alice was more ready with a response.

"I will say 'no' to that," she responded. "I have made financial provision for myself this year so that I can focus on my own work without the need for additional earning."

"I'm sure you have," Breen said and, whatever that comment meant, Alice knew her refusal to be compliant had caused some displeasure.

She had replayed the comment to herself several times and failed to understand the implied familiarity with her or her circumstances. She was slightly unnerved by a sense of Breen's desire to control her that lay thinly veiled behind a seemingly indifferent exterior.

Alongside the extreme response that she now knew

Helen Breen evoked in Ralph Wilson, Alice was clear that she herself had caught a glimpse of something fundamentally unpleasant in Breen's character. She had determined then to give her as wide a berth as possible and to keep her focus on her own work rather than becoming embroiled in the battle that was being played out in DePRec around the forthcoming promotion. She knew that academia could be a hostile place to be and wanted none of that to intrude on her own goals for the year ahead. She had given the lecture with a good grace and otherwise tried keep out of harm's way.

Back at her desk and gazing out over the Belfast landscape Alice became immersed in contemplating what she knew about DePRec. She realised that in her interview with Caroline Paton she hadn't thought to mention that the conference she'd attended in Dublin had been organised by the founder of DePRec, Tara Donnelly, whom she had found to be interesting company. The annual Harm Convention had been a small and congenial gathering with none of the pomposity and posturing that often accompanied such academic events. They had eaten an evening meal together at the end of each day's proceedings and the conversations there and later in the staff common room bar had been lively and thought-provoking. During these evenings, Tara Donnelly had been especially hospitable to her and had been interested to hear what was happening in DePRec, where she had her own history. She had talked freely about her early shared work with Ralph Wilson and Jackson Bell but had not made any comment about Helen Breen even though their paths must have overlapped. Alice had noticed that omission at the time and reconsidered it now in the light of Helen Breen's killing.

Alice and Tara had quickly established an understanding based on a shared view of the world. On a personal level, they had spent a pleasant day hillwalking together during Alice's holiday sojourn in Manor Kilbride. Tara had driven up to meet her on a bright frosty morning towards the end of the year and they had climbed Djouce together. The sky was ice-blue and there was a weak low sun that didn't really give off much warmth but was uplifting nonetheless. The air was chill and there was little wind. Apparently this was a rare blessing as often you could lie into the gale with your full body weight and be held firmly upright.

The two women were both fit and managed to sustain a good stomping pace whilst chatting amicably at the same time. The ground was frost-hardened and the going rendered even easier by a boardwalk made of railway sleepers laid lengthways, side by side and covered with chicken wire for enhanced grip. This created a one-man's pass over the boggy terrain. Tara explained that it was a popular walk with Dubliners and the pathway had been introduced to protect the local flora that was threatened by the route being overwalked. The views over Lough Tay and the Powerscourt estate were breathtaking. As she took in the impressive landscape, Alice had reflected on how much had happened since her first aerial view of these brackeny Wicklow Hills when she had approached Ireland for the first time, four months previously.

After their walk, in Alice's rental cottage, they had shared a pot of tea and toasted some bread on the open fire. The toasting fork had beckoned from the hearth and the woman of the house's blackberry jam completed the simple but scrumptious food. Alice was interested in the accounts of DePRec's beginnings and the picture she formed, from Tara's descriptions, of Belfast back in those days was gripping. There had been the tantalising possibility of peace alongside continuing, horrific sectarian and state terror.

Gradually, Tara had relaxed enough to share some of the story of her hasty departure from DePRec. Back in the day, when Tara had been pivotal in its formation, all shades of opinion had been keen to influence the direction taken by the new centre. The weight of academic opinion was viewed as credible and convincing and published work was seen to provide a solid evidence base and some degree of moral endorsement.

Every shade of opinion, political or dissident, wanted to have such academic validity given to their standpoint and DePRec was pushed and pulled in many directions.

Research carried out often involved deep immersion in local communities to ascertain the impact of the Troubles on day-to-day life. For example, a study of local women might uncover sensitive details about behaviours within families and localities that would be of interest to those in the establishment from whom such detail was concealed. The confidentiality and anonymity assured by research ethics protected disclosure of such findings in ways that would identify individuals and place them at risk from the authorities. But the intelligence forces charged with discovering what happened behind the scenes in communities found the work of DePRec of very great interest.

As well as the official collaborative work undertaken by DePRec in the public eye, Tara explained that there had been other parties whose interference had been more coercive than cooperative. Some of those keen to enlist the services of the head of DePRec had wielded more power and influence than others. Dependent on funding and on community research partnerships, Tara Donnelly had found herself in an increasingly precarious employment climate and despite her commitment to the work had finally decided to call it a day. Without specifying the exact detail, Tara had made it clear that more than frustration, it was actually terror that had made her leave the North and seek a more tranquil existence on the other side of the border. Not for the first time, Alice Fox was reminded of the disturbing covert forces that were operating in Northern Ireland, some of which were undoubtedly state sanctioned. She sensed that this was an exercise of power that was utterly chilling and potentially life-threatening.

It had been completely dark by the time Tara stood up to head for home and Alice had been glad not to have to leave the warmth of the log fire to make the dark drive back down into the city. On her own again, she had reflected on what Tara had shared about the shadowy history of DePRec. She had the distinct impression that there were still more upsetting elements of Tara's story in the North that she hadn't yet disclosed. For her part, Alice respected people's privacy probably more than most and she was able to let that rest. People revealed themselves at their own pace in relationships and it was not Alice's way to push against that.

21

What made academia tolerable to Alice Fox was the potential it offered to introduce the realities of people's experience into what counted as significant knowledge. She had listened long enough to those deemed to be knowledgeable and those whose views were not valued, to know where she placed her trust and confidence. Now that DePRec was a crime scene in its own right Alice saw with even greater clarity the irony of how crime was perceived by most people. They had no hesitation in accepting that the young people in the EXIT project were at risk of becoming offenders but met the possibility that the trusted academic elite might be involved in crime with widespread shock. She struggled with how the glaring prejudice and hypocrisy of this was not often seen. Alice believed deeply that most people did their best in life but that some were much better resourced to deliver on those aspirations and that was where the great injustice lay. So far, Belfast had proved to be a fascinating place to continue her study of restorative justice and her first three months had been fruitful in terms of the progress she had made.

She remembered clearly the evening back in September when she had first visited the EXIT youth project. It had been a significant journey in many ways. She had left the generously redeveloped Titanic Quarter, crossed the Lagan Bridge and made her way to the Castle Street area of the city from which she would access a black taxicab to West Belfast. Here there was no sign of investment and renewal. There were street vendors selling fruit and vegetables and some cheaply packaged plastic children's toys. They stood behind their carts calling boisterously to each other and anyone who showed any interest in buying. Here there was no gloss and glitter but ebullient humanity in abundance.

Alice had read the history of the Black Taxi movement and approached the central terminus with interest. In the early 70s the public bus transportation system was often disrupted. Buses and other vehicles were hijacked and burned and roads were often impassable. The London hackney cabs were introduced as an alternative form of local transport. They came to be known as the Peoples' Taxis and were shared by those travelling different routes in the west of the city. Each person paid a small sum of money and taxis picked up and deposited passengers on request. Initially formed on the nationalist Falls Road, the system was later replicated in the neighbouring loyalist Shankill area. Subsequently, with the advent of peace, Black Taxis continued to serve travellers in poorer communities and had diversified to offer guided 'political' tours to those visiting Belfast in the wake of the Good Friday Agreement.

That first evening, Alice had arranged to meet the DePRec student representative Liam Doyle outside the entrance to the Falls Cemetery and he would accompany her to the location where she would have her first face-to-face meeting with the local youth and community group. Doyle lived locally and knew the project from his own research. He had been accommodating of her need for some local knowledge and had arranged to meet her at the end of her taxi journey. She had taken her seat in the back of the black cab wedged between a woman with a child on her lap and a girl in a brown school uniform. An elderly couple sat on the fold-down seats opposite. They were heatedly discussing something but the accent was strong and Alice soon zoned out and focused on observing the urban landscape that they were passing through. In the background, the driver's radio was broadcasting a local news programme but distinguishing any coherent message was virtually impossible. They made slow progress in the evening rush-hour traffic and at certain moments they passed by wall murals that might well have featured in Jackson Bell's popular photographic studies of political wall paintings.

The woman beside her noted her interest. "Yer not from here, are yeh, love?" she announced more than asked.

"I'm from Massachusetts, ma'am," Alice replied, meeting the woman's open stare with a wide smile. "I am in Belfast for this year to study some of your projects."

"Oh, is that right? There's a lot to study here for sure." She laughed at her own comment and Alice understood the sarcasm and joined in.

"Massachusetts has a lot to learn too," she said. "I'm going to visit a youth club on your Glen Parade. I hear it is well known for making a difference in the local community."

"It would take something to sort out some of them young fellas!" the woman quipped with conviction. "Just mind your purse while yer in there. They'd take the eye outta yer head and come back for the other one. I'll let yeh know when we get to yer stop."

With that she turned her attention to the child on her lap who was whinging constantly and clutching at her mother's hair. The woman produced a soother from somewhere, sucked it in the interests of hygiene and lodged it in the child's open mouth. Her small lips closed around it and she settled into her mother's arms.

"She's starvin'," the woman announced. "I was out longer than planned and now the tea's gonna be late too."

The statement begged no response and Alice returned to looking at the passing views. Small shops and poor-looking side streets sat alongside large hospital buildings and what might have been a school or religious community, in leafy grounds surrounded by substantial stone walls. It was warm and just a bit smelly in the taxi and Alice was relieved when the woman leaned forward and tapped the glass between them and the driver with a coin. The driver pulled in immediately.

"Get out here, love," the woman instructed Alice. "Glen Parade is over there on your right and up a wee bit."

Alice unfolded herself onto the pavement and waved to the woman as the cab moved off again.

"You made it unscathed," she heard from someone wearing a hoody leaning against a nearby wall.

It was Liam Doyle, waiting as arranged outside the cemetery. At first glance, the graveyard seemed extensive, spreading over several levels as far as the eye could see. He noted her interest and said, "Oh! That's another day's work if you want the tour of the Fall's Cemetery. We will have to start that earlier in the day too before the local spooks take over for the evening shift."

She wasn't too clear what he meant but assumed it to be a reference to the popularity of cemeteries everywhere for young (and older) people who liked to gather out of sight for purposes that were not always entirely legitimate.

"Let's get you delivered to Glen Parade for now. Their evening programme kicks off about seven and Hugo will want to have a chat with you before that." Liam's long red curls escaped attractively from his hood and he reached amicably for Alice's arm. He led the way across the road and up a laneway that looked like a dead end. About halfway along they came to a red wooden doorway that had a small plaque that cryptically read '*EXIT – the way in*'.

Liam rang the doorbell and stood back.

"I'm just going to leave you to it," he said. "You don't need me crowding you out and you have my number if you need to call me about anything. I don't live too far away and can come to the rescue if need be."

Alice laughed. "I'd say I'll manage OK by myself. I know I'm a bit green on the local cultural stuff but I'm sure the core issues are universal. I'll be quite at home."

With no further ceremony Liam had turned and headed swiftly down the alleyway, turned right and was out of sight. Almost simultaneously the red door swung open and a large man about her own age, or maybe a little older, filled the space left by the opened door. He was clean-shaven and dressed in jeans and a black T-shirt. His slight paunch hinted at a liking for beer or chocolate or maybe both.

"You'll be Alice Fox, I assume." He extended his large hand and delivered a firm but surprisingly gentle handshake. "I'm Hugo." He smiled and stood aside, motioning to her to come in. "We'll have time for a chat before the guys start to roll in. Come in and have a look at the place. We were lucky to have had a good amount of EU peace money when we were setting up and that allowed us to get a firm base in place before the outside money dried up. We take care of maintenance ourselves now with some support from local sponsors."

Hugo led the way along a short entrance hall that had no source of external light and was a grim taster to the project. Alice had seen grim before and wasn't overly disturbed by the prospect. With a bit of a flourish Hugo opened the door at the end of the hallway and light from an atrium filled the large circular space. The walls were curved and brightly coloured and contained a number of alcoves off the main space that were obviously intended for quieter moments. The common central area had about ten comfortable seats set out in a circle and, to the side, a table held mugs and biscuits ready for the arrival of the evening group. In the farthest corner, near a door marked with a large 'H', hung a red leather punch bag and a sizeable area carpeted with thick matting. Alice recognised the de-stress zone and time-out corner where someone who was in a bad place could work out some frustrations without coming to or causing any harm.

"The 'H' is a local historic thing," Hugo smiled broadly. "During the Troubles, when the Maze Prison housed quite a number of the local male population, the republican political prisoners were housed in an area known as the 'H' Block. It was called that because of the shape of the building and you'll see lots of aerial photos that show that. There was a big emphasis on education and making use of the time inside to catch up on missed learning opportunities. The Open University delivered degree modules in Sociology and Women's Studies and such like and many of the local men, including my da, were educated there." He chuckled again. "There are a lot of hard men on this road who are committed feminists and not many working class areas in the world can boast that one. Anyway, my hideaway is known here as the 'H' Block. Obviously 'H' for Hugo but also, I hope, for the emphasis here on self and community development rather than the connection with incarceration. We are trying to avoid that."

He stopped and turned to face her.

"I'm gabbling on because I'm a bit nervous. I've read what you sent me about your work and it's not the same showing someone round who knows what they're at. We have done our fair share of tours with EU funders and such like but they just want the short version of everything and no detail. They want to meet the obvious success story and go away feeling virtuous for having funded us in the first place. It's rare to be hosting someone who actually cares about the work so, as I say, it makes me a bit antsy. You know, like 'ants in your pants' antsy. Does that translate?" He mimed a bit of a jitterbug hop and laughed heartily at himself.

She immediately appreciated his honesty and returned the open smile. She liked when people could allow themselves to be silly. It demonstrated a certain easy self-assurance that was easy be around.

"I'm here to learn too, Hugo. We can ditch the pressures on that score right off. No place for performances in this line of work. We can agree on that one from the outset."

She saw his shoulders drop and his movements become looser. She noted that he had a strange gracefulness that hinted at a man who liked to dance.

She took in the familiar set-up and inhaled the lingering smell of youth. "Actually, it's the first time I've felt at home since I arrived in Ireland over three weeks ago today."

She followed him to an alcove with two armchairs and a small table that held a box of paper handkerchiefs. She could sense the remnants of the heart-to-heart conversations that had happened there and the revelations about family life that didn't match any of the manuals.

"I think we can do the abbreviated version of the niceties." Hugo sounded very pleased about that. "We clearly speak the same shorthand and God knows that doesn't happen too often. Let's get straight to work, Alice Fox!"

The young people arrived around seven and the

group session opened with the young people accounting for their presence in EXIT. Some were excluded from school at an earlier age and had filled their days with petty crimes. These were mostly robberies in the local area and some shoplifting to order that took place in the city centre and suburban shopping complexes further from home. In one case this had been a family business, which further complicated the process of withdrawal from that lifestyle. There was some previous involvement with drug-taking and distribution but EXIT members had to be clean to attend the centre and so these references were all in the past.

Both the young woman and a few of the young men had spent time in a young offenders' centre and had a history of violence. Hugo had made contact with them when he went to speak about alternative ways ahead to individuals and groups ready for release. Almost everyone was now involved in further education and two were apprenticed to local craftspeople. One young man, Jed, talked freely about his literacy issues and the support he was getting from another person in the group. Another revealed his family involvement in dissident republicanism and the hazardous position this placed him in both with his family and the authorities. It became increasingly clear why the confidentiality clause in the group contract was so important.

Alice already felt a connection to the EXIT group and relished the idea of hearing more of the detail of their restorative work. She knew from her discussion with Hugo before the session that he facilitated some direct sessions between victims and perpetrators. They had both agreed to discuss the detail of these sessions further whether or not their collaboration proceeded.

Hugo had taken his turn in the circle and repeated some of the detail he had mentioned when they had talked earlier. He came from a local republican family and had been born at the beginning of the Troubles and lived in the area throughout the worst of things. Much of his childhood had involved travelling with his mother, in a crowded minibus, on weekly visits to his father in the Maze Prison.

"As I said, my da was educated inside and so maybe I learned about the importance of learning and freedom at the same time. I didn't follow in his footsteps in terms of ending up incarcerated but I did inherit his sense of justice and that there are many ways to work at changing what you don't like in your life. I went to college in Belfast and witnessed the beginnings of the Peace Process. There were a lot of conversations going on in this area that never reached the media but we learned a lot about reflection and consultation and being an agent in your own future. That's what I'm interested in here today … avoiding violent conflict, avoiding prison, deciding what needs to change and talking to everybody involved in making that change happen."

The respect of the young people for Hugo's honesty

was clear in the faces of those listening and nodding as he spoke. Alice felt the parallels in their two lives. Their realities were poles apart in many ways but they both traced their major life choices to elements of their fathers' legacy that had led them to taking on the challenges of life in a very particular way.

She had been relieved when she had received a call from Hugo some days after that first visit. He had told her that the group were pleased at the idea that she would join in their work. He added that he too was happy about the prospect of no longer working alone. She had suggested that they might take on the idea of 'self-defence' not just in terms of learning some martial arts but also from looking at how to make their relationships with others less confrontational. Now, several months later, that learning journey was proving interesting for all involved and enhancing Alice's data collection on the benefits of all aspects of restorative justice work. She resolved, perhaps with too little conviction, not to let the business of murder derail her main focus and to make sure to keep her work on track.

22

Later that Thursday afternoon, at the first available opportunity between her interviews with staff, Caroline Paton printed off three copies of Dr Cynthia Boylan's autopsy report and passed copies on to her colleagues. They would have a better conversation later on, when they reviewed progress, if they had all absorbed the detail. No surprises in the cause of death. They had been very abundantly clear. They were also hopefully a little closer to finding the scene of the crime but very much at the beginning of identifying the killer. Boylan's paperwork confirmed that the process of freezing the remains had muddied the waters about the time of death but hopefully there were other ways of coming at that puzzle. She had asked for a report from college security for the period from the Thursday before the end of term until the body was discovered. If that could tell her which personnel had been in both the Human Sciences and the Shipbuilders campus it might give them something useful. Of course not every visitor to the buildings signed or swiped in as was required, particularly if their absolute intent was anonymity. Another complication would be the inevitable slackness that accompanied the holiday period when people could desert their post to attend impromptu celebrations or even do the odd spot of Christmas shopping.

Ralph Wilson was Burrows and McVeigh's last interview of the day. He arrived promptly at five and appeared anxious from the outset. Ralph and his ex had spent a lot of time walking in the Scottish Highlands and years later his appearance still reflected this. He wore collarless shirts and tweed waistcoats in which he stored his pipe and smoking accoutrements. He exuded a pleasant aroma of aromatic tobacco. His shoulder-length curly hair was grey with just a hint of the original dark-brown showing through. He was unkempt and consistently trying to subdue the streeling locks that fell across his face as he talked and moved with characteristic exuberance.

"Tell us about your relationship with Helen Breen, Dr Wilson." Burrows launched his question almost before Wilson had time to sit down.

Ralph spluttered and tossed his head agitatedly from side to side.

"I wouldn't be known as her greatest fan ever." He

looked directly at Burrows, almost as if he were issuing a challenge as he said this.

His mind had been in turmoil since Bell's announcement as he tried to come to terms with Helen Breen's murder and the position in which that placed him. He had been nothing but vitriolic about her to most of his colleagues and had not made any secret that he despised her. He tried to remember if he had ever, even euphemistically, said he would harm her but couldn't be certain. Phrases ran through his head like '*butchering would be too gentle for her*' and '*I wouldn't be seen crying over her coffin*'. He was prone to such exaggerated pronouncements and he could imagine some of his typical colourful utterances coming back to haunt him.

Burrows raised a questioning eyebrow and Ralph continued.

"I have made it plain repeatedly, both privately in conversation with colleagues and publicly in meetings that will be on record, that I did not hold my deceased colleague in high esteem." He paused for breath. "My dislike was both ideological and personal. She epitomised everything I hate about educational trends at the moment. She lacked conviction and commitment and shirked work whenever she could find someone else to do it for her." Wilson realised that he was warming too enthusiastically to his subject and paused suddenly. "Anyway, you will hear that from many colleagues but hopefully you will also hear that I am not the murdering type." He looked nervously at Burrows, aware that his dislike of Breen had placed him pretty high up the line of suspects.

"Have you ever visited Dr Breen's home?" Burrows asked. He was asking all interviewees that question in an attempt to find out about her life outside work.

Wilson looked aghast at the question.

"I barely spoke to her in work and I certainly never met her outside of it." He shuddered as if the idea was repulsive.

"Tell us about your application for the new post of professor in DePRec. I believe Helen Breen would have been your only adversary in that competition."

Burrows watched closely as Wilson felt the evidence against him accumulate. He flushed red and his temper flared.

"I have never concealed my dislike of the woman. We were as different as chalk and cheese in terms of how we would fill the new position. I want to make things better, more just. Her only concern has ever been her own aggrandisement." He flung his arms about as he spoke. "I am under no illusion that I was not the favourite for the post – in fact, there are those who would say I was wasting my time even applying and I was mad to contemplate putting myself through the charade. There is no way they would choose me over Breen. She toadies up to Bell and Hartnett and anyone with any influence. I speak my mind and people don't respect that anymore. It's all about being businesslike and helping Belfast City College up the university league tables." Saliva flew from Wilson's mouth as his anger took hold. Burrow's lack of reaction eventually led him to stop in his tracks and realise he was making matters worse for himself.

"Would it be fair to say that your colleague, Helen Breen, provoked you to anger, Dr Wilson?"

"Probably more like rage," he admitted, "but I am not a violent person. I lose my temper and rant on about things but I am harmless. I wouldn't hurt someone." He was almost pleading by this stage.

Burrows asked Wilson about the end-of-term drinks at Professor Hartnett's. He was baffled by the question until he realised that he had been rather drunk leaving and might well have said some unfortunate things that could come back to bite him.

"I don't think it was anything other than the usual exercise in showing some scant appreciation to the masses ... an opportunity to mix with colleagues ... and probably drink too much free wine." He laughed feebly and tried to cover his tracks as best he could.

Burrows nodded and the younger fellow just kept writing and eyeing the screen of his mobile phone He was recording everything.

Wilson gathered himself together and added, "I know I don't come out of any of this smelling of roses but I swear I am not a murderer. The idea is preposterous.

When was she killed anyway? I am sure that I will be able to show I wasn't even anywhere near where it happened."

"Thank you for being so frank with us," said Burrows. He was as calm as Wilson was distraught. "We are obviously just in the early stages of gathering evidence. I am sure as we piece together the details surrounding the death of Dr Breen we will indeed be coming back to people to verify where they stand. We will no doubt be speaking to you again, Dr Wilson. Thank you for your time."

With that he stood and made it clear that it was time for Wilson to leave. Wilson did this hesitantly and without any grace.

Burrows and McVeigh exchanged knowing looks but said nothing. There would be time later to give voice to their impressions.

DePRec staff who overheard the six o'clock radio news would have recognised the details that had become all too familiar to them during the course of the day.

"*The PSNI have begun a murder inquiry following the discovery yesterday of the body of a woman in a building of the Belfast City College. For operational reasons the precise details of the discovery are not being disclosed. The body is believed to be that of Dr Helen Breen, a legal scholar and a senior lecturer in the Department of Peace and Reconciliation, known locally as DePRec. Dr Breen's family was informed of her death early this morning. A PSNI press conference is scheduled for tomorrow morning when it is hoped further detail of this killing will be made public. Anyone with information should contact the PSNI ..."*

Radio and television news bulletins also carried a recording of Professor Giles Thompson making a statement on behalf of the university. He spoke of immense sadness at the demise of a valued colleague. He stressed how eager the college authorities were for the PSNI to rapidly identify whoever had committed this odious crime so that the normal, nonviolent business of learning could be continued.

23

That evening, pushing her bicycle, Alice walked home from the Titanic Quarter to Botanic to give herself additional thinking time. The clashing of her previous and present worlds was niggling at her and she needed to have some serious words with herself. Detective or scholar? Was it possible to be both? Was that even the right question? Why was she now so drawn back towards the role she had consciously separated herself from all those years back?

She had already crossed the Lagan Bridge and passed by the Waterfront Hall before she became conscious of her environment. On her right was a well-restored Victorian covered market that promised a host of interesting things to eat and see over the weekend. Even now, when closed, St George's Market had an air of vitality and history that suggested it had strong, lasting community roots. Alice liked such places a lot. They suited her very well. It was possible to wander anonymously and glean indispensable cultural data unavailable in any other form. She liked this way of absorbing information and trusted her intuition about such things. She had been a savvy detective who tried hard to recognise the context of crimes as well as their perpetrators. Neighbourhoods needed to be understood in police work and that had become even more pertinent as she had moved from crime detection into the field of restorative justice.

In the Markets area through which she now passed and, in fact, every time she made her way around Belfast, she was constantly brought face to face with evidence of the legacy of the Troubles and the sectarianism of a still-divided community. The colour scheme here was the green, white and orange of the Irish flag signifying unity between South and North, orange being the colour associated with the Protestant North for centuries. There were also signs displaying a language that she now knew to be the marker of a nationalist area – there was nothing in it that she could recognise or make any meaning of and, because of that, it was a little intriguing. The modest houses were relatively recently built and surrounded by commercial streets and fading industrial development. It was a tight, residential enclave with stone bollards positioned across roads to restrict movement. She recognised these as a security force mechanism with which she was familiar in the poorer areas of Lowell, where police wanted to limit potential rat-runs and easy escape routes. Noticing such detail, she told herself now was congruent with both Alice the detective and Alice the academic scholar. Both needed to be alert to the detail and track it back to the structures where it was generated. She was a blend of both of these things for which there was no label as far as she knew.

She weaved in and around people on the busy pavement and soon turned right along the less populated Donegall Pass. In the space of a hundred yards, the landscape shifted sharply to become dominated by building-size paintings unequivocally claiming the territory for those with pro-British politics. An entire gable wall held a painting of a lifeless Union Jack flag and declared Donegall Pass as the terrain of the Ulster Volunteer Force (UVF) 1913-2013. Red, white and blue paint daubed the kerbstones and bedraggled flags flew from lampposts. On the external wall of a pub called 'The Hideout' a mural featuring a lone piper commemorated members of the '2nd battalion' of the Ulster Volunteer Force who were killed during the 'Troubles'. In some side streets Alice glimpsed smaller murals of masked men carrying machine guns and a longhaired man in archaic dress astride a white horse rearing up on its hind legs. She recognised the form of the seventeenth-century King William of Orange, colloquially known as King Billy, from the research she had done to prepare for her time in Ireland. At first, being in such close proximity to these robust cultural declarations had caused a chilling effect on her and her more blasé response today was a sign that she was no longer such a stranger in this place. She was beginning to settle into her surroundings.

As she moved along the Pass by small antique and bric-a-brac shops that were good for foraging expeditions, familiar odours of Chinese food filled the air and Alice was instantly transported home to the China Star where she had been a frequent customer when working in and around the Acre area in Lowell. Belfast's Chinese quarter was small but ample and Alice had rapidly found her favourite place to eat when she didn't feel like cooking.

Botanic Station disgorged a rush of people just as she passed by. Some were chatting loudly in that strange flat accent with its distinctive narrowed vowel sounds while others were solitary and had the grim-faced expressions of the discontented worker. There was a whole new music to the English language here and Alice Fox found it easy on the ear. Along Botanic Avenue the traffic was bumper to bumper and the broad footpaths were full of people making their way home from work via the supermarket or the bar. There was a general air of pleasant chatter and people open to casual exchanges with passers-by. A number of people made eye contact

149

with her and uttered a shy greeting – 'Hiya' or 'Hello there'. Belfast still retained a friendliness that other places she knew had long ago lost and she liked that hint of innocence.

By the time she reached the left-hand turn into her road she had come to a few conclusions about the demise of Helen Breen but she would keep them to herself until she had a chance to test them more thoroughly. Being a detective and being a social researcher were both about gathering data so that you could get a clearer picture of the truth. She would agree to settle for both those inclinations coexisting in her for the moment and see where that got her. She smiled to herself and felt relieved to have come to a resting place in that struggle.

By way of a reward to herself, she dropped into the local bookshop that had an excellent selection of crime reading and replenished her stash of murder mysteries that had been depleted during her Wicklow stay. She smiled as she reflected that for the moment she was more than amply preoccupied with the real thing.

Installed in her rooms just off Botanic Avenue, Alice sat quietly in her easy chair with sonorous cello music playing through her excellent sound system. She reflected on her day and on the inevitable chain of thought that the revelation of Breen's murder had sparked. There was no point in ignoring her inclinations to be drawn into reviewing the facts as she saw them. It wasn't possible to be in DePRec and not hear the ongoing chatter about the inquiry nor was she able to stop her mind thinking of all the possibilities. Caroline Paton's apparent openness to her contribution had perhaps been the defining catalyst in that it seemed as if it was almost required of her to use her skills and experience to help in whatever way she could. Anyway, at this degree of proximity she found it impossible not to be drawn further in. She closed her eyes and allowed the music to calm her busy mind.

She was just beginning to feel some sense of relaxation when her doorbell buzzed. She had very few callers and her initial reaction was to ignore it. It was probably someone proselytising on behalf of a religious group that she could live happily without. After a brief interlude the bell buzzed again, more insistently than the first time. She went to the window and looked down into the street. The January wind whipped through the trees and played with the streetlights to create a raft of agitated shadows. Two figures stood outside the gate to her building looking up at the windows. She realised that Mairéad Walsh and what looked like Ralph Wilson were staring up at her. She waved to them to come up and moved across to the door to release the remote locking mechanism.

A few moments later they arrived, windswept and anxious, at her first-floor entrance.

"Apologies for invading your privacy," Mairéad said, engaging Alice with a look of genuine regret. "I know you like to be left in peace, Alice, but we are desperate for some of your advice," she faltered, "in fact we are here to ask for your professional services." She registered Alice's look of bewilderment. "Look, lovey, just give us a few moments of your time and we'll explain. I promise we won't outstay our welcome."

Alice moved aside and showed them into her peaceful living space. The cello music played on and Alice reduced the volume.

Ralph produced a bottle of cold white wine and said apologetically, "Any chance of a corkscrew and a few glasses?"

At this moment in time, the opportunity of discussing the murder of Helen Breen was not something Alice was opposed to, and she produced three wineglasses and handed Ralph a corkscrew. Thinking they might not have eaten very much, she put some cheese and crackers on a plate on the table between them in case anyone wanted to nibble at something.

Mairéad looked around the room and smiled at the book-lined wall and orderly workspace.

The old oak partner's desk and office chair were part of the furnishings provided in the apartment rental and matched the high ceilings and simplicity of the Victorian building. The good taste with which the place was decorated had been a pivotal influence for Alice's choice.

She liked classic design and quality over tasteless modern ideas of comfort.

"This place suits you very well, Alice Fox," Mairéad said, nodding approvingly. "I hope you will excuse our intrusion."

Alice dismissed her concerns with a wave of her hand and a sideways smile. Ralph opened the wine and poured three glasses. They all sipped and then he began to speak in a gentle tone that Alice hadn't witnessed as part of his public, work persona.

"The fact is that I think I am very much in danger of being suspect number one in the murder of Helen Breen. If I wasn't sure of my innocence, I would suspect me too." He was clearly overwrought and Mairéad looked on with concern as he spoke. "You see I spent a lot of the holidays alone and have no one to vouch for my whereabouts except for a few evenings with Mairéad that I don't really want to make public knowledge."

"Well, more importantly," Mairéad interrupted, clearly wanting to move along from any insinuations about their relationship, "Ralph spent a lot of time verbally attacking Breen to other colleagues. They were usually in agreement with him then, but now that circumstances have changed he's coming up against a lot of suspicion and amnesia about all that. Their version of the truth for the detectives will be unlike what really happened before the killing. We can see that a case will be building against him and want to ask you to help find out what really happened. You are a professional, Alice, and know how this all works. You also know the Department and all the characters involved. We are lost in the face of it."

She looked older slumped against the sofa and Alice felt an urge to make everything better.

"In fact," Mairéad continued, "we are paralysed with fear and dread. This whole business is going to cause havoc with lots of people's private lives. Not just ours." She widened her eyes, clamped her lips in an expression of resignation and nodded repeatedly.

"I hear you," Alice said kindly, "but it's probably better not to rush ahead." It was the obvious truth, however, that Wilson was likely to be mentioned in many interviews as someone known to be antagonistic towards Helen Breen.

She sipped the wine thoughtfully and realised she was really enjoying herself. "There will not be much definitive police action until there is a time and place of death and then it will be important to be able to show that you are not someone who had opportunity to commit the crime. Also many people have rivalries and even enmities at work but that is not usually a motive for murder." She paused. "If even a fraction of negativity directed at people in the workplace actually led to murder then we would be looking at a boom in Crime Detection vocational training courses."

"But will you help him, Alice?" Mairéad insisted.

"Will you do some investigating of your own and see if it is possible to prove that Ralph is beyond reproach in this matter?"

They both looked at her with such a sense of despair that Alice felt her sympathies begin to slip in Ralph's direction.

"I have no role in this investigation and I don't think it's a good idea to aggravate the detectives by setting up an alternative inquiry. But I have got off to a good start with DI Paton and might be able to offer her some insider support that I think she would be open to." She was already seeing a way of both serving the interests of the investigation and Wilson's need to have someone looking out for his interests. "Let's calm down here and get systematic. We can pool what we know so far and see where that gets us."

She placed her phone on 'voice record' on the table between them and chaos gradually gave way to concentration.

By the time Mairéad and Ralph left her, Alice was convinced that Wilson was not the culprit. She was also already significantly invested in finding out more about what had motivated someone to brutally eliminate Helen Breen from the land of the living.

24

While Alice was warming to her challenge, in the Grosvenor Road police station DI Caroline Paton and her team were settling in for a thorough review of the first day's findings. They were joined by Sandra Woods who had managed to find an hour of carer-time for her elderly mother and was eager to get started and home as quickly as possible. Mugs of tea and coffee, a large plate of filled rolls and an equally generous basket of muffins sat temptingly in the middle of the table around which they all sat. An A4-size facial image of Helen Breen was already affixed to an electronic whiteboard that had the facility to print out a copy of its contents at any point in time. They would fill it many times over in their search for Breen's killer. Each dated printout signified the most recent point in their thinking and also allowed the possibility to review hypotheses in the light of new information.

"OK, Sandra!" Paton began with gusto. "You have the most pressing time limit so let's hear from you first. We will just do sound and paper notes for now and Bill can play with the Etch-a-Sketch later when we have a clearer picture of what's been happening here."

Bill was a big fan of the technology and loved that their rough mind maps and random scrawlings could all be captured with such ease.

Paton raised her eyebrows slightly to signal to Sandra that she could begin. McVeigh started his recorder and they all made dated, pen-and-paper notes to supplement the evidence base. Paton knew from experience that people retained very different details from the same evidential accounts and from their three versions she hoped they would cover most bases.

Sandra held her notebook in one hand and with the other rubbed a piece of Blu Tack between her thumb and first two fingers. The constant movement helped her to think and she always had some handy. "I arrived at the home of Agatha Breen just before 9am. Lisa, the elderly woman's resident carer, admitted me. She is from the Philippines and has been with Mrs Breen for six years. I could see that Lisa was a little anxious about my appearance in her home but when I got the chance later in the kitchen, I reassured her that her status was not of any interest to us. She has a clear overview of family business and relationships, which I'll get to in a bit. Mrs Breen is in her 80s and her mobility is restricted. Her mental capacity on the other hand is sharp and she has developed a tough exterior by necessity, I'd judge. Her relationship with her children is distant and I got the distinct impression that Helen was emotionally detached from her family. Mrs Breen was shocked by the news of her daughter's death but she talked about a relationship that was quite atrophied really. It had little currency. I was given the impression of Helen Breen as a woman who was self-interested and whose connection with her home and family was entirely functional and self-serving." Sandra paused to sip her tea. "The husband is dead about twenty-five years and the mother said that Helen was very close to him. She was about sixteen when he died and apparently felt abandoned by the father whose favour she was very much invested in gaining. She and the mother were never close and, in recent years, Helen only used the house as a postal address for work-related things. The phone contact for DePRec was also the mother's house and the carer, Lisa, was tutored in taking messages for her and passing them on, usually to an answering machine. The messages were never acknowledged. Helen collected her post on Sundays and otherwise did not have much contact with the mother. For some reason she didn't give work her actual home address, which is in Hillsborough. She appears to have been hyper-vigilant about her private life. Neither the mother nor her carer, Lisa, had ever been to her place in Hillsborough, which is a good indicator of the degree of distance in that relationship. I do have the Hillsborough address which is in my written notes and a spare key that was kept at the mother's."

Woods always made impeccable records of her findings and Paton and her team had learned to trust her judgment and to rely on the accuracy of her paperwork.

"I was struck by the irony that the family business was refrigeration. I even wondered was her death part of some vendetta against the family but there was nothing else to suggest that might be the case. Still, I thought it was worth mentioning."

"There's another icy connection in the fact that DePRec is in the Titanic Quarter," said Burrows.

This was greeted with smiles but no one was quite sure if these links were humorous or not.

Sandra continued. "When the father died the business was sold as none of the three children of the family were interested in keeping it on. It sounds as if it was a successful affair and I expect that they all benefitted financially from the sale. I saw and heard no evidence of anything but a very comfortably well-off family." Sandra took another mouthful of her tea and proceeded uninterrupted. "Michael Breen, Helen's younger brother, arrived not long after he was telephoned. He runs quite a large tile-importing business and again appeared affluent and described his business as 'flourishing'. On his part, there was little display of affection or emotion towards his mother or distress about his sister's murder.

He was shocked by the manner of her death but he actually said to me that he had never liked his sister and that they had little or no contact. He had called to her house in Hillsborough once, in the past, to discuss the fact that their mother was no longer able to live alone and that he had employed a residential carer. He said she didn't even invite him in." Sandra flicked over a page in her notebook and continued. "I left him alone with the mother for a bit and sat in the kitchen with Lisa. She had a good handle on the whole family. The oldest son, Frank, although he lives in Australia, has more contact and shows more concern for his mother than his siblings ever did. He phones every week and his children communicate regularly with their grandmother on Skype. Lisa found the behaviour of Helen shocking. She was less judgmental of Michael because her expectation was that a daughter would be more caring towards her mother than a son. She said that Helen was cold and seemingly heartless. She talked about her as if she had some kind of emotional disability and said several times that she didn't feel comfortable with Helen. She could see that Mrs Breen was lonely and hurt by her children's neglect of her but the old lady maintained a façade before everyone, including Lisa. The mother talked about them as if they were just very busy and Lisa did not ever want to add to her hurt by showing that she thought of their behaviour in any negative way. She said to me that she thought it was sad that she, who loved her family, had to leave them so that she could care for someone whose children didn't want to spend any time with her at all. I said nothing but I got her point."

At this point Woods closed her notebook and looked around the room at her colleagues. They were all nodding in approval at her initial report.

"I will be going back to check in with Mrs Breen tomorrow and see what else I can discover. Any suggestions of what might be useful to your inquiry?"

"Really great progress to get the address and keys for Hillsborough, Sandra," said Paton. "We'll get someone out there tomorrow early and give it a good going-over. Ian, maybe you can call in a few lab boys and head out there first thing. See what you can pick up in terms of computer, phone and observations from neighbours. Maybe talk to the local police and see what they know."

She turned back to Sandra who was gathering her things to leave.

"Thanks for all that, Sandra. I'll know better if there are any particular areas for poking at tomorrow when we have done with our review this evening. Bill will be in touch with any questions we come up with but otherwise just do what you always do and we'll be happy with what you uncover. I will get there tomorrow evening to interview Mrs Breen and Lisa and probably Michael as well. You might flag that up so that the brother is there too. Let's say six o'clock. It sounds to me as if Helen Breen may have had some kind of personality disorder or something like that. Maybe see if the mother will spill the beans about any possible psychiatric issues. Let's look at school records, college, GP and see if there is anything there. Helen obviously really annoyed somebody so anything that might shed light on her relationships even going back a bit could be helpful. We'll talk more tomorrow, Sandra."

Sandra nodded and left without any further comment.

Paton refocused on her two colleagues. "So let's begin with the autopsy report – Bill, any of your observations of that process?"

They extracted the copy of the report from their papers and Bill started the discussion.

"Well, the bad news is that the refrigeration has meant that we can't get very precise info about time of death – but the point at which the freezing became effective at arresting degeneration suggests that it took effect probably in and around ten hours after death. So she was killed and then her head was wrapped in plastic sheeting and she was moved fairly quickly to the place where the body was found. As I suspected, the forensic sweep in her office indicated that some altercation had taken place there. It looks like a fairly professional clean-up was done but there is always a trace or two of body fluid – or in this case blood-and-brain matter – that gives it all away. I am going back to the college later to talk to the night security staff and see what I can pick up there. I've asked for a look at any logs they keep and

CCTV from the car parks and surroundings. That's just in the unlikely case they walked rather than drove from one building to the other. Better cover all possibilities." He reviewed his notes and had a bite of a ham roll. He chewed quickly and carried on with his input. "In terms of the autopsy, cause of death was penetrating brain trauma. Her head was pounded repeatedly against what forensics and the autopsy will show was a concrete pillar in her office. The deed was done by someone who was really determined that the victim was not going to survive. Cynthia was clear that she continued to be battered some time after her life had stopped. It was as if the motion of beating became almost hypnotic and the perp lost sight of the fact that death had occurred before he or she actually stopped. Now we need to establish when this might have happened and who was around that might have seen or heard something. The last night of evening classes was the Thursday and as far as I can gather, Helen Breen wasn't seen again after that although her passkey was used to sign out on Thursday evening at nine thirty-six. Lectures finish in and around nine twenty to allow time for the buildings to be clear for nine thirty. I suppose we have to consider that someone else may have used that passkey to create uncertainty about the time and place of the killing. I'm hoping we will be able to piece all that together to get a clearer picture of the possible timeline."

Ian McVeigh was fishing through interview notes.

"On the Thursday before term finished up on the Friday," he said, "Jackson Bell asked Helen to cover evening duty for him as he had another meeting to attend outside the college. They had all been at Professor Hartnett's on the Wednesday for a Christmas bash and Breen was alive and well at that event. She was observed by several colleagues to have been deep in conversation with …" he shuffled through his notes, "yes, here it is … she was seen talking with Liam Doyle, the young buck who looks after student interests. We have him coming in tomorrow for interview after the Press Conference."

Paton raised a hand to indicate she was going to comment. "Just while you're on the subject of interviews, let's see where we are with the staff. We got through most of the DePRec staff more quickly than I had imagined would be the case. The admin and part-timers were pretty consistent. Helen Breen wasn't well liked. She invested nothing in establishing relationships with her peers, aside from her superiors, whom she seemed to cultivate fairly earnestly." There were nods of assent to that. "Jackson Bell bucks the trend in that he thought very highly of her. He spoke of her as his most trusted colleague. They seem to have had a steady and mutually supportive relationship. Let's find out what the motivation behind that was when we talk to him tomorrow. He's either a poor judge of character or there was some understanding between them that suited them both."

She was working methodically down her mental list and Burrows and McVeigh knew the form and remained quietly attentive.

"We didn't learn very much from the interviews in Marine Biology. The maintenance were worried about causing damage to the contents of the freezers and called in a staff member. Dr Baker saw that there was what looked like a body in the freezer and rightly called the President who alerted us. She had nothing to add really aside from a little context about the contents of the freezers, which is no use at all to us. Hard to get excited about different sponge varieties I'd say, even when you are not preoccupied with a murder." She grimaced. Paton had a low threshold for anything not directly relevant to her case. "We didn't get far with security as the right people weren't available. I asked for various reports and video footage to be gathered and said we would call back later tonight." She raised both eyebrows in the direction of Burrows who nodded agreement. They were both on the same track there.

Burrows allowed a small pause and then launched into the void. "Ian and I had an interesting conversation with Ralph Wilson. His name cropped up in a good few interviews as an obvious antagonist of Breen's and he lived up to his reputation. He was beyond nervous and really lost it when he was describing his reasons for disliking Breen. He demonstrated that he has quite a temper and he didn't seem to be able to keep it under wraps at all." Ian nodded in agreement. "When we asked if Helen Breen made him angry he replied that it would be more accurate to say that she provoked him to 'rage'. At the same time, he was so open about how he felt about her that it was hard to think that if he was the one who harmed her he would actually be that obvious."

"I agree with Bill," said McVeigh. "He kept insisting that he had a fiery temper but was not a violent person. But then again he would be aware of his reputation and there would be no point in trying to conceal that. I think we need to see how he matches up with times and locations when we have those pinned down."

"Bell was fairly damning about Wilson as well." Paton had briefly talked informally to Bell earlier in the day and found him a bit of a paradox. He was open and helpful in response to questions about the workplace and even his visual research interests in different communities but there was something not entirely authentic in his demeanour. She had not eliminated him from her list of potential suspects by any manner or means. Perhaps his admiration of Helen Breen was such that any betrayal of him could provoke a violent response. "Wilson is obviously a thorn in Bell's side, critical of his decisions about the future of DePRec and a constant dissenting voice at staff meetings. I think we need to talk to Wilson again, maybe in the station to ramp up the pressure a little. I can do that tomorrow afternoon before going to the Breen family. We'll wait until the afternoon and contact him then to request he comes in here to assist us. Ian, will you look after that?"

McVeigh was tapping some interview notes with his pen and interjected. "When you said about personality disorder, DI, you reminded me of another conversation that backs that up. There was a part-time person who had a specific personal gripe with Breen. Most of them just disliked her at a few degrees of separation. This guy, Neil Larmour, had covered some classes for her and yet she had seemed unwilling to approve his legitimate pay claim. A month elapsed without him being paid and, when he asked her for an explanation, she offered to give him book tokens in lieu of payment. He was furious at the time, mainly at her lack of understanding that his payment was needed for his rent and other bills. He said he had challenged her rather forcefully saying, 'Do you think I can pay my bills with fucking book tokens?' He said he was angry at how casual and disregarding she was about his needs. He described her total lack of empathy as shocking." McVeigh was good at holding on to useful pieces of the overall picture that might easily get lost. "Larmour was illustrating something dysfunctional in Breen's personality but, I suppose, he was also putting himself on the list of those with some motive for harming her."

"Good thinking, Ian. I feel we are really making progress with the victim profile and are at least getting some insights into the possible character of our offender." She seemed to be considering whether to add something and that sharpened their interest. "I interviewed the visiting scholar from New York City university this afternoon – one Dr Alice Fox. It is always interesting to get the outsider's perspective. Anyway Alice Fox confirmed a lot of the stuff we've mentioned about Breen being disliked and even had her own experience of being used to cover Breen's class for free. But more importantly, before becoming an academic, Alice Fox was a detective in the Lowell Police Department in Massachusetts. She knows the business of detection well and might be a useful insider viewpoint for us to consult if need be."

Burrows and McVeigh were giving only slight signs of agreement with that idea and she left it at that for the moment. She knew not to push some ideas too hard until they came around to her viewpoint in their own time.

"Who's left on the list of DePRec personnel that we need to talk to, Bill?"

"We still have Bell's official interview, then the faculty head, Professor Janet Hartnett, Liam Doyle the student rep and Mairéad Walsh. That's it for the staff. If Ian goes to Hillsborough I can get started on those in the morning once Sandra is briefed. I'll head straight to DePRec this evening when we finish up here and hopefully they'll have the security reports you asked for ready and waiting. I want to check out about college cleaning procedures too. I'd say it's a sub-contract like the security but I'll check it out anyway. I'll keep in touch about any outcome from that."

Paton added to the list. "I need to update the President too at some point, out of courtesy at least, not to mention he needs to know that the murder took place on college premises. He won't like that one little bit. In fact, I'll phone him when we finish talking here so that he is up to speed before the press conference tomorrow morning. I think the Super wants me to take the lead on that although he will also be present to show that we are treating this as a priority. We are on at ten o'clock in HQ so make sure that Sandra is with Mrs Breen at that point in case it provokes any new media disclosures."

DC Ian McVeigh was charged with contacting the Hillsborough police that evening and finding out if there was any local knowledge on Helen Breen. He could follow up then the next day when he went to examine Breen's home. Because of its security priorities during the Troubles and even now, local police were vigilant about anything that might jeopardise the security of Hillsborough Castle and those who lived there. As the home of the Secretary of State for Northern Ireland and any number of high-profile visitors, it meant that there had not been the same relaxation of security measures in Hillsborough as elsewhere in the province.

They spent some time pooling the most burning questions that presented themselves. Who was known to be on DePRec premises on the Thursday when they now deduced that Breen been killed? How had the killer cleaned up after the killing and how was the body moved to the nearby Maritime Studies building? It was clear that someone must have seen something unless the removal of the body was purposefully designed to be congruent with everyday college activities. What was to be learned from Helen Breen's Hillsborough home that apparently none of her colleagues or her family had ever visited? Was Breen a recluse or were her chosen associates entirely outside her work colleagues? If Breen was killed at work what had become of her car? College Security held records of all vehicles so they might be able to help Burrows answer that one when he spoke to them later that evening. Who had removed her belongings – her bag, laptop and phone from her office and why? What information could college IT systems provide in relation to Breen's College account and computer usage? Could the mobile phone company she used be requisitioned to provide account details and printouts of user history for the past six months? Any CCTV footage from the MI motorway between Belfast and Hillsborough was to be accessed and indeed footage from around the Titanic Quarter on the Thursday evening and into the following day would be worth studying. The list was always long at this point in an inquiry.

As they approached the end of the first full day of investigation, they had made some progress but a lot was left to do. These were the crucial moments in detection when most clues were available for discovery. With every day that passed getting results became more difficult and valuable impetus ebbed away. Caroline Paton was plainly aware of these time imperatives and she knew that Burrows and McVeigh would not be found wanting in their drive to solve this case as quickly as possible. They would each spend another several hours that evening working on the tasks they had identified and would be on call if any important new evidence required their attention, even throughout the night.

Paton reached for a second muffin and nodded to the men to help themselves. They would need any energy boost they could get tonight to keep them going for another few hours.

25

After their briefing in Grosvenor Road Barracks, Bill Burrows made his way back to DePRec and his prearranged meeting with College Security. During Paton and McVeigh's earlier meeting with security staff that morning it was clear that the right people were not on the premises to consult. The provision of college security was through a private company and although it was part of the oversight of Estates Management, college staff did not carry out the actual tasks. It was much harder to pin down these private outfits, Bill thought as he drove towards the Titanic Quarter. All these subcontracts meant that staff members were moved about frequently from one organisation to another and people were no longer familiar with their colleagues. It was cheaper to work in that way but Burrows doubted it did much for staff morale or team spirit, never mind basic efficiency. His expectations of getting any solid evidence from the college systems were not high.

He parked in the college underground car park and went straight to the security desk located in the main foyer. The uniformed man was obviously expecting him and said that the security manager was waiting for DS Burrows in the operations room in the basement. Burrows returned to the lift and followed the directions to find Matt Gillespie of HiSecurity Services. A young man in his mid-to-late thirties was waiting in the room where a line of monitors flashed everchanging views, both internal and external, of different areas in the college.

They sat at a desk to the side of the monitors and Gillespie passed a folder of prepared data to Burrows. "This is what DI Paton requested," he said, pleased with himself for having delivered on the task. Bill scanned the cover sheet and was impressed at the comprehensive contents.

"This looks good," he said, and the younger man appeared grateful for the praise. "I'd like you to talk me through it all, Matt, but first tell me how the security system here is set up and who oversees the staff that come and go. I am assuming that there isn't a great deal of continuity and people can potentially work a number of different company jobs in the same week?"

Burrows expected to hear a lot of business jargon and assurances that HiSecurity Services was all things to all people, but Matt Gillespie was personable and plausible and gave no impression of whitewashing the facts. He explained that the College had twenty-four-hour security with a series of motion-activated cameras recording comprehensive visual information on an ongoing basis. "A staff member sits at a desk in the foyer throughout this period and has access to immediate back-up if an incident occurs. All staff members are fully trained and many are ex-police or armed services personnel. The visual data is stored digitally and archived for twelve months at which point it is deleted."

Matt Gillespie was impressive in his matter-of-fact description of the system, thought Bill.

"We are not big on cyber-security, firewalls and anti-hacking as that is a specialised security business very different to what we do. On the other hand we have secure cyber archiving systems that mean within a given twelve-month period visual data will be safely stored. More importantly perhaps it can be easily retrieved. Things have moved on a lot from the days when information was recorded on video cassettes that would be randomly taped over or lost."

"What would be the perceived security risks in a place like this?" Burrows asked out of genuine interest.

"Well, that's one of our fundamental questions when developing a customised organisational system." Matt warmed to his subject. "There is a staff-monitoring and supervisory element to our systems here based on the idea that when people know they are being kept a check on, they modify their behaviour accordingly. They police themselves in other words. We would occasionally have a student who gets obstreperous either with a staff member or another student and security might be called to control that situation. A lot of emphasis is understandably on protection of property and equipment. The library has its own book-protection system but we are constantly vigilant about other items – computers, furniture, stationery – even toilet rolls are a valuable commodity that increasingly needs to be locked up securely!"

Gillespie explained that the passkey system was not a foolproof method of tracking staff behaviour but was liked by organisations like Belfast City College because it placed responsibility on academic, admin and ancillary staff to be accountable for their movements. Of course people forgot passkeys or could ask a colleague to swipe them in when they were elsewhere but generally it was sufficient for a low-security educational establishment.

"I guess you just need one murder on the premises to dispel that myth." Burrows could not resist stating the obvious but he got Gillespie's point. At the same time he understood that every organisation could not be expected to guard against every risk. Armed guards on schools in the USA did not seem to him an example of progress but it was useful when detectives could access good quality data from those they collaborated with in solving crimes in the community.

When they got down to specifics, Matt Gillespie demonstrated that he had a firm grasp of his business. Paton had asked for a breakdown of the staff present in the building on the night of that Thursday in December. The first printout in the folder provided showed the arrival and departure times of all staff that had used the passkey system that day. This included the fact that Helen Breen's key was used to swipe out at nine thirty-six that evening. Ralph Wilson had been present until seven-thirty, Jackson Bell until five fifty-five, Liam Doyle was not registered on the system that day and Janet Hartnett had left the building at nine-thirty.

The second sheet provided similar details of those who had been working in the Maritime Studies Centre on the same evening. None of those listed had any links to DePRec that Burrows could identify but he would check thoroughly for any overlap.

The third sheet in Gillespie's folder gave the contact details of the security staff that had been on duty that evening. He reported that he had talked to both of them and they had not observed anything out of the ordinary on the Thursday evening. It was the final session of evening classes and there was some revelry amongst the students but nothing that merited being recorded on the digital incident sheet. The cleaning staff had arrived in the evening as usual at nine forty-five and again neither security guard had noticed anything untoward. The guy in Maritime Studies Centre had been called to the front door to deal with a noisy incident but he was only away from his post for five minutes during which time everything was quiet aside from the usual cleaning and maintenance activity.

Gillespie had personally reviewed visual data from all cameras in both buildings between six on the Thursday evening until six the following evening. He had sent copies of these files to the email address provided by DI Paton so that they could be further scrutinised by the police. His own review had shown a number of facts that he thought would be of interest. At this point he activated the monitor on the desk where they sat and loaded an image of the car park adjacent to the operations office. The date confirmed the date and time in December.

Gillespie moved the image to another angle in the car park and indicated a Mazda car that was still parked there at eleven-thirty and five o'clock next morning. This was identified as the vehicle registered on the system to Dr Helen Breen. The sensors, activated the following morning at shortly after eight, showed the same car being opened by a male person and driven from the car park. An image of the driver was recorded at the exit barrier and replicated in the folder. It matched the logged ID picture of the Student Representative, Liam Doyle. Cameras in the post room to monitor access to mail showed that Doyle swiped in just before eight, went to the post room on the ground floor and then directly to the car park.

Burrows felt the familiar lift that accompanies a breakthrough in an investigation. Several people in their interviews had mentioned Liam Doyle as linked to Helen Breen. There had been implications of a sexual liaison and a closer-than-might-be-expected relationship between a senior lecturer and a student representative. He would pass this on directly to Caroline Patton this evening.

Burrows listened as Gillespie talked him through some other reports and demonstrated how to access other material on the visual data files. He would get someone onto a thorough review of the video footage first thing tomorrow before going to DePRec to conduct the final interviews there. The interview with Doyle would be best kept until Caroline was done with the Press Conference. He would begin with Mairéad Walsh who had indicated she was available from eight-thirty, and then he would talk to Jackson Bell and Janet Hartnett. By that stage he hoped that Caroline would be there to interview Doyle with him. Two heads were definitely better than one in that instance. As he headed for home he noted that the time on the Albert Clock was ten twenty-five. He would just check in with Caroline Paton and then call it a day.

26

On Friday morning Alice Fox ran along the Lagan towpath with greater vigour than usual. The rhythmical movement and breathing stilled the chatter in her head and restored her sense of composure. After a shower and breakfast she got on her bike and headed for EXIT where she had arranged to meet Hugo and plan the forthcoming term's activities for the group. The feedback from their paper at the conference that had seemed high on her agenda had slipped a little, overtaken by the murder of Helen Breen and the concerns of Ralph Wilson to which she was giving some attention.

Belfast seemed to be ill at ease this morning. The day was dank and bitterly cold and around the university area students huddled into their winter attire and moved quickly towards the shelter of campus buildings. This was no climate for hanging around and chatting in the open air. Drivers too seemed inclined to irritation with one and other and Alice took heed and did what she could to protect her vulnerable status as a cyclist.

Cycling through the Village area towards west Belfast, the dilapidation in some quarters seemed to overshadow signs of development and regeneration. Alice realised that she was projecting her own unsettled feelings onto the entire environment and worked hard to shift her attitude into a more positive place before she arrived at EXIT.

Hugo opened the familiar red door and welcomed her with a concerned smile. "I've just heard the ten o'clock news about events in DePRec. Are you alright, Alice?"

She wheeled her bike past him, stored it in a recess beyond the de-stress zone and turned to face him.

"Well, it has been a quite shocking turn of events really. You can imagine what the atmosphere is like in the college with everyone being interviewed by the police and the unrestrained speculation of some who are getting high on the drama."

She followed him to his office and allowed herself to settle into the battered armchair facing his desk. He started to make her a coffee without needing to establish her preferences. Alice felt herself ease into the reassuring sense of belonging in this place.

"It's a strange melding of two worlds for me. I'm having to work hard to establish a new equilibrium that takes account of having a murder inquiry added to my list of daily distractions. It's hard to completely ignore old patterns when you are so up close to what is happening." She lapsed into silent consideration as Hugo watched and waited. She shook her head as if to dislodge a bothersome insect. "What did they say at the press conference?"

"Oh, they named the victim as Dr Helen Breen and said they were conducting a murder investigation that centered around the Belfast City College, and they named DePRec in particular, where she had worked. They said the inquiry had begun on Wednesday evening after the body was located in the Titanic Quarter. A journalist asked them if it was true that the body was found in a freezer in the Maritime Studies Centre. The woman detective who did most of the talking refused to give any detail of where the remains were found – you know – 'for operational reasons' or some such phrase. She asked for consideration to be given to Breen's family and for anyone with any information to come forward. I suppose it's early days if she was only located on Wednesday evening."

Something in Hugo's matter-of-fact tone and attitude reminded Alice that violent death was a more familiar topic in Northern Ireland than in many other places. In the past there was nearly always the question of a political motive associated with violent death. She wondered how policing had changed for DI Caroline

Paton and her colleagues since the Troubles had ended and crime had become more to do with ordinary, everyday social conflicts. And in terms of their work in EXIT, did the context of a murder make any difference to the nature of reparation and justice?

"I can see that you have a lot on your mind, Alice," Hugo gently cut into her rapidly spiralling train of thought. "Would you like to postpone this planning session?"

She realised that she had been totally distracted to the point that when he spoke she was surprised to find there was someone else in the room. She mustered all her powers of concentration and met his questioning look straight on with her determined response.

"I would not, Hugo. We have a lot to talk about. I want to hear about your break and I definitely want to tell you about the conference and the reception that our paper received. I am even more enthusiastic than I was before about being aware of social harm in the work we do. The group are absolutely right that only one set of people are expected to make reparation and their own harm is rendered invisible by current structures." She realised she was gabbling and reined herself in. "And before all that I want you to bring me up to date about how everyone is in the group. I hope there were no crises over the Christmas spell. I know it can be the worst time for many people. Then we have a plan to make for the next few months." She smiled convincingly to show him that she was able to pull it all together. "Where will we start, Hugo? Just as well we have the whole day." She stood up. "First of all let me wish you a happy New Year," and she moved around the desk and hugged him enthusiastically.

27

Despite a disturbed night with the new baby, Ian McVeigh was leaving his home not long after eight o'clock on Friday morning. He had made sure that his appearance communicated competence and authority in an understated manner. Nothing too flashy, just quiet tasteful clothes and excellent grooming. Sally had wolf-whistled when he came into the kitchen to say goodbye and he knew he had hit the right note. He liked to get a chance to take charge of some aspects of an investigation and Paton and Burrows had grown to trust him. He was meticulous in his attention to recording findings and his instincts were sound. Although it didn't show too much, he was quietly ambitious about his future in the force.

Ian had called Hillsborough Police Station the previous evening and explained that he would be in the village on Friday morning as part of the investigation into Helen Breen's murder.

The night duty sergeant had been very affable. "I wondered how long it would be before we heard from you guys," he had quipped. "There's quite a stir in the village already since the news began to leak out. Once the press gets a hold of the details I'd say we'll get a bit of spillover attention here. Of course it goes without saying that we'll be happy to support your inquiry any way we can."

Ian made a mental note to check with DI Paton about involving the local force in some house-to-house calls. The familiar trusted face often gathered more useful information than the stranger could.

He had asked for any help they could offer in terms of background knowledge on Helen Breen as a local resident and any known relationships she had in the area. He explained that the following morning he would be bringing some forensic people to look at her house and car if it was available and that he would call at the local station before meeting the lab guys at Breen's house at ten. The sergeant said he would get a local patrol car to drop past that evening and see what was to be seen from outside. It would take a day or so to pull a report together for them but he would set the wheels in motion straight away. He would also leave a note in the station log so the daytime squad knew to expect him.

McVeigh took the rural Hillhall Road out of Belfast towards Lisburn in the hope of avoiding the morning motorway traffic. He wasn't long on the road, singing happily to Cool FM, when Burrows phoned to update him on developments. He could expect the car to be at Breen's house as they had CCTV of Liam Doyle driving it there on the Friday morning after Breen's killing. That was quite the turn-up! Doyle was moving centre-picture now alongside Wilson and the pace of the inquiry was picking up. The 'boss' was gathering information on Doyle and she and Burrows would interview him together later on Friday morning.

"You and the lab boys can check for any signs of Doyle in Breen's house or the locality," Burrows continued. "Gather up any laptops, mobiles or interesting paperwork and ask the local force to check back on their CCTV for the period before and after the Thursday when we now know she was killed."

"Bill, what do you think about asking the locals to do some house-to-house?"

"Good idea. I'll get the boss to set that up with her counterpart in Hillsborough. Best to follow the procedures. Good thinking, Ian. See you back at the Barracks this afternoon. Things are finally beginning to take off, I think."

Burrow's quiet excitement was infectious and Ian braced himself to give his part of the picture his best effort. He switched off the radio. Bill's call had totally re-engaged him and he wanted to give it his full focus.

There was a bit of traffic mayhem in Lisburn and it

was nearly nine when Ian pulled into the car park in front of Hillsborough Police Station. The surroundings were very different to the Belfast stations. Unlike the often run down urban settings, this was an affluent leafy suburb. Ian was impressed by the size of the houses round about. Even the new build near the station consisted of enormous detached houses with big gardens and double garages. It was a radically different work environment to the one he was used to in Belfast City Centre.

The difference wasn't only outside. Hillsborough Station had an impressively comfortable reception area that obviously catered to its more genteel victims of crime.

The duty sergeant showed Ian into a small room off the reception area and gave him an envelope that had been left for him by the night staff. "That's a short account of the patrol car officer's observations of the property and the vehicle parked outside. The fuller report is in hand." He settled himself on the edge of the table and motioned to Ian to take a seat. "The old Manse is on the southern side of the village and relatively discreet from other dwellings. Your victim didn't show much interest in integrating into the community here. Quite the opposite actually." It was clear that Helen Breen had not scored many points for social interaction. "There is a recent development of about eight town houses near Breen's place, but they are all facing away from her. I'd be surprised if there was any contact."

"We are very grateful for any local knowledge you can share with us that is pertinent to the case." Ian wasn't sure that what was forthcoming was fact or local fiction but either way it would have some bearing on the victim profile and he needed to pay close attention.

The local man appeared to be intent on giving Ian a thorough cultural briefing. "We make it our business to know our community well, DC McVeigh. We have ongoing security issues here because of the Big House."

Ian nodded to show he was up to speed with the local territory and policing priorities.

"Our chaps on the ground know more about local residents and their frequent visitors than they would ever imagine." He raised his eyebrows and looked meaningfully over the top of his glasses. "We need to know if anybody at all who spends time in the Village is a potential security risk. We may need to do background checks on people visiting locally to ensure that they are not just positioning themselves to carry out a terrorist attack in the future."

His pause here seemed to be for dramatic effect and Ian kept his face open but expressionless.

"If someone, like Dr Breen for example, has unusual habits that are legal between consenting adults and pose no security threat, then we cease to be interested and people are free to do as they wish in the privacy of their own homes. Nevertheless, we remain vigilant and well-informed." He grinned smugly and Ian refrained from any response. "We don't broadcast that our surveillance is as thorough as it is, but it may be that in this instance our observations of Dr Breen may be of some interest to your inquiry."

"Thank you, Sergeant. We would be more than grateful for any information you can share about Helen Breen and particularly her recent visitors. We believe that a young man called Liam Doyle may be on that list and any details you have about him would be much appreciated." He handed the sergeant a card that had the email contact details for the detection team and his own mobile number.

The local man stood up to his full height, indicating that he was finished for the moment and Ian rose too, glad to be able to head off and meet his colleagues outside Breen's house.

"I will have an extra word with the person who is preparing that report for you, DC McVeigh." He nodded conspiratorially. "I hope we will be able to provide you with something of use to your investigation."

Hillsborough village centre took in a steep hill with tasteful small shops, pubs and restaurants on either side. At the top, off to the right, was the entrance to the Castle – an attractive soft sandstone building behind high railings and with sentry boxes at the gate. With a population of less than four thousand and some fine Georgian architecture, Hillsborough was a well-regarded place to live. The Castle, known locally as 'the

Big House', was the Queen's residence in Northern Ireland and there was the sense amongst quite a number of the residents that they were courtiers just waiting to be called to the royal presence. A terrace of three houses in the village square had their doors painted consecutively red, white and blue. In the North, this clearly articulated the political identity of the area to all with eyes to see.

The main road followed the castle wall and just a few minutes further along this treelined road Ian drew into a short driveway that led to the Old Manse. He could see Breen's Mazda parked outside the house which stood well apart from any other places of residence in the immediate area, facing the stone wall and forested grounds around the Castle. As the local sergeant had said, there was indeed a small new development to the rear but the houses faced away from the Old Manse and there was no shared access road.

It was clear, even from the outside, that Helen Breen had bought this fine old property on the outskirts of the village and tastefully renovated it to be her escape from all those who would relish a glimpse of her private life. She had definitively ensured that her personal life was exactly that.

As he was a little early, he decided to write up some notes from his meeting with the station sergeant. He had definitely been saying that Helen Breen had visitors whose sexual interests were somewhat unusual and that was a significant element to add into the victim profile. The envelope he had handed over contained details of the vehicle parked, unmoved, outside the house since Friday 20 December. Local patrols had noted that the house seemed uninhabited over the holiday period but this was not seen as unusual since so many local people travelled abroad for Christmas.

Ian was lost in thought when a familiar face peered in the side window at him, pulling a comical expression. Tim Bryson was the same vintage as Ian and they had attended some elements of the police graduate programme together. Tim had studied science and Ian and he had hit if off in those early days. Ian was inclined to be overly cautious and Tim's inclination to play the clown had helped him relax and they had remained friends even after their career paths had become quite separate. He got out of the car and greeted his friend warmly. Tim's assistant was a trainee and she stood shyly by as the boisterous reunion played out.

Minutes later when they were all suited up, Ian led the way towards the house. "Let's go inside first and if the car keys are obvious maybe you would have a look at it afterwards."

As Ian opened the front door with the key provided by Breen's mother, a local patrol car drove slowly by.

Once inside, his first impressions were of a tasteful yet lifeless scene from an interior design magazine. He was involved in creating his own first home at the moment and Sally and he chose everything together. They had spent several weeks recently selecting a fitted carpet for the hallway and living room and he knew what a lot of time and cost was invested in these decisions. He reckoned that Breen's home was a study in careful style choices alongside the expenditure of a lot of money.

The entrance hall was light and uncluttered. Where you might expect some outdoor clothes abandoned inside the front door there was only a full-length mahogany mirror and a semicircular glass table that held one small, but probably very pricey figurine. He noted that Helen Breen's home was furnished with high quality pieces of furniture, discreet electronic devices and several expensive-looking artworks around the walls. Nevertheless, to Ian's mind, it lacked any sense of being a home where day-to-day life happened.

The forensic duo was waiting for his guidance so he pulled himself back into the moment and looked carefully around. There was no sign of any disturbance and Ian didn't think that there was any direct link here to the actual murder. He looked around for the kitchen and any more sign of life than had been evident to date.

At the rear of the house, a covered glass walkway of about fifty metres connected the main house to a reclaimed two-storey outbuilding. Downstairs had been converted into a large kitchen, dining room and casual seating area. There was a wood-burning stove and a manicured log pile that filled a custom-built alcove. The whole space was open, reaching from the floor to the exposed rafters. Here at least there was some sense of a life having been lived whereas the main house suggested only a life concealed.

In the kitchen area there was an unwashed cup in the sink and a handwritten note on the table. McVeigh was immediately alert. "The note is from 'Lx', which we can assume is Liam Doyle. '*The guy collected the laptop. I Waited for a while but guess you have been delayed. Talk later.*' It's dated Friday 20th December so the day after the killing. I'm interested to know if there is evidence of Doyle anywhere else. We'll check out here and the bedrooms and bathroom in the main house too."

Off the kitchen to the rear of the building there was a sizeable utility room. A large freezer was stocked with pre-prepared meals and a collection of fine wines filled a large wine rack. Helen Breen liked to eat and drink well for minimum personal effort.

Tim Bryson and his trainee set to work while McVeigh studied the lay of the land. Since their arrival the trainee had been taking photographs throughout the house. He would make sure to have them uploaded onto the shared drive and these would be useful for sharing with his colleagues later. "Bag and dust in here too, please, Tim, and I'll have a look upstairs. I'm looking for any devices – PC, laptop, mobile phone or maybe even some written evidence from a study, a filing cabinet or anything like that."

He ran up the open-tread staircase that led to a mezzanine area. A big skylight dominated the area and otherwise there were no windows. One wall was lined with books and files except for a large rectangular space into which an oak desk was set. There were three desk drawers on each side and a high-backed cream leather chair sat in between. An outsized bed was centred on the second wall. It had an impressive black iron headboard in the shape of a spider's web. The bedclothes were plum-coloured silk or satin. On the third wall a large screen television was angled towards the bed. A half-wall overlooked the lower part of the building where Tim and his colleague could be heard going about their task of gathering evidence.

To the left of the bed a door led to a walk-in wardrobe and dressing room. Here, all was impeccably ordered with military precision. To the right of the bed, a door led to a bathroom which had a large bathtub and a separate walk-in shower. These two rooms had an interconnecting door. Up here, Ian thought, there was the first real sign that Helen Breen was not a total automaton but what the space said about its owner was not entirely clear. She had gone to enormous lengths to hide her real life behind the façade that the front of the house presented to the public. He had noted the implication of what the sergeant had said earlier about her covert pastimes but was slow to jump to conclusions without evidence.

He pulled his latex gloves more securely over his hands and moved towards the desk. The top was bare except for the wires that had once attached to a laptop. A double socket also held a mobile-phone charger but there was no device present. The top righthand drawer held some college stationery and a handbook for a MacBookPro. Ian searched methodically through the remaining desk drawers and in the final one found a diary and an address book, both of which contained handwritten data and some printed business cards. He bagged these for scrutiny later. Then he turned to the shelves and the box files in particular.

After a couple of hours more spent in Breen's house, McVeigh transferred his findings to an empty evidence chest and carried it to the car. The forensic team had their own case of carefully labelled samples already stored on the back seat of their vehicle.

"We will get reports to you as soon as we can, Ian, and Myrtle will load the images as soon as we get back. Nice to catch up with you, mate." Tim pulled one of his classic faces and winked exaggeratedly. "We must do this again soon, sir," he said in his best lord-of-the-manor voice, jumped into the passenger seat and gave a regal wave as he was driven off.

McVeigh turned his car towards the M1 and headed back towards the station where he had plenty to occupy himself with until the planned review that evening. He had uncovered a considerable amount of evidence to add to the victim profile and potentially point to motives for her murder that had nothing to do with the workplace. He felt pleased with his morning's work.

28

That same morning, at exactly eight fifteen, DS Bill Burrows sat down in the comfortably upholstered chair at the end of Mairéad Walsh's large office desk. It was here that she entertained Ralph Wilson when he came to call. It was also where overwrought staff and students experienced her soothing powers. Burrows had brought a coffee with him and Mairéad lost no time in proffering a selection of rice cakes as a possible accompaniment. He politely declined and hoped that Caroline Paton never discovered them – he greatly preferred Paton's idea of a snack. Mairéad had asked that they speak in her office so that if she were needed she would be on hand. She had explained that her colleague who occupied the inner office was working off campus for the day so they probably wouldn't be disturbed.

"This is a shocking business, Detective Sergeant," Mairéad began imperiously.

It was as if the peasant class had behaved even more outrageously than might be expected and Burrows was inwardly amused by her manner.

"Mrs Walsh, I realise you are in a very privileged position in DePRec in that you see and hear a wide range of opinions and accounts of events. Have you formed any view of who might have a motive for harming Dr Helen Breen?"

"I would be extremely surprised, Detective, if this event were related to the workplace at all. I have worked here for decades and I have seen all types of rivalries and conflicts," here she took a long meaningful breath, "but it has never resulted in this, or any other type of violence." She paused and then added, "Once a long time ago a young female lecturer slapped the face of a senior male colleague at an end-of-term drinks 'do'. She was disciplined on her return to work but otherwise we have remained as peaceful as our title would suggest." She took another thoughtful moment, this time accompanied by an eye roll, and then she took off again with renewed vigour. "You see, Detective Sergeant, academics are all about words and talk. They love nothing better than to hear themselves pour forth at great length on any subject whatsoever. It might be the weather, the restaurant menu, the state of the college lavatories. I have had all the lectures and more, delivered as if there were an Oscar pending for the performance. But I would say that the idea of moving far enough outside themselves to become active, never mind violently so ... well, that just does not match with my experience."

"How well did you know Dr Breen? What opinion had you formed of her?" Burrows launched his questions and waited.

Mairéad Walsh considered her answer and examined her fingers at some length before responding. "DS Burrows, my role here means I see and hear much that I am never expected to divulge. My opinion of my colleagues is not a relevant part of my role in managing the smooth administration of the DePRec's day-to-day business. I know many things, all of which are confidential. I attend all DePRec staff meetings and I write letters and minutes and private documents for Professor Bell and others. I have full audio and written records of all meetings going back over a number of years. Whatever opinion I formed of Dr Helen Breen is neither here nor there."

The woman's bluster was convincing but Burrows was experienced at being played and had his own strategies.

"But, Mairéad," he coaxed, "I just want to know if you liked her."

"I did not," she responded without hesitation. "I treated her with the respect due to a colleague and another human being but I did not like anything about her."

Burrows remained silent and Mairéad continued.

"I felt she was a heartless woman entirely motivated

by her own self-promotion. I don't think I ever saw her show a genuine emotion about anything." She took a breath and looked at him over her glasses. "She put me in mind of a wicked puppeteer ... always scheming and manipulating so as to raise herself up higher in her own estimation. I don't think she really cared about anyone or anything."

"That's a very definite position to have taken, Mairéad. I wonder if Helen Breen was close to any of her colleagues? You might have been in a position to hear chat about such friendships. Would people have visited her home for example? Did she invite people for meals or did she ever have a party?"

"No. I never heard about such an event ever taking place. She kept very much to herself. She was here but outside in a way. You would feel she was always watching and calculating. She would have gone for a coffee or lunch very occasionally with Professor Bell and she emailed him very frequently but more to keep herself at the forefront of his mind than out of any sincere closeness, in my opinion. Part of my role is to monitor Professor Bell's work emails and I can assure you that she was forever bolstering the idea that she was DePRec's most devoted supporter. And for some reason that very clever man fell for it all – hook, line and sinker."

Burrows changed tack a little and asked about the forthcoming contest for the new professorial post.

"DS Burrows," she said as if speaking to someone

who has missed an obvious item of information, "it is no secret in DePRec that I am a close personal friend of Dr Ralph Wilson, who would have been Helen Breen's only competitor in the professorial appointment process. Much of Breen's time was spent discrediting Ralph and spinning opinion against him. In fact, she was very effective in doing that and she would more than likely have been DePRec's next professor." Mairéad stopped as if suddenly aware that she was creating a clear motive for Ralph to wish his opposition out of the way.

Burrows nodded and probed a little further.

"How did she go about that? Have you an example?"

Mairéad restrained herself from launching into a rant about the machinations of Helen Breen. She calmly recounted the episode of Breen's lunch invitation to the new faculty head, Professor Janet Hartnett.

"They knew each other at school apparently and Breen was not going to miss the chance to swing influential opinion in her direction. It was stomach-turning to watch her operate with such brazenness right outside my office door. It was quite the performance, I can tell you." She paused to purse her lips and lower her eyelids in disdain. "And it was even worse to witness how effective she was ... and at the same time others further down the food chain she would treat like dirt." She had said more than she intended and wasn't too happy with the impression she had communicated of her own clear bias. "Look, I am not really sure why Helen

201

Breen aggravated people so much but a big part of it was her obvious unshakeable confidence in her own worth." She smiled at some internal image. "I had an old aunt in Dublin who had a phrase she used when people got above themselves. She'd roll her eyes and say 'delusions of adequacy!'. I think it's a concept that suited Helen Breen very well."

Time was getting on towards nine o'clock and Burrows gathered his papers and thanked Mairéad for her time. He said he would come back to her if he had any further questions and left to go to the boardroom where he had an appointment to talk to Jackson Bell at the top of the hour. He liked Mairéad Walsh and her direct approach to giving her views. At the same time she had unintentionally added detail to the case against Ralph Wilson and he felt that they were right to have a second, more insistent chat with him later that day.

29

On Friday morning at precisely nine fifty, DI Caroline Paton was shown into the Detective Superintendent's Office in PSNI Headquarters. As the head of the Murder Squad, Paton commanded considerable respect but she did not take any of that for granted. She knew the tide could just as easily turn against her and was mindful of that, without allowing herself to be fawning or sycophantic toward her superiors. She worked as hard as she could and then some, and preferred to steer a small efficient ship than the showy self-aggrandising alternative. Detective Superintendent Graham McCluskey was a canny Scot who appreciated this approach to policing. Caroline had observed that he was as careful of his immaculately groomed appearance as he was of his untarnished reputation for good policing. She delivered the kind of results for which he was happy to accept overall responsibility and in exchange he did not meddle in her case management. She had sent him the necessary briefing papers the previous evening and knew he would rely on her this morning to field the press enquiries and provide judiciously framed responses.

He stood as she came in and extended his well-manicured hand. "Good morning, DI Paton. Any significant overnight developments that I need to be aware of?"

Caroline noted his ability to politely cut straight to the chase.

"We have made some progress since I wrote your briefing, sir. Nothing which I would like to make public at this point but enough to be able to honestly say we are making progress in our enquiries even at this early stage." She hesitated and then decided it was best to be completely candid with her concerns. "I feel there is a distinct possibility that the press may have got hold of the details of the location of the remains. There were too many maintenance and security staff involved to be able to control that information and it's the kind of thing they'll go for. However, I would like to try to shut that line down for the moment in the hope that we can still use some of the detail to catch someone out in our questioning. There are some important staff interviews still to be completed today. I have a number of responses prepared that will support that position. We can give them a little more detail once we have the weekend behind us."

At one minute to ten the office door opened and a young uniformed constable announced that it was "time to raise the curtain". The two senior officers proceeded to their prepared places at the front of the Press Room like performers secure in their grasp of the current script. As they sat down calmly on the podium, their audience gave them their unfaltering attention.

30

In the home of Helen Breen's mother, PC Sandra Woods sat in the warm kitchen and helped Lisa as she prepared a tray to bring in to the elderly woman. She had reportedly slept soundly the previous night.

"She is not very much an emotional person," Lisa said by way of explanation. "I think she has got used to being by herself and she has stopped expecting to feel things for her son and daughter. They don't give her any reason to feel anything … and so she doesn't any longer have the habit."

The presence of Sandra Woods was perhaps a relief from the solitary nature of Lisa's task and she continued to voice her long-observed opinions of her employer's disposition.

"She is very different with her son in Australia and his children. Usually when they call her on Skype there is laughing and chatting and then she is a little sad afterwards when the call is finished." Lisa smiled to herself. "I have even heard Mrs Breen singing to the smallest child."

Sandra revised her view of Mrs Breen upwards.

The kettle boiled and Lisa made the coffee in a cafetière and set it aside to brew. Sandra asked if there had been a Skype call with Mrs Breen's son Frank and his family since she had left yesterday afternoon but then realised that with the ten-and-a-half-hour time difference that was unlikely.

"Michael was going to email them and Mrs Breen will call them this morning. I will put the Skype call through for her once I have served the coffee. You will see that Frank is the most friendly of all the Breens."

Sandra held the door open for Lisa to carry the tray through. Mrs Breen greeted the constable in a reasonably friendly manner and waited patiently as her coffee was poured and placed on the small table beside her chair. The morning paper was opened at a small piece about the emerging murder investigation.

"I wanted to show Frank the item about Helen in the local paper," she explained with a certain innocence. "Maybe you would like to have a few words with him too, officer?"

Sandra wondered if Mrs Breen had after all been given some type of relaxant, given her apparent calm acceptance of her daughter's murder. Perhaps it was more to do with remaining in the moment, a capacity that the constable had remarked in other older people with whom she had carried out her Family Liaison role.

"Thank you, Mrs Breen. I will happily have a few words with Frank and address any queries he may have." Sandra would be able to flag up a future interview with DI Paton and her team as she was sure that was somewhere on the schedule.

BBC Radio 3 played classical music soothingly in the background as the women sipped their coffee.

Mrs Breen smiled faintly. "This is almost quite pleasant," she observed. "I am so used to being alone that I forget that company can be quite agreeable."

Lisa made brief eye contact with Sandra with a look that suggested the surprise she felt at this uncharacteristic declaration.

"If you are ready, ma'am," she said, "I will begin to dial Frank's number. Sometimes it takes a moment or two to get the connection."

Sandra's role didn't usually extend as far as Australia but she was open to the possibilities offered by meeting another member of the Breen family who seemed to be outside of the regular, rather frosty family mould.

31

By the time that Caroline Paton had extricated herself from PSNI HQ and returned to DePRec, Burrows had finished his interviews with both Bell and Hartnett and was having coffee and a scone. Caroline helped herself from the table at the side of the room and sat down beside Burrows.

"Nothing out of the ordinary at the Press 'do' aside from the fact that news of the freezer is already out there," she said. "I hedged that question but by Monday they will expect a fuller account of the inquiry. What about you, Bill? Anything talking back to you yet?" She was adding copious amounts of butter and jam to her scone and looking pleased with herself.

She loved sweet things and Burrows admired her capacity to balance that with remaining fairly trim. He supposed it was the large amounts of energy she put into her work that helped burn the calories. He didn't see her as the gym type but maybe she was a secret exerciser. Without any concerns for his own weight, he swallowed his mouthful of scone before he answered.

"Well, now," he said, "both Bell and Hartnett were interesting to talk to in their own way. I'll give you a full account later of course but they both have some kind of history with Breen that is not entirely clear."

Paton gave him her full attention. She trusted his investigative instincts which had paid off several times in the past.

"Bell had an inexplicable trust and loyalty to Helen Breen that is at odds with the opinion almost every other member of staff recounted to us. He comes across as a strange fish ... somehow otherworldly or old-fashioned or ... I haven't quite managed to figure him out yet. In terms of opportunity it struck me ... the night she died he had asked her to cover for him as the senior manager on duty in DePRec. That means that he knew where she would be at a time when others would not be expecting her to be there. He claims he was out and about reviewing political wall paintings and was alone so his story can't be corroborated. We need to check cameras around the college to see if he may have returned and simply omitted to swipe in. I doubt that security staff, who are used to seeing him about, would really notice him. On top of that, the last evening of term is messy and the unusual is almost expected."

Burrows was visibly computing information and Paton was used to his thorough approach and enjoyed seeing the signs of his mind at work.

"I asked him if he wasn't surprised that Breen was not in work on the last day of term and he answered very promptly that he wasn't. He had received an email from her the previous night saying that she had to stay at home during the day, as her mother's Filipino care worker was unexpectedly unavailable during the day. Bell had no idea that Breen did not live at her official address on the college records. He had accepted her email without question but now the times are not matching up. What we know about time of death doesn't tally with the victim sending emails after ten o'clock. I'll check the story out through Woods but it rings hollow to me."

Caroline reached for a second scone. "Will you have half of this, Bill, and save me from myself?"

"OK, go on. We can both feel virtuous. Anyway, what I'm saying is that Bell is still in the loop for me although his behaviour the night the body was located suggested he was genuinely surprised."

Caroline nodded. She knew they would visit all this in detail later in the day but could see that Bill was processing and allowed that to finish uninterrupted. "And Professor Janet Hartnett?"

"Well, she is relatively new. She only took up the post of Faculty Head in September, having been in a college

211

over the water prior to that. She lives in Crawfordsburn in a large property that is shared with her parents. They are getting on in years and she needed help with her young adult son who has quite considerable intellectual disabilities. Anyway, their arrangement suits everybody. She was a few years older than Breen at school. They were not friendly as such but since she has arrived Breen has been quite affable and they had been to lunch a few times. Hartnett was in her office on the Thursday evening and swiped out at nine thirty. She went straight home as her parents like to go to bed early and the son needs constant care. He has some kind of neurological disorder." Bill swept up some loose crumbs and tipped them into his mouth. "It doesn't seem, on first reflection, that she would have had time to kill Breen and get away home so quickly … but her earlier relationship with Breen merits a little more investigation. Mairéad Walsh told me that Breen was courting Hartnett's favour with gusto."

Paton nodded in agreement. "We will have a lot to sift this afternoon. The weekend is falling well for us in terms of the college being closed and giving us a few days' grace before the next meeting with the press on Monday. I have some hope that we can make some real progress over the next few days …"

Burrows understood from this that they would be working through Saturday and Sunday but he would have expected nothing less.

There was a knock on the door and Liam Doyle

stepped sheepishly into the room.

"Just give us five minutes, please, Mr Doyle." Burrows extended his large palm as if stopping traffic. Doyle withdrew. "Let's have a quick recap on what we know so far about Doyle. I sent a message to Ian to check if there is any sign of Doyle being a visitor to Helen Breen. I want to know exactly what we have on this guy."

When Liam Doyle came back into the room, at Burrows' invitation, his handsome features were pinched and distorted with worry. He sat opposite the two police officers who purposefully left a few moments' silence before beginning the interview. It was clear from Doyle's demeanor that he was very much on edge and Paton and Burrows both sharpened their antennae for what might be revealed. They could instinctively sense the potential in the moment.

Doyle broke the silence with an explosive statement. "I know that I should have come to you myself as soon as I heard of Helen's death but I was in a bit of a fog and didn't realise the significance of what happened ... I don't mean what happened to her. I mean what happened to me and how it will look when I explain." He looked at them with some desperation but neither offered him any relief. "Historically, my family doesn't have a good relationship with the forces of law and order and I'm sure that held me back from being more insistent about having an earlier appointment to talk to you ... I just want to get on with my job here and not make any waves." His voice had all but petered out as he tried to justify himself, but Paton and Burrows had let him carry on uninterrupted.

Eventually Paton spoke calmly, making direct eye contact with Doyle. They had agreed that she would lead the questioning and Burrows would observe.

"We know that you are the student representative in DePRec, Mr Doyle, and that role has been fully outlined to us by Professor Bell. For the record, he spoke very highly of you and your attentiveness to your role ... but that is not what is at issue here, as you know. What we would like to focus on now is your relationship with the late Dr Helen Breen. And as it seems to be the case, when did your connection with her move from a professional concern with student welfare to a more personal liaison?"

Doyle looked at Caroline Paton as if he was struggling to understand her question or to grasp the context in which it was being asked. "I have always liked her since I did my Master's here. I suppose since she showed an interest in me and my work. I know that other people don't ... I mean didn't like her but she was always considerate of my interests. She made me feel as if I was important and she was not known for taking a lot of interest in people. In fact, I think that it was because of her recommendation to Professor Bell that I was offered the post of student rep. She told me that herself. I was very grateful to her and tried to show my loyalty by defending her when her colleagues were critical of her. I said clearly that I supported her in her application for the new professorship. I was on her side so I hope that makes it clear that I would never hurt her." All of these statements were delivered in a hesitant, emotionless voice. "I was in love with her but we were not lovers. She was in a different league to me. Why would someone like her be interested in an orphan from West Belfast whose parents had blown themselves up planting an IRA bomb? It would have been against all her professional aspirations. She could have been with anyone she liked. You don't get to be professor by messing around with a student or someone who had just graduated from that role." His arguments were accurate but not very convincingly made.

"Some of your colleagues noted that you had become increasingly close in the lead-up to the Christmas break. You were together at the Christmas drinks party ... only had eyes for each other apparently. It has been said that your behaviour towards each other the night in Crawfordsburn was overtly sexual." Paton paused to let that message hit home.

He looked forlorn. "Sometimes I thought she did like me that way," he said very quietly. "Like, she sought me out to do stuff with her. Small stuff ... carry heavy things out to her car, move furniture, open boxes of books she had ordered and put them on shelves. Help clear up after student evenings when she needed to rush off to look after her mother."

Paton and Burrows watched as Doyle revealed the small uses, some of them obviously fabricated, that Breen had put Doyle to and how grateful he was for being the subject of her demands. The familiar grooming process resonated with both of them.

"I was at her house in Hillsborough a few times and I don't think she asked people there really. She was a very private person ... a mystery in lots of ways. I've been thinking about her constantly since I heard the news and I realise I know very little about her." He faltered. "Like I know very little about her personally. I never met any of her friends and apart from her mother, she didn't talk about family really. The only photo I saw in her house was of her father but she didn't talk to me about him other than to let me know he had died suddenly when she was a teenager."

"Where were you on Thursday evening, 19th of December, Liam?" Paton enquired whilst turning her pen over and back between her two hands. "Were you in college for the last evening of classes?"

"No. I should have been here but I was needed at home. I live with my nan and she needs help in the evenings. The woman who usually helps her to bed wasn't available because of her Christmas work's 'do', and there was only me free. It doesn't happen very often but I knew that the last evening of the term it was unlikely that there would be a crisis that couldn't wait until January."

Paton intervened. "Who did you let know that you couldn't be at work that evening? Did you know that Dr Breen was covering for Professor Bell on Thursday?"

Doyle answered immediately. "It isn't like that. I don't really report to anyone. I manage my own time and people know they can email me if I'm not about and I'll get back to them." He thought further about the question. "I might have known that Helen was working. She might have mentioned it the night before but it wouldn't have made any difference. My nan comes first. She raised me after my parents died and I wouldn't leave her without the help she needs."

Burrows fixed Doyle with a steady stare. "I want you to think very carefully when you answer my next question. When did you last see or hear from Dr Breen?"

Doyle looked bewildered. "I don't remember if I saw her on the Thursday during the day but I got an email from her on the Thursday evening. It was a bit strange actually and I'm worried about it now that I know what happened." He looked anxious as he continued. "I would need to check back and see what time I got that. I'm not even sure I kept the email but she asked me to pick up her car keys in the college on Friday morning and drive her car to Hillsborough. She'd left the keys in an envelope in my mailbox in the post room. She said she had to stay at her mother's unexpectedly on the Thursday and someone was calling at the house early on Friday to collect a laptop that needed repair. I was to go there and let the guy in and she said she would see me there later. I went there as she asked. I let the guy in and he seemed to know what he was at. He collected the laptop and then I waited, and I tried to phone her but she never came and I got a bus home eventually ... in the afternoon." He looked at them as if he was aware of how farfetched this story sounded.

Burrows furrowed his brow and looked incredulous. "I'm not sure how that all adds up, Liam. Take us through it all again from Thursday afternoon onwards."

With the morning's interviews completed, Paton and Burrows met with McVeigh on his return from Hillsborough for a late and fairly unappetising lunch in the station canteen.

"I'm not sure, if this was a blind tasting, that I'd have detected either the chicken or the curry element of this dish," quipped Burrows.

"Just as well then that your forte is detecting murder and not flavours in haute cuisine," Paton said with her customary dry humour.

They all three ate in companionable silence for a few minutes.

"So we have a lot of catching up to do that will mostly have to wait until this evening when I get back from the Breen household," Paton then said. "Let's eat this and then grab half an hour in the office to get a grasp of the basics before we get on with the rest of the day. We have Doyle here being processed for some further inquiries this afternoon and Wilson coming in at three."

McVeigh interrupted. "I have a box of stuff to go through from Breen's house. There are files and photographs that I'd like to make sense of before I share them later."

"OK," said Paton. "So probably best if Bill and I continue with Doyle and Wilson for the moment. While I'm out with the family later on I think the two of you might have a look around Doyle's house. We have enough to justify a warrant. Then we'll meet up back here about eight and decide what we've got and where we go from here. I am hopeful that by Monday we can begin to see a much clearer picture of this whole affair."

The men nodded in agreement while intently chewing large mouthfuls of food.

"I'm sure I'll have a number of things to get up onto the shared drive before we meet later," said Ian, "and the few hours this afternoon would be more than useful." His head was buzzing with his discoveries from the morning. "I'll get Doyle's prints over to forensics to see what sort of matches that throws up from the Hillsborough search."

"OK. Let's hold steady, guys. We have a busy afternoon and evening ahead and we need this small break to rest and replenish the little grey cells. Pudding, anyone?"

They nodded in unison and DI Paton rejoined the canteen queue to collect three bowls of apple crumble and custard.

32

To the DePRec admin manager, it already felt like a very long day. Towards the end of lunchtime, she and Ralph Wilson sat in the corner of the college canteen in deep conversation. A skin had formed on Wilson's untouched milky coffee and the packet of ham sandwiches in front of him was barely touched. As he wrestled with what he saw as his desperate plight he emitted the occasional whine as if in physical pain.

Mairéad drew herself up into a more upright posture and breathed earnestly through her nose. "You know, Ralph, this is all quite pointless until the detectives do their job and gather in the evidence. You feel like you're an obvious suspect but you don't need to rush ahead always expecting the worst. Lots of colleagues despise each other without resorting to murder. I'm prepared to bet this is about something much bigger than a staffroom tiff."

He looked at her from beneath his brows, willing her to be right.

"Let's put some faith in Alice Fox," she said. "She knows what she's about and she'll do what she can to help."

His hair straggled across his eyes and he pushed it back in exasperation. "I just feel like every way I turn my life is a disaster. My academic work holds little or no influence any more, my home life has crumbled away to nothing but grubby solitude and now I am likely to be a suspect in a murder case. Even from the grave Helen Breen is managing to bugger me up!" He met her gaze. "I don't know how you can be bothered with me."

Before she could retort that he was an utter Drama Queen, his mobile phone rang and he looked at it in alarm.

"Who can that be ... unknown caller?"

He lifted the phone to his ear and muttered his name by way of greeting. His expression of gloom intensified as he rested his head in his free hand and listened to the caller.

"Yes, detective," he said, "but can you tell me exactly why ..." He was listening again and looking defeated. "Yes. OK. I'll be there for three o'clock."

Mairéad looked at him questioningly and stretched her upturned palms towards him to emphasise her query.

"They want me to come in to the police station for further questioning." His bottom lip slackened and his

222

shoulders slumped. "There are matters with which they feel I can be of further assistance. What under God might that mean?"

Mairéad too was taken aback by this development but said nothing.

"I'd better get it together anyway. I've to be there by three o'clock. Don't want them coming looking for me." He began to gather his belongings.

"Ralph, I will try and contact Alice and see what she thinks. They may just want to rule you out of the inquiry. Try to keep your cool and phone me as soon as you get out."

They stood and she placed her hand a little helplessly on his.

"I will try my best to get Alice Fox ... " she said as he turned despondently and made his way towards the exit.

As Mairéad approached the departmental office she saw that the door was open and someone could be heard moving about inside. She hoped against hope that Alice Fox had returned unexpectedly from her scheduled day in the EXIT project. That would be a stroke of luck. As she pushed at the door her heart fell when she saw the back of Jackson Bell who was using the departmental phone. He was replacing the telephone as she made her way to her side of the desk and sat down.

Bell's anxious expression had become a fixture in recent days and Mairéad knew better than to ask any specific questions. "May I help you with something, Professor Bell?" she said efficiently and opened her drawer to check that her supply of rice crackers was sufficient to the afternoon ahead.

"I was trying Liam Doyle's home number but there was no reply. I know he lives with an elderly relative and I wanted to make sure that … Mrs Walsh, Liam Doyle has just been taken into the Grosvenor Road Police Station for further questioning. I have no idea what's going on but I feel responsible for letting his family know."

For reasons that Mairéad could not have elaborated on if asked, she found herself remaining quiet about Ralph's invitation to the police station. Instead, as soon as Bell left, she texted Wilson to say that he was not the only person who was being questioned. She hoped that might help him to remain calm and not contribute any further to a negative image of himself. Then she turned her attention to tracking down Alice Fox.

33

Hugo and Alice worked companionably through the day, finishing in the late afternoon with a hearty plate of fish and chips in the local café. By the time they had closed the red EXIT door behind them, they were both fully up to date on the conference and on each other's holiday period. Alice had enthused about the walks in Wicklow and Hugo reported that he had made strides in his culinary adventures with his son. He said they were nearly ready to experiment if she could think of anyone who might be willing to take a risk. She had laughed and said she would give that challenge careful consideration.

The group had not raised any urgent issues at all over the break, which they agreed was a sign of their growing maturity. They had a solid plan for how to extend the new work with the group around social responsibility, agency and the role of state bodies and representatives. This would be the term of critical citizenship in practice. They had a series of viable suggestions to discuss at their meeting with the group the following week and they had totally earned their hearty Friday evening tea.

The local chipper was owned and run by an Italian family and Hugo was evidently a frequent customer. Several generations of the Fusco family sat at a table towards the rear of the eating area and little by little they all found a reason to stop by and exchange some chat with Hugo and this interesting new woman.

A grandmother figure with a definite twinkle in her eye enquired if Alice was going to be a regular customer. She winked shamelessly at Hugo who accepted the banter with ease.

"Alice is much too fit and healthy to be eating chips every night of the week, Nonna," he parried with her.

The woman patted Alice's shoulder and reassured her with mock sincerity. "I make you a perfect green salad next time you come, signorina. Hugo needs to have a good example too."

There was no telling where this was all going but the scene was disturbed by the entry of Gary from the EXIT group who was clearly looking for Hugo. The nonna faded towards the back of the room and rejoined her family who were eating and watching a TV affixed to the wall above their table.

It was clear that the young man was agitated.

"What's up, Gary?" Hugo asked calmly. "Sit down and let us hear your news."

Gary remained standing, shifting about nervously from foot to foot.

"The cops have just come to our Liam's house and are talking about searching it," he blurted all in one breath. "They said it is about the murder of the woman in the college where Alice and our Liam work. He isn't home and I was looking after the old lady till he gets back. I panicked a wee bit and ran. I didn't know what to do so I just left them there with her and came looking for you." He waited wide-eyed for Hugo to provide a solution.

"Well, let's go around there and make sure old Mrs Doyle isn't too freaked out by her visitors. Or more likely that they aren't too freaked out by her! Then we can see what else needs to be done about Liam." He turned to Alice as he was standing to leave. "How do you feel about coming along, Alice?"

"Sure," said Alice, wondering if it was appropriate for her to be there but surmising that as a co-facilitator of the group she was well within her rights to be part of the salvage mission. "Lead the way, Gary!"

"I'll settle up with you later, Domenico!" Hugo called back as they left the café.

They crossed the main road in the direction of the EXIT premises but took a left turn along a small cul de sac, just before the EXIT alley. There were eight or ten small terraced houses on the street and two police cars were parked at the far end facing outwards. One car was empty except for a uniformed driver. The other had two uniformed police officers sitting in the front.

Hugo knew where he was going and headed straight through the open door without knocking. An elderly woman sat in the corner of a small living room beside an open fire. Although her hair was pure white, Alice could straight away see the family resemblance to Liam Doyle. The glorious red hair and fine features were obvious in a number of the family photos placed around the room. Two detectives sat on a small sofa facing the woman. The older of the two was holding some papers.

"Hi, Mrs Doyle," said Hugo, bypassing the men and going straight to the old woman to give her a hug. "Have you been causing difficulty to the forces of law and order?"

She laughed heartily but the laugh became a barking cough that lasted until Gary got her a drink of water from the small adjoining kitchen.

Hugo turned to the detectives, both of whom Alice recognised from Caroline Paton's team that had spent the previous day in DePRec.

"I'm Hugo Ramsey, a local community worker and this is my colleague Dr Alice Fox who is a scholar in DePRec and works with us locally. Can we help you at all?"

A flash of recognition crossed the older man's face

when he heard Alice's name. This was Caroline Paton's insider contact. He stood up awkwardly and shook hands with both Hugo and Alice, introducing himself as Detective Sergeant William Burrows and the younger man as Detective Constable Ian McVeigh. McVeigh, unable to easily free himself from the low, cramped sofa where he had become ensconced, nodded in greeting.

"We have a warrant to search this house as the home of Liam Doyle who is assisting us in connection with an ongoing inquiry. We didn't want to proceed until there was someone to look after Mrs Doyle."

Alice registered the careful approach taken by the detectives and wondered how the same scenario might have played out back home.

Mrs Doyle's strident voice broke in on her reflections. "I keep telling them there must be a mistake. My grandson Liam is a good wee lad who has never been in any bother. He has a job in the college looking after the young students." She paused for breath and then took off again. "His ma and da both died in the Troubles and he has lived with me since then so I know what I'm talking about. I looked after him and his sister and now he's looking after me." She turned to Hugo. "Hugo, tell them Liam is a good lad that wouldn't be mixed up in anything like this."

All this time Gary was standing nervously just inside the kitchen door, watching closely what was happening.

Alice sat down next to Mrs Doyle on a small stool

and placed a comforting hand on the old woman's arm. She could feel the woman begin to relax.

Hugo was looking at the papers that Bill Burrows had been holding. "This all seems in order. I guess you'd better go ahead," he said tentatively. "Gary, go and see if Shane Ramsey is home and could drop down to give us a bit of advice. Sounds as if Liam may need a solicitor anyway so I'm sure Shane will oblige."

Gary left immediately.

By way of explanation to Alice, Hugo said, "Gary is Liam's young brother-in-law so he's part of the Doyle extended family now." He and Mrs Doyle confirmed the veracity of this with an exchange of nods. "Shane is a cousin of mine from the intelligent side of the family. There's a small enough gene pool in this area!"

Burrows interrupted this account of community relationships. "Doyle hasn't been charged or arrested but you are welcome to provide a solicitor if you wish. We will just proceed with our search now that you are here to watch over Mrs Doyle."

With that the two detectives went to the front door and signalled for the two officers in the second car to join them.

Burrows allocated distinct areas to each man and they began their search. Within less than ten minutes every inch of the small house was being combed. Gary returned with a middle-aged man in a grey suit and an open-necked shirt. He first greeted Mrs Doyle and then turned to the others in the room.

"What's going on here, Hugo? I was just through the door and had taken my tie off ready to have a Friday evening beer."

Hugo introduced Alice, explained the situation and Shane agreed the warrant was in order. He said he would head down to Grosvenor Road Station and see if he could be of use to Liam and would let Hugo know what was happening.

"I'll send our Colette down here to stay with Mrs Doyle," he said. "Gary, I'm sure your ones will be wondering where you are. You go off home now. Well done on organising us all."

He saluted Gary who left willingly.

"The poor lad is very nervous around the cops," Shane explained and headed off with every sign of efficiency to arrange care for Mrs Doyle and legal support for Liam.

Alice was fascinated at the ease and good humour with which the local community network was mobilised. Hugo emerged clearly as a pivotal and respected figure in that process and her appreciation of him increased accordingly.

From the moment Gary had arrived at the café she had been thinking about how Liam Doyle could be implicated in Helen Breen's death. She'd been surprised when she'd discovered that Liam Doyle was a supporter of Breen. It seemed out of kilter with the views of most of his colleagues. When she had evaluated the class she covered for Helen Breen the students had said it was interesting but not part of their course and therefore not very useful. They had seemed generally discontented with their learning experience and she had suggested they should talk to Doyle in his capacity as student rep. They had rolled their eyes and laughed and implied that there was a sexual relationship between Doyle and Breen and that Doyle was unlikely to accept any criticism of his beloved.

On another occasion, Liam had made supportive comments to Alice about Breen's suitability for a management role, which had surprised her a little at the time. Mairéad and Ralph had talked about the close conversation between Liam and Helen Breen the night of the Christmas drinks party in Janet Hartnett's. None of that really suggested a motive for murder only a short time later and she would need more detail to understand what was going on. She reminded herself that she was a bystander rather than a detective in this case but her instincts were driving her to try and make sense of what was happening.

Hugo was closely attending to the activity of the police and, when they returned to the living room holding a laptop and some diaries, he immediately stood up and asked what they were removing. The younger detective handed over a handwritten list. They politely thanked Mrs Doyle and apologised for the disturbance to her evening and then they left.

232

Almost immediately a young woman in her late teens arrived.

"Here's my favourite baby-sitter," quipped Mrs Doyle who was beginning to look a little weary. "Make me a cup of tea and a wee bit of toast, love, and I'll go to bed quietly."

Colette laughed skeptically and went straight into the kitchen.

"We'll be off, Mrs Doyle," announced Hugo, "but I will call by later to see what's happening. I'm sure Shane will bring Liam back with him."

The old woman's eyes were cast downwards towards her hands, which moved busily in her lap.

Outside they headed for EXIT. Alice needed to collect her bike and she had a few questions to ask Hugo about Liam Doyle and if there were reasons, apart from the obvious fact that he and Helen Breen were close, why he might have landed himself straight into the middle of a murder investigation.

34

In the town of Holywood, situated along Belfast Lough between the city and the coastal town of Crawfordsburn, Janet Hartnett had stopped mid-afternoon on her way home from work to collect some groceries. It had surely been some eventful return to work after the Christmas break. It was Friday afternoon in a week that had been dominated by a mighty storm, the discovery of Helen Breen's body and the fairly constant presence of the PSNI in the college. Janet had had her own interview with the Murder Squad that morning. Detective Sergeant Burrows had been pleasant enough. She had explained that she was new to the college and that her role as Faculty Head meant that DePRec was only a fraction of her responsibilities. She was not, for example, up to speed on all of the intricacies of inter-personnel rivalries. The recent revival in her

234

connection with Helen Breen, she had explained easily as a desire on Breen's part to establish a positive link with her in her new role as Head of Faculty.

"She was obviously an ambitious woman, Sergeant, who had her sights on the upcoming professorship in DePRec. I am not a stupid person. I knew what she wanted and, frankly, she struck me as a better prospect than her opponent who was known as quite the firebrand."

Burrows had been most interested in the fact that she had been at the same school as Helen Breen and had poked about in the detail of their connection back then. She had explained that because of the three-year age gap their relationship had been limited. They had met socially a few times through mutual rugby connections but they couldn't ever have been described as friends. He had made a note of her maiden name and she had wondered a little about the significance of that. It was decades since she had been called Janet Baldwin and that person had long ago become a stranger to her. She and Burrows hadn't talked for long and she felt sure that she had not emerged as someone who was of any great interest to their inquiry.

As she toured the shelves in Tesco she filled her trolley with her son's favourite produce. This was indeed a labour of love. At seventeen, Rory was now her main man. He had suffered brain damage at birth and required fulltime care. She had split up with his father several years earlier and had made a valiant effort to

235

balance job and home-care responsibilities by herself until the strain became unbearable. As Rory outgrew school and day-centre care proved unsuitable, she had no option but to abandon her career in London and head home. There at least she would be able to call on support from her parents and try to make the best of things. The post in Belfast City College had been opportune and for the first time in years she felt her life was getting back on track. She could finish up her working life quite happily back in Northern Ireland and her pension alongside her substantial gains from the divorce would make for a secure future for Rory and her. She wasn't going to let anything disrupt that plan now that so much effort had gone into putting it in place.

As she headed for the car she saw that there was someone in the passenger seat. She was sure she had locked the car but here was the reminder that this man was no respecter of boundaries. She loaded her shopping into the boot and slipped into the driving seat.

"What an unexpected pleasure, Alan," she said sweetly. "That's what you want to be called now, is it? One of the real perks of being back in the North is knowing that I can see you as often as I want. Takes you back, doesn't it?"

"I got your message," he said. "I thought I said that I wanted us to keep contact to a minimum until the interest in our little clean-up project blows over. It's actually better if you don't know what's happening and then you can play dumb with greater conviction." He kept a sharp eye on her reaction to this remark and was pleased to see he hadn't pushed too hard. He met her gaze with all the mock sincerity he could muster. "After all, there needs to be a bit of trust between us now that we have resurrected our old relationship."

Her response was scathing. "Let's not wander off into La La land, Alan. You're much more spook than trusted contact to me. Just keep me in any loop I need to be in. I don't want any unexpected callers at my door."

"Understood, Professor." He tugged his forelock subserviently. "The forces of law and order are too preoccupied with Doyle and Wilson at the moment for you or me to be even slightly interesting. Go home and have a large Friday G&T and leave the case management to me. I've got this."

Without any further attempt at dialogue, he opened the passenger door and melded into the busy throng of shoppers.

35

It was six thirty before Alice looked at her phone and saw five messages from Mairéad Walsh. They went progressively from urgent to fairly desperate. By the time she cycled back across town she had already texted Mairéad to say she would be home by seven thirty and could talk then. She knew now that both Liam Doyle and Ralph were on the police radar in relation to Helen Breen's murder and she had heard from Hugo the story of the violent death of Liam Doyle's parents when he was still a child. As she cycled, some of her lengthy discussions with Tara about the complexities of Northern Irish life came flooding back. So many things had a tailback into the recent past and it was clear that sectarianism, and the complex web of events that was called the Troubles, was more than just a bygone memory. She could see the ever-present theme of sectarian conflict in her knowledge of the lives of the young people in EXIT. It emerged like fossils in old rock in the areas she passed through daily, in the multidisciplinary elements in DePRec and in almost all the people she encountered in this new life of hers. She wondered in what way DePRec's areas of concern might somehow be linked to the murder of Helen Breen. It seemed that despite all the efforts at peacebuilding, everything in this place was still in some way under that historic cloud of division and dissent.

By the time she reached her flat and settled into her easy chair, Alice had concluded that life in Northern Ireland seemed complicated in a way that it wasn't back home. Then again she knew that might be a case of the devil you know being easier to understand than the unfamiliar demon.

She dialled Mairéad's number and relaxed back into her chair.

"I am so glad to finally get you, Alice," Mairéad exclaimed. "I didn't know what else to do other than keep leaving messages and I knew you would get back to me as soon as you could."

"Things got a little busy in the west of the city this afternoon. I didn't get a minute to look at my phone." Alice avoided getting into detail about Liam Doyle. If she was going to have even a peripheral role in this investigation it couldn't be one of gossip and scandal-monger. She waited for Mairéad to speak.

"Ralph was asked to go in for more questioning and he was in such a state. I am so worried about his negative frame of mind at the moment. He isn't used to being on his own at home yet and then to have all this fuss going on as well ... I fear for his mental stability."

Alice said she was sorry that Mairéad was so worried.

"All I could think of was to say was that I would call you and that you would do what you could to look after his interests." Mairéad sighed deeply. "In any case, he phoned me just now to say he was home and that he thought that he had dealt more calmly with the questioning this time. It was the woman detective who interviewed him and that seemed to suit him better. Thanks to your advice the other evening, he didn't allow himself to get so riled when talking about Helen Breen."

As well as pooling their knowledge on Helen Breen when they called with Alice the previous evening, Alice and Mairéad had tried to get Wilson to see that his wild and reckless presentation of himself was adding to his problems. He was doing quite a lot to create an image for himself of someone who could easily get out of control and it wasn't too many steps on from that to believe that he could be a killer. Wilson had taken it all on board.

"DI Paton seems to be a soothing influence, sure enough," said Alice more by way of encouragement than anything else.

Mairéad had almost regained her usual control by

this point. "Quite a lot of his time was spent waiting around, I think. They had Liam Doyle in there as well and he kept them busy it seems. I heard that they were going to search his house. Poor lad. His family background won't gain him any favours with the police."

"I'm glad that Ralph is home and feeling a little more positive. Try to get him to take it easy over the weekend and we'll see how things have developed by Monday. I plan to do likewise." Alice did not allow herself to be drawn into discussing Liam Doyle's dilemma.

"Oh, me too, Alice! That's more than enough excitement for one week and that's for sure."

As they said their farewells Alice's phone buzzed to indicate she had a new message.

"Liam Doyle home and under orders not to leave the country! Thanks for being there. H."

She allowed herself a few slow, deep breaths and then reached for some paper and a pen to gather her thoughts.

36

Just after six that evening, Caroline Paton rang the doorbell at the Breen residence and focused her thinking on the areas she wanted to probe further. In some ways she was there out of respect and courtesy because Sandra Woods was as likely to find out any important information as she was. However, it added immensely to her understanding of the victim to meet the family and spend time in the home where the person was raised. She had a personal belief with regard to murder investigations that, within the limitations imposed by time pressures, nothing was wasted. Every moment spent learning about the detail of a victim's life contributed to her knowledge of the person and also therefore to solving a case.

A woman whom Caroline deduced to be Mrs Breen's Filipino care worker, opened the door.

"I am Detective Inspector Caroline Paton and I think you must be Lisa," she said, smiling and extending her hand. "I think that I am expected."

Lisa took the detective's hand shyly and nodded in affirmation. "Mrs Breen is waiting for you in the living room."

She opened the door off the hallway and stood to the side to allow Caroline to pass.

"This is Detective Inspector Caroline Paton to see you, Mrs Breen. I'll bring in some tea."

"Please call upstairs to Michael to come and join us, Lisa, if he can bear to be separated from his work emails for just a few moments." Mrs Breen's tone was not quite caustic but rather one of resignation to competing for attention with her son's work priorities. She smiled meaningfully at Caroline and waved her hand towards the sofa to invite her to sit down. "DI Paton, I am glad that you could make time to call when I know that you must be extremely busy. Your Constable Woods has been a great support to me since this dreadful business has happened." She paused and then took off again. "I only have one child who has a heart and he is in Australia. Helen and her brother Michael, whom you will meet shortly, favour their father's belief that emotions are for the weak. As such, imperatives other than relationships drive them and we have not been close since they took control of their own lives."

"I am sorry for your loss of your daughter, Mrs

Breen. Sudden and violent death is always shocking no matter what …' Caroline stopped what might have sounded like a judgement on the deceased. It was clear that Agatha Breen had lost her daughter a long time ago. "I am sorry too that I need to intrude on your grief but we are eager to make progress in our inquiry as rapidly as possible and perhaps you or your son will be able to help us with that."

Mrs Breen mumbled something inaudible that merged into a sharp cough. She sipped some water. "We are not a close family, DI Paton. There is no point in trying to appear otherwise. My husband was against any displays of emotion and Helen was the most strongly influenced by him. She wanted nothing more than to win his approval. He was an amateur scholar of Machiavelli and above all, he admired the art of manipulation. His daughter was his avid acolyte. When he died suddenly she was angry and then withdrawn and then it was as if she determined to take over the role of arch-schemer for herself. Her brothers and I were her laboratory rats for a while until she decided the outside world offered more scope to her and she left us in relative peace. Frank left Ireland as soon as he finished college and Michael found his own furrow to plough in pursuit of money and becoming a chip off the old block to his own family … It's not the most edifying of family histories, DI Paton." She looked more than a little downcast. "I'm afraid I chose self-preservation over any good fight to try and change things."

She did not make her final remark apologetically but Caroline was not sure that it wasn't tinged with just a hint of regret. She was spared making any response to Mrs Breen by the door opening and Lisa wheeling in a trolley that held an array of small sandwiches, savouries and a collection of cakes. Michael Breen followed in her wake.

Caroline stood to help with the distribution of plates and cups but Mrs Breen hastily stopped her. "Do sit down, DI Paton. This is my son Michael who is sufficiently housetrained to help Lisa. You are our guest, after all."

Caroline couldn't help but reflect on the extent to which Mrs Breen's comment about self-preservation meant she was implicated, albeit unwittingly, in sustaining the pattern of family hostilities. She greeted Michael Breen and sympathised with him on the loss of his sister.

"We weren't close," he replied as if to explain his lack of distress, "but murder is always a bit out of the ordinary, I suppose. We have no prior experience to draw upon."

The Breen family lack of emotion was truly remarkable, thought Caroline.

Lisa handed around food, tea and coffee. Mrs Breen and her son showed no loss of appetite and Caroline found it was difficult to reconcile this almost festive interlude with the violent demise of Helen Breen.

After an interval she asked, "If I might ask you both

245

to think about whether there was anyone in the past who might have a reason to be angry with Helen?"

Michael shook his head almost imperceptibly. "As I said we were not on friendly terms for as long as I can remember. She was older than me and quite dominant." He stopped momentarily, lost in some recollection and then began again with more feeling. "I mostly stayed out of her way to avoid being on the receiving end of her vitriol or being manipulated into doing something to advance one of her schemes and ending up in trouble for that." He looked at his mother then who was seemingly entirely focused on the contents of her small plate. "Really since she left school and went off to college I have had as little to do with her as possible. There was the odd Christmas meal or something like that but aside from finding her to be a quite an unpleasant person, I wouldn't have known anything about her life or her associates. Frank was a few years older than Helen and might have had more of a chance to know what she got up to when we were all in school."

Mrs Breen shook her head. "DI Paton, Helen did not bring friends home either from school or college. She kept everything compartmentalised and secret. It was as if she didn't ever want the separate parts of her life to converge." The old woman turned to look at the garden behind her as if watching some reel from the past.

Caroline finished her tea and waited for Mrs Breen to come back to the moment.

"Come to think about it," Mrs Breen continued, "she very much related to one person at a time and when that ceased to be her father she became even more distant from the rest of us."

Caroline turned to Michael again. "Mr Breen, have you been in touch with your brother Frank? Did he have any new perspective on who might have wanted to harm your sister?"

"I spoke to Frank this morning, DI Paton," Mrs Breen said before Michael could begin to formulate an answer, "and he had of course been shocked to get Michael's email. He and Constable Woods had a good chat about school days and she asked him if he knew Janet Hartnett. It took us all a while to realise she was talking about Janet Baldwin, as she was then. She was in Frank's class in sixth form. I didn't know Helen and she knew each other but Frank remembered it all in more detail. I'm sure the Constable will pass on his recollections. She made a careful note of them, as you would expect."

"Thank you, Mrs Breen. That is very useful indeed." Caroline rose to go. "I don't want to take up any more of your time but if you think of anything that might be useful to our inquiry, please do get in touch."

As she drove back to the station, something that had been said in the Breen household was niggling at the back of Caroline's mind, just beyond reach, but she couldn't retrieve it.

She thought about the woman she had first encountered under a sheet in the morgue. She was emerging as a fairly unpopular person both at home and in work. But that was the nature of the task. Even when the victim turned out to be seriously unlikeable, she had to continue to seek justice for them and disregard how unsympathetic they had been to others in their lifetime.

As she neared the end of the second full day of inquiry she hoped that tonight's review would bring significant advances towards finding their killer. She had texted ahead to say they would start as soon as they all got back. No point in hanging about when they had the wind at their backs.

Caroline was known for being both an intuitive and a methodical investigator. So it was that as she sat in the evening traffic she decided to make a call to Alice Fox and arrange to talk to her when the evening briefing was done. She needed some perspective on this case and if she had judged her correctly, Alice Fox might be the one to give her that much needed outsider viewpoint.

With any luck they would be done with the review by nine o'clock and there might even be time for a late bite to eat. Friday night was lively enough in the Chinese quarter up around Shaftsbury Square and they might well be able to mix business with a little culinary pleasure. It was worth a punt and she would make the call as soon as she got into the Grosvenor Road Station car park. Then she would harness every ounce of energy she had for that crucial session when all their findings and hunches could be pooled. She had a good feeling about the progress they were making and by the time she made her way through the foyer of the station she was whistling optimistically.

37

Earlier in the afternoon DI Paton had interviewed Ralph Wilson at some length and then left him for Burrows to process and let go. Wilson was angry by nature and probably more harm to himself in terms of raised anxiety levels than he was to the rest of humanity. At the same time, Burrows had interviewed Liam Doyle and then left him to cool in the interview room while he and McVeigh searched Doyle's house for signs of Helen Breen's devices. In the end, both men were released under caution to remain accessible should they be required for further questioning. They were both worth keeping an eye on but neither had given the impression that they could be driven to murder. Doyle was young and impressionable and Burrows suspected Breen had systematically groomed him as a convenient minion who was easy on the eye. He would wait to hear later what

McVeigh had in terms of supporting evidence before he settled definitely for that position.

Ian had spent the afternoon making phone calls and sorting through the material he had brought from Helen Breen's house. When Burrows had seen him at his desk earlier, his brow had been furrowed in a way that led Bill to hope there would be something worthwhile to discuss later. It seemed as if suddenly they had amassed a quantity of new information and he recognised that as a phase in all inquiries where progress might be accelerated. Just after five o'clock the two men headed westwards to the home of Liam Doyle. In their chat in the car, they didn't stray too much into new areas of evidence keeping those for the disciplined environment of the review meeting later that evening.

When they returned to the police station Burrows spent a little time preparing headings on the electronic evidence board so that they could share their findings as rationally as possible. Sandra Woods had emailed a written report and said she would be available by phone if they needed any clarification. He had shared other reports throughout the day as they had come in and he saw that Ian had also added some files to the shared drive. He would wait to hear his verbal report before starting to wade through all that.

His phone buzzed. It was a text from the boss to tell him to order in tea, coffee and snacks and that she would be ready to start in ten minutes. Ian was already gathering himself together to join him at the meeting-room table.

"Hey, team!" Caroline said as she made her entrance with a little more than her usual gusto. "We have a lot of evidence to get through but this is our process and we have shown it works. Careful step by step through the detail is what exposes the connections that lead us to our killer. It's not the stuff of TV drama but then who would cast us as the Dream Team?" She was in buoyant mood. "I have a good feeling in my bones about this meeting. Let's get started."

Gathered in the Murder Squad offices, Burrows gave an overview of the report from DC Woods. She had elaborated further on the Breen family relationships. Her discussion with Michael Breen had revealed that his sister had bossed and bullied him and generally made his life a misery. He had related an incident soon after the father's death when she had implicated him in the sale of her father's expensive wristwatch. Helen had sold it and left the jeweller's receipt in her brother's room where their mother discovered it. Michael was not able to convince her that he was not the guilty party and, when Helen had covertly given him a new pair of pricey trainers, the case against him was compounded. He said that he thought Helen's motivation in such actions was not to get money but to bring the wrath of his mother down on him and find pleasure in watching his misery and helplessness.

Wood's discussion with the older brother, Frank, had been a little more useful in that he remembered Janet Hartnett from his class at school. He didn't remember Helen being friendly with her but they did both hang around the rugby crowd and so may have known each other then. Janet Baldwin had been a popular party animal, Frank remembered, whereas Helen was younger and had been more peripheral to that social circle. Like Michael, Frank had avoided contact with his sister whenever possible. He had a theory that she wanted to prove herself to be the child who was made most in the likeness of their father. While he was alive, her efforts to win the father's admiration had been extreme and often involved discrediting Frank and Michael to add to her own kudos in their father's eyes. After his death her behaviour had become centred on pleasing herself and much less predictable.

Burrows placed the report at the bottom of the pile of papers in front of him. He looked at his two colleagues. "From the evidence collected in DePRec and this family contribution we are getting a clearer profile of our victim. With the exception of Bell and Doyle, who both found her charming, Helen Breen was universally disliked." He referred to the notes he had gathered on the victim profile and continued. "Breen's family describes a self-centred, emotionless and manipulative person who delighted in scoring points over others. Her brothers both independently used the term *sociopath* to describe her. They had evidently gone into researching her characteristics in some detail. Her mother claims the pattern was originally begun in the relationship with her father and became exaggerated and deeply entrenched after his death. From then on, her desire to acquire and maintain power over others is what motivated her." He paused to sip from the mug in front of him. "Her mother maintains that Helen's behaviour was irritating and sometimes shocking, but it never became an issue that caused ripples at school or prompted psychiatric testing. Helen Breen managed perceptions of herself as carefully as she did everything else and succeeded in remaining just beyond categorical disapproval. She was a smart operator even at an early age." He glanced at his colleagues to confirm they were still on board with his theorising and continued. "Calculating and executing the steps in a power game is evidently where her satisfaction came from. In the context of DePRec, it may have been about avoiding doing aspects of her own work by getting others to stand in for her – if possible without any payment. Or again about irritating an academic competitor, like Wilson, to the extent that the rival's erratic behaviour meant that she became the more desirable candidate for promotion."

Paton and McVeigh were making moderate signs of agreement and Burrows persisted in presenting his profile.

"I think we can deduce that she had groomed Liam Doyle to use for her own ends. It's not quite clear what the full extent of her plan for him was but it definitely included fetching and carrying and cleaning up after her." Burrows facial expression showed contempt for Breen and a certain sympathy for the young student rep. "He was her ardent advocate amongst the student body and Professor Bell heard that praise as confirmation of his own conviction of her great worth. She had positioned her supporters carefully to reinforce her desired perception of herself."

He could see from his colleagues' body language that he was becoming too long-winded and tried to summarise what remained in his notes.

"I know that we will work through all these witnesses systematically but I think it's worth articulating this personality type at the outset and we can test it against the rest of the evidence. Sandra's work with the family has been vital in establishing a pattern that I think was also a core feature of her work life."

Caroline had been absorbing all this input with concentration. "Sociopaths don't really endear themselves to many people, do they? They are the classic target for murder, if we can say that such a thing exists."

McVeigh held his had proprietorially on the pile of papers in front of him and said, "My trip to Hillsborough links very closely to what Bill has said, in terms of the victim profile. I don't know if you want to hear that now or if you want to go through the latest interviews first."

"Let's take today's evidence one step at a time," said Caroline. "We'll take the interviews chronologically and then we'll look at your findings from the victim's home place, Ian. There will inevitably be some toing and froing but we'll try to keep it straightforward and crucially we'll try not to lose any detail." Her expression sought assent for the plan and the men nodded agreement. They were used to this sifting and analyzing and keen to get on with it.

"OK!" began Burrows, trying to maintain the energy in the room. "Yesterday evening I had a useful meeting with Matt Gillespie, one of the local managers of HiSecurity Services. He had done his homework well and had a file ready for me. You have copies before you and I'll talk us through the important detail." He flourished the file to show the section he was referring to. "He had taken all the DI's requests on board and provided what answers there were. As we deduced the passkey system is far from foolproof. If somebody has a pass card belonging to another member of staff then they can make it appear that someone has swiped out when in fact they were not even present. It is possible therefore that our killer took Helen Breen's passkey, swiped her out at nine thirty-six on Thursday 19th December, leaving the body in the office to be dealt with later that evening. I will come back to that." He turned a page and continued. "In terms of security, there is a desk presence in each building and some strategically placed cameras that record movement and store the digital images in a cyber archive for a full year. All that material has been made available to us and I have had someone checking through images from the Thursday evening at six until six on the Friday evening. Gillespie has prepared lists of staff who had checked in and out on those days and they concur with what individual people told us about their movements. So... there is no sign of Bell on the premises after six o'clock on Thursday evening but he is clearly there all day on the Friday. So too, Wilson's claim to leave at seven thirty and Hartnett's nine thirty exit are not contradicted. Helen Breen is visible in footage on a number of occasions between six and seven forty-five and then not seen thereafter when we can assume she is in her office. There was nothing remarkable in the passkey detail from Maritime Studies on any of those days. All that suggests that the murder, the clean-up and the relocation of the body to Marine Biology all took place within the expected routines of the college." He paused for a mouthful of coffee.

"Meaning what exactly, Bill?" Paton queried.

"By that I mean that the actions used by the murderer fitted in with expected college activity. Nothing took place that raised any suspicions or attracted undue attention. There was nothing that seemed out of the ordinary."

She nodded and signalled for him to proceed.

"Cleaning staff, who are part of a separate contract to security, arrive in and around nine forty-five after the building is cleared of evening classes. They clean first in the library building and then move to the Maritime Studies building. They are mostly part-time, precarious migrant workers who change from day to day and are managed by one person who allocates people to each floor and leaves them to it."

"OK," interrupted Paton. "Lots of scope for messing with the system."

"Exactly," agreed Burrows. "And given this was the last night of term there was even greater laxity than usual in the oversight of what was happening on each floor."

Paton and McVeigh were nodding in understanding now as it became clear what had potentially taken place.

"One of the guards was away from his desk dealing with some students outside the building. They had been celebrating the end of term a little boisterously and it is possible he missed the arrival of some additional personnel but nothing out of the ordinary shows up on the video footage. By ten forty-five when the cleaners move to the second building all was as normal." Here Burrows smiled sardonically and nodded to emphasise his point. "This is how easy it was. As it was the end of term there was some movement of large containers of materials for shredding. This process takes place in the basement of Maritime Studies and unfortunately there are no security cameras there aside from the foyer where nothing untoward showed up. It is entirely likely that

Helen Breen's body was wrapped and placed in a shredding bin or maybe even a cleaning cart for movement to Maritime Studies." Again he indicated the report from Gillespie. "Based on the video footage, her office was cleaned by two men wearing baseball caps and standard cleaner outfits, who attracted no attention from their peers. They are all used to paying no heed to anything outside their own tasks. There are no facial shots of these two mystery men." He closed the file he was holding, indicating that he was almost finished. "What we can say is that a great deal of planning and organisation went into the office-cleaning operation and movement of the body. Although the actual murder appears to have been somewhat risky in terms of taking place while work in DePRec was ongoing, the subsequent operation to cover up the crime, or at least delay discovery, was calculated and meticulously carried out."

Paton and McVeigh both wore puzzled expressions as they contemplated what Burrows said.

"So we may not be looking at a single perpetrator here," Paton mused. "Or at least a killer equipped with their own cleaners and removal persons. How very organised! A murderer with staff indeed! We'll have to think through the relationships between staff members for signs of a potential double act – or even a group effort."

They all gave this new information some silent consideration and then set it aside until they were up to date with the rest of the data.

"Good work, Bill," said Paton. "Do you want to fill us in on the final revelation from the security manager?"

"Well, as you both now know, Gillespie had located some interesting footage for us on the Friday morning. This showed Liam Doyle collecting a message from the post room, going to the underground car park and driving Helen Breen's car from the building directly to her home in Hillsborough. Needless to say, DI Paton and I followed up on this matter with Mr Doyle in our subsequent interviews with him this morning and this afternoon."

"Let's get Walsh, Bell and Hartnett out of the way now, Bill," said Paton, "and then we can home in on the more detailed second interviews and Ian's findings from the leafy retreat of Hillsborough. I am not suggesting for one moment that we relax our gaze on these three just yet but I know we have more concentrated findings from Wilson and Doyle and from the search of Breen's and Doyle's home."

"Well …" Burrows smiled kindly, "Mrs Walsh is a formidable woman but I'd not stake any money on her being a killer. I'd say she is made of finer stuff than that. She is however a shrewd observer of all that happens in DePRec. She has audio and paper records of all meetings and she operates a form of confessional in her office where all members of teaching staff collect paper registers, laptops for lecture presentations and other such things. She hears a lot of day-to-day departmental chatter and her perspective is invaluable in relation to operational routines and interpersonal staff relations." He shuffled his papers and unearthed notes of Mairéad's interview. "Mrs Walsh did not like Helen Breen. She found her devoid of emotion, self-interested and manipulative. She thought Breen had an unjustified high opinion of herself and cared about no-one. In short, her views concurred with those of Breen's family and other colleagues." He reached for a chocolate biscuit and unwrapped it as he spoke. "Walsh was of the opinion that Breen spent a lot of energy ensuring that Jackson Bell held her in high regard and Mairéad was shocked that she had duped Bell so effectively. Breen had a similar strategy in relation to Janet Hartnett apparently and Mairéad Walsh had witnessed some of her overtures to the new professor." He ate some of the chocolate off the biscuit in his hand. "Mrs Walsh didn't hold back on her negative view of Helen Breen. She admitted that she, Mrs Walsh, was a close friend of Ralph Wilson and that she was obviously biased against Breen because of that. She felt that in her experience of working with academics, Breen's murder was unlikely to be a work matter. She had witnessed numerous academic disputes but they almost never progressed beyond verbal sparring. I wondered if she was trying to deflect attention from Wilson in that regard."

"Good point, Bill. What about Bell and Hartnett?" Paton was keen to keep the meeting moving forward but was nonetheless attentive to the details.

"Bell and Hartnett are both interesting. Bell because he was such a devotee of Breen despite others being convinced that she was a charlatan. Breen obviously devoted a lot of attention to keeping Bell believing in her worth. He said she showed more interest in departmental matters than all the other staff put together. He was unfaltering in his certainty of her loyalty to him personally and to DePRec as well. When I said others didn't share that view he swiftly put that down to jealousy because of her outstanding academic prowess making others feel inadequate. His confidence in Breen seemed utterly unshakeable. He was sure she would have become the next professor and indeed spoke of her as his obvious successor."

"And on the actual night of Breen's death?" Paton prompted.

"He said that he phoned her after eight thirty to make sure that nothing untoward had arisen while she was covering his evening duty. She assured him that all was well. He used his mobile phone so we can check his side of the story anyway. Short of his having discovered some great betrayal, it's difficult to see any motive he might have for wanting Breen out of the way. We all saw his dismay the night the remains were found. He would have to be quite the performer to have faked all that and his demeanour is in fact quite devoid of any dramatic content. He comes from a very strict religious background and I can't see him convincingly behaving in such a duplicitous way."

"And Janet Hartnett? Anything of interest there?" Paton pressed forward.

Bill thought before answering. "She is a relative newcomer and slightly removed from the day-to-day DePRec business by having a responsibility that extends across all the social sciences. She and Breen were at the same school but she is several years older and didn't make much of any previous friendship. She did find that Breen was being friendly towards her since she had arrived in the college but didn't attach much weight to that either. I wasn't sure that she was all that relevant to the inquiry but I also wasn't convinced that I had got to the bottom of her – so to speak." His expression assumed an element of aversion to the topic. "Her area of academic interest is the caring professions so she makes great eye contact." He laughed at his own dubious opinion of counsellors and the like. "She says all the right things but there's a hollow ring to it. And she was on the premises at the time we think the murder took place but was home in Crawfordsburn just over an hour later so that doesn't add up really. I think we keep her in our sights until she merits being crossed off."

"Thanks, Bill, for all that," said Paton. "We are still only on the second full day of inquiry and we have made good progress. We know where and when and how Helen Breen was murdered. We know how the body was moved and we have had second conversations with some people who emerged as potentially of interest. OK. Let's look at Ralph Wilson now. Maybe I can give some views on that one and as we have all interviewed him at least once we can compare impressions. Dr Wilson struck me this afternoon as a man who has made a supreme effort to bring his thoughts and feelings about his deceased colleague under control. As we know, the inside of a police station has that effect of introducing a good dose of reality into even the most unreasonable characters."

Her colleagues responded with knowing nods and murmurs of affirmation.

"I interviewed a much more docile character today than you both met yesterday. I'm sure you noticed that when you set him free later in the afternoon, Bill."

Burrows nodded in agreement.

"The bluster was extinguished," she said, "and I think he has moved from the habit of stating his views with undiluted passion to a more diplomatic version of himself. I left him to stew for quite some time and that too may have activated his more rational side." She looked around at Burrows and McVeigh to see how they were buying this new reading of Ralph Wilson and continued with some supporting evidence. "I accept that Wilson had an extremely acrimonious relationship with Breen but that has been the case for a considerable period of time and he has never attacked her, other than verbally and always in an effort to justify his ideological standpoint." She paused for possible dissent and when none came continued. "Might the approach of the professorial competition have pushed him over the line into violence? I saw nothing this afternoon to suggest that was the case. I don't think he really cares about promotion. His wife has recently left him and he is desolate about that and the prospect of being alone. He has a friendship – perhaps a little more than that – with Mairéad Walsh, but that is not going to ease his lonely nights in any permanent kind of way. He is passionate rather than violent, I think. He wasn't in college late on the Thursday evening, having left and gone home where he remembers making something to eat and having a lengthy conversation by Skype with his ex – Angela. That can be easily verified." She passed a phone number to McVeigh who added it to his 'to do' list for later that evening. "We might argue that he had means and motive but opportunity appears to be missing."

Burrows was nodding thoughtfully. "I did think that he was a little too obvious in expressing his hatred of Breen but it was worth pushing a bit harder to see where it took us. He is an old school, trade-union type who is used to making fiery proclamations about things but more of a serial demonstrator than a violent killer. Mairéad Walsh was talking this morning about how academics like to talk about things and enjoy grandstanding when they can get an audience. Wilson fits that bill well but could he be as well organised and proactive as our killer? Perhaps not. What do you think, Ian?"

McVeigh was ever practical. "I will check out the timing of the Skype call. It will be in his records and, if the ex saw him in his house at that time, then he's in the clear ... unless he employed someone to do it for him." He smiled wryly and Burrows threw a tightly folded chocolate wrapper at him.

"So ... let's see what we have on Mr Liam Doyle," said Paton. "Bill, do you want to take this one as you have interviewed him twice and visited his home?" She sat back in full-on listening mode.

"Doyle is an interesting one alright." Burrows repeatedly flexed his fingers as he spoke – a familiar sign that he was fully engaged in his thought processes. "He clearly carries the legacy of his parent's IRA involvement and their sudden death when he was a child. As we know the paternal grandmother brought Liam and his sister up. Mrs Doyle is now elderly and quite incapacitated and the tables have turned. He takes care of her along with his married sister and her extended family. The old lady is a bit of a character and the family has a complicated relationship with the forces of law and order. That said, Liam Doyle had never been in any trouble with the law. He has a good reputation in the college both as a postgraduate student and as the current student representative. All of those we spoke to acknowledged his good work on behalf of students. His post gives him privileges like access to staff common rooms and connections with lecturers that other students would not have. Hence the scope for the relationship with Helen Breen."

He paused and considered the timeline that he had sketched on the whiteboard.

"His story that he was at home on the Thursday holds up. He didn't appear on any of the video footage for that evening and his computer showed that he received an email from Breen at ten-twenty. It was very much along the lines he described. She had to stay unexpectedly at her mother's. The car keys were in an envelope in his postbox and would he go to her house and facilitate the guy coming to collect her laptop for repair." Burrows' sympathy for the duped young man was clearly apparent but he didn't let it cloud his judgment. "He was so flattered to be asked to service her needs that he didn't think. Like, why would she not bring her car to her mother's house? Why was it necessary for him to be called in to open the door for a repair person? Why didn't she just change the appointment to a time that suited her? And of course we know that Helen Breen was not on care duty at her mother's on the Thursday evening, or any other evening for that matter. At the time that the email was sent from her account Helen Breen wasn't even alive. After pushing at Doyle quite hard, both this morning in DePRec and this afternoon here in the station, I am not convinced

267

that he was anything more than Breen's obedient servant." He shook his head in exasperation at how Doyle had let himself be taken in by Breen. "He seemed quite gormless at times during our questioning ... as if he wasn't capable of thinking critically where Breen was concerned. He claimed to be in love with her and he didn't question anything she said or did. She had the measure of him, I'd say, and played him royally. My question is ... why would someone use the dead woman's email account to send messages to Bell and Doyle?"

Paton answered quickly. "In the case of Bell, they wanted to play for time. If Breen wasn't expected on the last day of term because she was needed to care for her mother, then it would be January before her death was discovered. Where Doyle is concerned, someone wanted her home computer taken out of the picture, and maybe a home mobile phone too. Her office was cleared of laptop, phone, and handbag and it would have been careless to leave the home stuff available for scrutiny."

"I get that," said McVeigh. "But why involve Doyle? If they had the car keys and keys of Hillsborough why not just go there directly and help themselves to whatever they wanted? They could have gone there on Thursday evening and there would have been no need for Doyle to be a player at all."

"These are good questions," mused Paton. "We have to assume that this was also a delaying tactic and also muddied the waters by putting Doyle in our sights. They succeeded in getting the car away from the building without having to deal with security cameras and distracted us with Doyle who was rumoured to be in a relationship with Breen. Then, without any prying eyes, they were able to take the items they wanted and dispose of whatever evidence they could have provided."

"It seems as if our cleaners did a very thorough job," said Burrows. "I did ask Doyle to describe the computer-repair person but he was very vague. Another guy with a baseball cap and driving a nondescript white van." He expelled air noisily through his pouted lips.

"Perhaps the local force will be able to help there," said Ian. "They keep a very close eye on traffic into and out of the village, for obvious reasons. I will follow up on that one too, later this evening." He added it to his list of tasks and underlined it with extra emphasis. "Our killer has been painstaking in covering his tracks and removing all personal devices belonging to the victim."

"You are right, Ian. Let's hold that in mind as we forge ahead here." Paton poured herself more coffee from the thermos on the table and checked to see if the others wanted some. "It seems as if we are discounting both Doyle and Wilson for the moment. Right, Ian, what have you got for us that might shed some greater light on things?"

He smiled with satisfaction. "Prepare for the cat to get well in among the pigeons now."

"One morning in the countryside and you've gone all rural on us," jibed Burrows playfully as he prepared to add to the detail on the evidence board while McVeigh delivered his report.

McVeigh took the floor. "I called first with the locals. I had forewarned them about my visit the previous evening and I was met by the duty sergeant who had a good handle on the situation. We were expected. Because they keep a close eye on movements in and out of the village he was aware of Helen Breen and happy to share. I received a verbal report from him on the spot and then a more detailed one by email this afternoon. There are not too many secrets in Hillsborough and local intelligence is sharp. You will see that what I've unearthed about our victim further complies with the characteristics of a sociopathic personality." He consulted his copious notes and continued. "Breen kept a low profile and did not mix socially in the local community although her superficial charm had been noted. The Sergeant was careful to tell me that Breen was not a lawbreaker ... and, as he put it, 'what happens between consenting adults is not our concern as long as the security of the Big House and its occupants is not breached'." He paused for a breath and continued. "When she moved there they had rapidly become aware that she had regular weekend visitors. They were usually but not exclusively male and coming from a range of EU countries. Occasionally it was a man and woman travelling as a couple. The visitors were mostly from a consistent cohort with only occasional changes. Now and then a new person would appear and a previous regular would no longer be seen. Guests nearly always arrived Saturday and left Sunday and were only very occasionally seen outside Breen's home, walking around the lake in the forest park or visiting a local shop. Hillsborough got 'Special' to look into this and they found that she was a member of what's called a 'Meet up BDSM' group." He glanced around his colleagues to make sure they were following.

"Interesting but not really surprising," said Paton. "Promiscuity is a classic part of the sociopathic persona. When was the last guest logged by the local police?"

"You're right, Boss," said Burrows. "That's not so interesting for us. It was two weeks before the murder so not a direct link. Though it might be connected if, for example, someone close to her discovered her pastime and was jealous or outraged, for example." He added some arrows and question marks to his whiteboard notes.

"Is there more?" asked Paton.

"Yes, ma'am," said McVeigh. "The report from Hillsborough contained contact details of the regular visitors and I made a few calls this afternoon to verify the facts. I spoke to one guy from Geneva and a couple from Copenhagen. Both had been in Hillsborough in the month of December. They were surprisingly open and willing to cooperate. Again the point about consenting adults was made by all of them. They were obviously fairly well off in that they could afford to travel quite often to satisfy their particular sexual preferences. I asked if Breen ever travelled to them, and they said that she did not. Group members with families were not always able to receive guests so obviously Breen was carefree in that regard."

Paton's reaction was, as ever, measured. "Let's not get distracted by the unusual sexual side of this other than to ask what it may contribute by way of motive. We can work through each of our known associates of Helen Breen."

They homed in onto Burrow's list on the electronic white board. "OK, so we'll take them in the order you have them, Bill ... Liam Doyle first. So he was in love with Breen and might well have felt excluded and been angry if he discovered her predilections and promiscuity. Would he have been angry enough to kill her? But then his alibi puts him elsewhere at the time ... unless someone in the family is covering for him. Ian, you take Wilson."

"Right you are. I don't think this new information adds to his motive other than it may have reinforced his negative opinion of her and further enraged him. All in all, I think he would have been more likely to see this as an opportunity to discredit her once and for all rather than kill her."

"I agree," said Burrows. "Moving on to Professor

Bell now. It's unlikely but if he did discover her tendencies his disillusionment might have been considerable. His family is Brethren and any sexual irregularity is viewed very severely."

McVeigh raised a hand to intervene. "I don't want to leap ahead but I have more to reveal, that will cast that viewpoint into doubt."

"We will stay with this train of thought first and then take any qualifying information," said Paton. "Who's left? There's the brother Michael, Mairéad Walsh, Janet Hartnett and sundry part-time lecturers and other staff. Any of those could have taken on the mantle of avenging angel. Remember that our evidence from the autopsy is that our killer was determined and insistent. This was not a wild frenzied attack. It was a concentrated, focused demolition of the brain of the victim with way over and above the effort required just to kill her. Our killer was not out of control. On the contrary he or she was focused and decisive in intent and action." She sat back and breathed deeply. "We are getting closer to the nub of things. I can feel it in my waters. Carry on, Ian."

"Hillsborough trawled through camera records and, aside from what we already know, there was nothing of note. No devices to be found either in Helen Breen's office or her home. I will follow up with the tech guys and the phone companies to see what they can unearth remotely but not much to be gleaned there I imagine. Nothing through yet from forensics on the house but what I did find was some paper stuff – background details and some information and photos that Breen had been amassing on her colleagues. Some of it vicious enough and some of it possibly libellous." He had his colleagues' full focus now as he opened a green manila folder and pulled the contents onto the table in front of him. "These are all scanned onto the shared drive so I can pull them up on screen for you."

They turned to face the other wall where McVeigh had pulled down another retractable white screen. He then put up three enlarged photographic images.

"I have filtered these as there were multiple copies of fairly similar images. The one on the left is a little dark but I have checked thoroughly and it comes from a series of photos Breen had of Ralph Wilson and Mairéad Walsh. They are dated and are taken in the Library Bar in the city centre. They do show a certain level of intimacy and were clearly being kept in case they became useful to Dr Breen. The photo on the right is of Professor Bell. There are a number of these also. They are identified as being in the Rainbow Bar and Club also in the city centre and a well known LGBTQ gathering place."

"Ah, that answers some questions!" said Paton.

"There was a lot of speculation amongst staff about the relationship between Bell and Breen. It was assumed by some that his unquestioning loyalty to her was motivated by a sexual connection. Now we can surmise that she had guessed his secret and controlled their relationship with the ultimate threat of disclosing his homosexual tendencies. Both in his private family life and his academic career, knowledge of his sexual identity would cause waves. In the first case because it would be seen as a betrayal of both the Brethren religious values and the marriage he had entered into with his wife, Hanna. His colleagues on the other hand might judge him for his denial of the rights of LGBTQ people to be visible and socially integrated. He would please nobody, poor guy."

"So she had him on a tight leash," said Burrows. "Maybe even literally."

Paton ignored this remark and just nodded thoughtfully. "And the third image, Ian. It seems more explicit."

"Yes, ma'am. That certainly is one way to describe it. It is a much older image and shows a naked young woman in the company of two similarly naked young men. There is clearly sexual activity taking place between them. The woman's face is entirely visible but views of the men are more obscured by the angle of the shot. I reckon we can enhance this one somewhat so that at least one of the male faces is distinguishable. It is a still image from a video, I am told, and most likely stored by Breen for its potential to expose the participants. I discovered this afternoon that in the late seventies and eighties, the paramilitaries produced pornography as a part of their fundraising machinery and possibly a more sinister community-control mechanism. This photo was inside a copy of the rugby magazine for the school attended by Helen Breen, her brothers and Janet Hartnett previously Janet Baldwin. We have to assume Breen got hold of it then and held on to it in case it became useful."

They gazed intently at the image and there was no doubt in anybody's mind that they were looking at a youthful photograph of the recently appointed Professor of Human Sciences.

"*Yes!*" said Paton through closed teeth as she punched the air with vigour. "I've been waiting for that connection to fall into place since earlier in the Breen household when it was mentioned that Hartnett's maiden name was Baldwin. When I was a rookie, back in the late 80s, there was a case that involved fundraising by various dubious means on the part of some East Belfast paramilitaries. It was a delicate affair as the reform of the Force was a good ten years ahead into the future and there were considerable pockets of sympathy within the RUC for the need to support and strengthen the loyalist paramilitaries. If my ageing memory serves me well, there was a small businessman named Baldwin implicated in that case. Ian, can you do some diplomatic digging into that? Professor Hartnett's father may well have had a family interest in that sordid business that never became apparent at the time. My recollection is that it was all brushed under the extremely lumpy carpet." She paused as she was drawn into the detail of the past. "Yes! I'm sure of it. My then Chief, sadly now deceased, was one of the good guys and he was spitting nails about the whole business. It was one of those memorable learning moments for me about the realities of the organisation I had joined." She looked crestfallen for a moment and older than her years. "We've come a long way since those days but there are sadly plenty of skeletons still to emerge. Ian, can you turn your fresh young eyes to this tomorrow?"

"OK."

"I think we can hold this new information close to our chests for this evening," said Paton. "Dig out what you can on the Baldwin affair and see if you can identify the two men in the picture, Ian. Look at some of those school journals with class photos and pay attention to the guys in the school rugby squad around that time. Bill, talk to Frank Breen and send a copy of the picture to see if he can identify any of his classmates from back in the day. Somebody knows more about this video. See if we can dig up a copy and see who was involved in the production and distribution. And let's have a close look at Professor Hartnett's career. How did she graduate from porn star to successful academic? Who was covering her back?"

They reviewed the rest of their evidence piece by piece from a fully loaded day of data collection. They agreed areas of priority for the following day and began to gather up and store the various documents that were strewn across the table. Paton knew that they would give their all to tomorrow's tasks and with some degree of satisfaction, just before nine, she called it a day for everyone.

38

Caroline Paton's call and suggestion of dinner and an unofficial consultation about the killing of Helen Breen had come as a bit of a welcome surprise. Alice had just been gathering her thoughts about the case when her phone rang and the idea of talking it all out face to face was appealing. She agreed to book somewhere in the Chinese quarter and text the details to Paton.

At nine fifteen she was sitting at a table for two in the Welcome Restaurant on the Stranmillis Road. Alice had changed Caroline's suggested plan slightly as the Chinese quarter was noisy on a Friday evening and this place was quiet and well regarded. It was a long-established business and there was an easy confidence in the calm created by friendly, experienced staff. The very pleasant décor included a lot of crisp white linen, abundant flourishing green plants and the restful sound of trickling water. She knew that a working murder squad detective might not be the most punctual of fellow diners and so was pleasantly surprised when Caroline Paton arrived not more than ten minutes later. They shook hands a little formally and then relaxed into choosing their food and ordering equal amounts of wine and water.

"I'm going with my gut here – although not completely." Paton looked mischievous. "I did check with Lowell's finest to make sure you weren't an axe murderer. They let me know that you come from the best pedigree so I was pleased I got that right."

Alice attacked a prawn cracker from the basket that had arrived in front of her and nodded with feigned seriousness.

"I'd have done the same thing myself if the shoe was on the other foot," she said with a smile.

"Good!" said Caroline, closing the menu in front of her. "I was going to order a vegetarian dish. What do you want?"

"That sounds good to me too," Alice replied.

"Will we share the 'abundant veggie special for two' and let them surprise us?"

Alice agreed and called a waiter and placed their order.

Without further delay Paton moved very directly to the subject of the case of Helen Breen.

"We will have time to reverse, I hope, and go through all the social niceties when this case is solved but for now can we cut straight to the chase? I'm assuming trust and confidentiality is a given, so I'll give you a quick summary of where we are and I'd really appreciate your perspective as an outsider/insider so to speak."

"I'm good with that as long as we can eat at the same time!" Alice was fully alert and suddenly ravenous.

Paton spoke quietly but with assurance. "Right so ... Dr Helen Breen was killed in her DePRec office on Thursday night of the 19th December. Professor Bell had asked her to cover as evening duty manager as he was busy elsewhere. Breen's passkey was used to check out of the building at nine thirty-six but there is no video evidence of Breen leaving and her car remained in the underground car park all night. Bell received an email from her account that same evening after ten saying she would not be in the following day as she was needed to care for her mother and would work from there. Liam Doyle received a message around the same time asking him to collect her car keys from his post box and drive her car to her home in Hillsborough where he needed to admit an IT technician who would be removing equipment for repair. Doyle seems to be the only one who actually knew where Breen really lived. Her official address was her mother's – and her childhood home. We can now assume that Helen Breen was already dead when these two messages were sent."

"How did Doyle think she would get to her home without a car?" Alice mused.

"I don't think he did that kind of lateral thinking. He was besotted and just pleased to be involved in some aspect of her life no matter how menial."

She paused as the food arrived and an array of steaming dishes was placed in the centre of the table for sharing. The waiter explained the contents of each dish and left them to it.

They filled their plates and Caroline continued with the contents of her mouth only partially eaten. Neither woman was concerned with the finer points of dining etiquette.

"According to Doyle, and the security footage from the college confirms this, he collected the car and drove it to Hillsborough. A nondescript man, driving an unmarked white van and wearing a baseball cap duly collected a laptop, and possibly a mobile phone and some other items. Several hours later when Breen did not arrive and did not respond to his text messages Doyle got a bus to Lisburn and then another one back to west Belfast. He did not hear from her again despite having made several attempts to contact her. Again his phone records verify this."

"So someone very carefully arranged that Helen Breen was not missed until all her electronic devices were safely removed – and they staged things so that possibly nothing would be discovered until the holiday period was over. Devious and fairly well executed by the sound of things."

Caroline continued. "We can see on college security

footage that two people presenting as cleaners transported something that might either be a cleaning cart or shredding bin from the DePRec building to the Maritime Studies Centre in and around eleven o'clock that evening. Two of the regular cleaners were phoned by someone purporting to come from the cleaning company and told they were not needed that night and so their replacements were able to blend in unnoticed with the rest of the squad. There was no docking of the original cleaners' pay so the message evidently had nothing to do with their employers." She refilled her plate and paused long enough in her account for Alice to comment.

"Someone has a fine understanding of the security and cleaning procedures in the college. I suppose these services are all privatised, which makes tracking individuals very difficult. The same challenges already existed in the States before I headed back to college. I guess we exported our precarious service industry model to the rest of the world. Nothing to be proud of there!"

"You are spot on, Alice. We are dealing with an experienced strategist here who went to considerable lengths to cover their tracks and delay discovery of the body of Helen Breen. I quipped to the guys earlier that it sounded as if we were dealing with a killer who had staff but maybe there is something to be teased out further in that."

They both were silent for a few moments, digesting the parameters of this possibility.

"I am sure you are building up quite the victim profile on Helen Breen," Alice mused. "What I was wondering earlier when you called me was what significance might DePRec and its work have in this case?"

Caroline was suddenly a fraction more alert. This was just the kind of sideways perspective that she had been hoping for from Alice Fox.

"Talk to me, Alice," she urged and sipped thoughtfully at her glass of white wine. "What were you thinking about in that regard?"

"Well, I am very conscious of the constant underlying politics that is part of the social fabric here. From my first day in Belfast I have been struck by the way that individuals and communities are defined by their different cultural identity. It's often unremarked but ever-present, in the background of so many aspects of everyday life … even on the walls, as Jackson Bell's photographic recording of political murals describes. I suppose when you have been here long enough, like anywhere I guess, you don't see that stuff as clearly any more."

"Yes, indeed. It just becomes like slightly tasteless wallpaper," Caroline mused.

Earlier when she had been thinking over the details of Helen Breen's killing, Alice had arrived at the conclusion that DePRec must be a significant part of the murder. Otherwise why not simply kill her elsewhere where a less elaborate cover-up was required?

"Since it was set up all those years ago," she said,

"DePRec taps into the underbelly of all those political aspects of Northern Ireland life in a whole range of ways ... like my own work in West Belfast with the EXIT group just to cite a small, recent example. In our research and local involvement of course we become privy to community knowledge ..." She hesitated slightly and then continued. "And we learn community secrets as well that are subject to our ethical guidelines about anonymity, confidentiality and protection of research subjects from harm. But here in the North the subject of such research relationships has an interest value beyond most normal research environments. I mean that there are people here, maybe more so in the past, who deal in secrets and will go to great lengths to capture them."

A light bulb went on full strength in Caroline Paton's mind and she clutched the table edge firmly with the fingers of the hand not holding her wineglass.

Alice noted the surge provoked in the detective's energy level and persisted resolutely with her line of thinking. She felt that she was edging closer to something important. "I met the founder of DePRec, Tara Donnelly, at a conference in Dublin before Christmas. In fact, I realise now it was exactly during the period when Helen Breen was murdered. I got onto quite friendly terms with her because of our common research interests but also primarily because of her history in DePRec. She told me a little about why she left the project to which she was so deeply committed and her story involved reference to very murky influences and pressures. They were not paramilitary in nature but part of the state machinery to get inside the communities that were of interest to them. She didn't tell me much really but I could see that she had been frightened off. I guess she doesn't know me well enough yet to open up fully, but I could see that whatever happened has kept her away from her family and northern friends unless they visit her south of the border. Anyway, I suppose what I am trying to say is that from my culturally distanced perspective, I can see that DePRec has always been open to being used and exploited ..." here she became even more serious, "and people who move in those undercover circles are not opposed to making their point persuasively, maybe violently, when they feel they have to. Might there be something in what you are looking for that relates to DePRec the organisation as well as to individuals within it?"

Caroline poured more wine and looked intently at Alice. "You have really helped me with that steer, Alice. Now I need to carefully think through a whole new set of connections so I am going to go home now and work through some of the possibilities here." She paused for thought. "I wonder if Tara Donnelly would talk to me. I'm guessing she has a bigger story to tell and maybe if she knew she would have a sympathetic ear she would be more inclined to meet with me. Would you be happy to explain the situation to her and see what she comes back with?"

"Perhaps she would talk to both of us," Alice ventured, lifting the last of the sauce from her plate with her finger and licking it appreciatively. "It's too late to phone now but I could email her and see what she says. I'm guessing you would have to travel if you want to meet her face to face."

"OK. See what response an email gets and you can call and let me know. We can take it from there." She waved at the debris left after their meal. She gave Alice a playful, apologetic look. "You must promise me we'll do this again and reprise the earlier conversation we skipped and even have some sweet course and coffee! I'd love to hear more about what led to you finishing up in Belfast when you had the world to choose from."

"I give you my solemn word I am up for that," said Alice with a laugh.

They split the bill and outside Paton hailed a passing taxi and Alice walked home past the softly lit Gothic and Tudor style buildings of Queens University. She felt a real connection to this area now and realised how lucky she was to have selected such a perfect place for herself from such a great distance away. Not too many streets off in several other directions and life could have been much less pleasant.

Alice sent off a carefully worded email message to Tara, asking her to call as soon as she could and began to do her end-of-the-day routine. She planned to run in the morning and then head west to prepare for a forthcoming martial arts session with the EXIT group. She would use the opportunity to call with Liam Doyle as well and see what she could discover there.

As she was checking the front door, her phone rang. She thought it might be her sister Sam who would just be getting home from work in Lowell – however, Tara Donnelly's soft northern voice was instantly recognisable.

As Alice had intended, Tara was intrigued by her email message and couldn't wait until morning to find out what it was all about. They talked for nearly an hour and ended by making an arrangement to meet in a hotel just south of the border at three o'clock the following afternoon. Alice had vouched for Caroline Paton's reliability and knew she was right in her judgment.

When she eventually said goodnight to Tara, Alice texted the detective with details of the suggested meeting. Caroline confirmed immediately and they agreed to meet at two o'clock next day when Caroline would drive them both to the Ballymascanlon Hotel, just over the border in the Irish Republic. The trip should take an hour each way, at the most.

It was almost midnight when Alice finally switched off her bedside light and focused very hard on emptying her mind so that there might be some hope of sleep.

39

The Murder Squad began their Saturday with an eight o'clock breakfast meeting that was charged by copious quantities of carbohydrates and coffee. They had all done some follow-up thinking on the previous evening's meeting and had lists that would keep them busy for the day. Paton told them about her conversation with Alice Fox and the plans to talk to Tara Donnelly that afternoon. They agreed on the division of labour for the day. Caroline would collate and analyse all outstanding reports: the forensics from Helen Breen's office and the Marine Biology Centre, the forensics from Hillsborough and the report prepared by the uniformed officer who had reviewed all the CCTV footage. She would go back to the college security footage from Thursday 19th December and talk to the cleaning firm to check if it was possible to find out who exactly had taken the place of the cleaners given the evening off. Ian would focus on uncovering the story behind the photo of Janet Baldwin, the original case in which Mr Baldwin might be implicated and any available info on Professor Janet Hartnett. Burrows would tie up loose ends in relation to Wilson, Doyle, and Bell as well as contacting Frank Breen and delving a little deeper into the school-time relationships of Breen and Baldwin.

They scheduled a review meeting for six that evening and Caroline said she realised that they had been full on since Wednesday evening and hoped they might get a few hours' family time that evening. She was good at sensing when the prospect of a small break might energise an investigation at risk of hemorrhaging vital stamina. She knew a few hours could feel like a holiday when you have had little respite for several days and she observed the proof in the renewed enthusiasm generated in the room.

"So let's just agree where we want to be by this evening ... and then onwards and upwards!"

Bright and early Alice Fox was on her bicycle heading across town towards the EXIT premises. She knew that on a weekend she could spend some time alone there with her thoughts and at the same time do some martial-arts training and prep for her session with the group next week. Tae Kwon Do had been a passion of Alice's since she discovered it as a police cadet. She liked the controlled dance-like quality of the set moves and the emphasis on blocking attack rather than aggressing an opponent. The complex series of punches and high kicks was exhilarating to perform and as a police officer had allowed her to be calm and effective in unarmed combat.

This morning as she did some heavy-bag training she relished her clear head and the ease with which her high kicks made contact with the weight of her target. She was light-footed and precise in her movement that in its advanced application had a very controlled quality. She wanted to share this type of confidence and self-reliance with the young members of the group. Most of them had some experience of street violence for which they were ill prepared. Her work with young people at risk in the US had shown her that the discipline required to develop skill in a martial art actually helped avoid violence. The holistic nature of Tae Kwon Do, based on ancient Korean values of peacefulness and rationality had captured Alice's respect all those years ago. It allowed the embodiment of the goals of a peaceful society and fitted harmoniously alongside the discussions about social justice that she and Hugo had instigated with the group. They had talked enough about self-protection. She was sure that now was the right time to introduce some physical action.

After over an hour of highly physical activity she showered and headed around the corner to Liam Doyle's house where she wanted to check out how he had survived his ordeal of the previous day.

She knocked the door and heard the old lady call out, 'It's open. Come in if you're good-looking.'

The effort left Mrs Doyle coughing strenuously and as she entered the small living room Alice responded immediately to the hand signal that she knew meant that she needed a drink of water. Once calm was restored Alice reminded the woman who it was had made free and easy with her kitchen.

"I know who you are," she laughed somewhat scathingly. "I'm not as doolally as I look. You were here with Hugo yesterday. The peelers let Liam home last night but he is in poor spirits. He got me up this morning and then went back to his room. You'll find him in the front room upstairs." She pointed to the stairs and then leaned her head back on the winged chair and closed her eyes.

Feeling a bit like a burglar, Alice made her way up the narrow stairs. The door of the front bedroom was slightly open and she tapped it and pushed it open. Liam Doyle was sitting at a small desk facing the window, which overlooked the cul de sac. His head was in his hands and a curtain of red hair covered his face.

"Sorry for barging in," said Alice. "I was round in EXIT doing some training and wondered how you survived yesterday's experience in the police station."

He turned his chair to face her and motioned for her to sit on the neatly made single bed, the only available place in the cramped room. He looked as if he had been crying and Alice felt a surge of sympathy.

"I'm sorry for all the trouble you've had, Liam, including the loss of someone that you cared deeply for."

He stared at her as if expecting there to be a sting coming after the kind words. When none came he relaxed a little and sighed heavily. "Well, I feel so confused, Alice. I think I have been a very stupid person but that doesn't make the feelings of grief and loss any less." His eyes filled with tears that he attempted to blink away. "And then to be a suspect on top of that is just shocking. It dawned on me as I was being questioned that I was probably being played not just by Helen, who clearly didn't have any genuine feelings for me … but by someone else … some spook who killed her and then emailed both Bell and me. In the case of Bell it was to gain time but I was implicated in an altogether different way. I guess they knew that with my background I'd be the cops first choice as a suspect."

"Tell me what you've been thinking," Alice encouraged him gently. "I think that you may unwittingly have some information that will help identify who did this. Why would someone want Helen Breen dead and be prepared to incriminate you in the whole affair? Where is the sense in that, Liam?"

Liam Doyle shook his head slowly from side to side and sighed repeatedly. "Of course I am racking my brain constantly, trying to remember anything that might answer that question. It's not helped by the fact that I was so besotted that I wasn't using my critical faculties very often when I was around Helen. I feel now that I was mesmerised by her ... like under a spell that stopped me seeing what was happening around me. How come others all saw her as one kind of person and I saw a completely different reality?"

"Well, I wouldn't be too hard on myself if I were you, Liam. Often we see what someone wants us to see and Helen Breen had picked you as someone that she liked to have around and she made sure that you saw a flattering version of her." Alice chose her words carefully so as not to add fuel to Doyle's self-deprecation.

He took solace from her words and continued with his reflections. "I did know that she was not as big a fan of Jackson Bell as she let him believe. She was usually careful about what she said but one day she made a remark that insinuated he wasn't as good-living as he made out to be. 'I've got his number,' she said, and she was quite pleased with herself ... and not in an endearing way. I asked her what she meant but she covered it over and moved on. I forgot about it then. Ralph Wilson was the usual butt of her rancour and she really was looking forward to annihilating him in the professorship competition. She knew I was on her side so I suppose she wasn't so careful about slagging off her competition to me." He took comfort from the recollection of that degree of intimacy and relaxed further into his musing. "The really funny one, now that I think about it, was the new Faculty Head, Professor Hartnett. Helen curried quite a bit of favour with her when she arrived first. They had been at school together and I think she thought that might be useful to her. When I think about her now I can see she was quite the strategist. I realised when the detectives were questioning me yesterday that I was a part of that strategy in some way that wasn't clear to me. Anyway, I once asked her how Professor Hartnett's career has been so successful. Like, was she very clever at school ... you know just making conversation really. That seemed to provoke something in her and she was quite vitriolic in her response. She said that Hartnett wasn't as flawless as she appeared to be and that she had undeniable proof of that should she ever need to use it. There was something too about Hartnett's father turning out to be more reliable than her own and that really seemed to rankle her."

He looked wrung out by all this soul-searching and Alice was sorry for this young man whose life journey had already been altogether too bumpy.

"You don't think I killed her, do you, Alice?" he ventured.

She answered without hesitation and with heartfelt kindness. "No, Liam. I don't think you killed her. I am sure you were more harmed in all of this than you were harming. What's more, I think if you stay close to home, near your very loving family, this will all be resolved before very much longer and all our lives will begin to get back to an even better version of what they were just a small number of weeks ago." She placed a comforting hand on his shoulder and headed for the door.

"Thank you, Alice Fox," he said and followed her downstairs.

As she closed the front door she heard him ask his nan if she fancied a cup of tea.

"I thought you'd never ask," she chuckled asthmatically.

40

At five to two Alice was ready and waiting at the interface of the Donegal Road and Shaftsbury Square where she had arranged to meet Caroline Paton. Belfast bustled past her as she stood just beyond the corner near the entrance to the International Youth Hostel. There was a tantalising aroma of fresh baked bread from the home bakery across the road mingled with some kind of strong disinfectant being used by a young man scrubbing down the pavement outside a pub on the corner of Sandy Row. It must have been a busy Friday evening.

Waiting at the side of the busy road, Alice reflected on what she had learned about the history of DePRec and Tara's virtually forgotten role in it. DePRec had been part of a rapid and financially generous response, in the North, to the IRA ceasefires of the early nineties. Pumped with funding and recognition by the EU, the

British and Irish Governments, DePRec had been one of those projects that had outlived the initial funding phase to become mainstreamed into the Further and Higher Education landscape. The interdisciplinary department was given firm footing by the then visionary young Head of Department. She was adept at developing viable cross-community research projects that attracted funding and seeded lasting peace-building structures. In the early days, she had been a legend in the academic world of Peace and Reconciliation but after her hurried and unexplained departure, her name was quickly forgotten by most. Such was often the case with prophets, Alice reflected.

Today the detective was a little early and they were soon on the M1 Motorway heading south. By the time they took the turn off for Hillsborough and joined the dual carriageway towards Newry, Alice had related the detail of her earlier discussion with Liam Doyle. They agreed that Helen Breen had clearly amassed information to discredit colleagues who did not comply with her strategic plans – a habit that could well have made her unpopular with someone. The stumbling block in this line of establishing a motive for murder was that none of those she had targeted appeared to have any plans to prevent Breen having what she wanted. Both appeared to support her candidacy for professorship and Bell evidently saw her as the most loyal and reliable member of his staff. Paton told Alice about the background detail that Breen had on Wilson, Bell and Hartnett and that gave her pause for thought as they drove through the bleak winter countryside.

Despite sounding expansive, the journey across the border was not much more than forty minutes and Paton took it at a leisurely pace. Alice asked her about the changes she had seen in the systemic shift between the RUC and the PSNI. Caroline Paton had laughed out loud and said they would need to be doing the European road trip for her to have time to cover that topic even minimally.

"For a young woman in the late 80s when I joined up, the RUC was sexist and sectarian and resistant to new ideas. Elsewhere the women's movement was flourishing but the Northern Ireland police force had long been a solidly male, conservative and secretive organization. It had more than its fair share of members of the Masonic order and a sizeable Special Branch that dealt with gathering strategic information from the various paramilitary groups. The whole intelligence system was complicated. There was the RUC Special Branch but there was also Military Intelligence run from the Army HQ in Lisburn and of course MI5 Security Services run from the Holywood Barracks. That's the one that's still running in its original form." Paton glanced at Alice to check that she was following and then continued. "RUC Special Branch was merged with Crime in the belief that peace would bring the need for a different kind of undercover work to do with ordinary decent criminals rather than terrorists. The military operation was wound down eventually but we still have our spooks." She interrupted herself in full flow. "Why am I telling you all this?" She laughed at herself. "And after I had said it was too long to go into!' She paused for a moment and then stole a sideways glance at Alice. "I think it's relevant but I'm not altogether sure why just yet."

"I'm fine with that kind of intuitive detective work," Alice encouraged her.

"Anyway, a decade later, by the time of the Good Friday Agreement and the Patten Report into policing, change was really long overdue," she said animatedly and obviously keen to explore the topic. "The RUC was described at the time in one report as 'bloated' and that always struck me as pretty accurate. Despite huge progress today and much more community inclusion, there are still threads of connection to the bad old days. There are still cover-ups and secret dealings in dark corners that the ordinary run-of-the-mill cop doesn't even know exists. I hope in my heart that it is just the remnants of something that is gradually becoming an anachronism."

"Are you sensing something of that nature in the murder of Helen Breen? Something that ruffled old feathers enough to make someone act murderously?"

"I'll know better this evening. I've asked Ian to follow up on a hunch for me today and it may well be that old wounds have been unwittingly scratched by Helen Breen."

They passed the turn off for Newry and merged onto the motorway towards Dublin. Here the landscape became more wild and mountainous and the cloud lifted as if a different climactic zone had been entered.

"I know it's not obvious but we have crossed the border," said Caroline. "I always think that the fact that it's barely noticeable has more significance than we realise."

Within moments they were speeding alongside a forested area that Paton explained was known as Ravensdale. She said it was infamous as the likely burial place of British Army Captain Robert Nairac. He was an agent in military intelligence who was abducted and killed by the IRA in 1977 and his remains were never located.

Caroline added, "Gruesome rumour at the time suggested he had been put through a meat processor and included in sausages and meat pies sold to local shoppers."

Alice once again got a chilling reminder of how little she knew in real terms about the Irish Troubles.

They drove in silence for a few minutes and then Caroline took a motorway exit for Carlingford and within a matter of moments they turned into the driveway for the hotel where they were to meet Tara Donnelly.

"The Ballymac has long been a meeting place for northerners who wanted an outing to the peaceful side of the border. Nowadays it's a golf and spa destination but there are all manner of North/South meetings that still take place in the bar and restaurant."

Caroline seemed to know her way around and parked not far from the door of what appeared to be the original Victorian house on a large estate. The building had been extended but the main house retained its quiet dignity. They had arranged to meet Tara in the bar and made their way there directly. It was just approaching three o'clock when they took their seats at a window overlooking some well-tended gardens that edged the golf course.

A few minutes later Tara arrived, looking flustered.

"Am I very late?" she asked. "I decided I would go for a walk up Slieve Foy before our meeting and forgot how long it actually takes to drive back here from Carlingford. Then I had to change my muddy boots. Sorry!"

Alice did the introductions and Tara extended her hand to Caroline Paton and gave Alice a hug before she sat down.

"It's funny to be so close to the North and not go that bit extra," she said with a heartfelt honesty that Alice recognised and appreciated.

"I guess that takes us straight to the point of our meeting," Caroline said gently. "I'm really grateful to you, Tara, for making the trip up from Dublin. My time is very squeezed just now and meeting halfway makes everything easier. I suggest we get some food and then talk. I'm sure you've worked up a bit of an appetite on your walk. I seem to remember Slieve Foy has a very steep side to it in Carlingford."

They ordered coffees, toasted sandwiches and a basket of chips to share and relaxed into the comfortable, well-worn armchairs that furnished the bar.

"Thanks for phoning so promptly last night," Alice said. "I didn't want to disturb you so late and thought an email was a safer bet. I know you don't talk easily about all this period in your life and I really appreciate you doing it now in such haste and with someone that you only have my word can be trusted." She accompanied this statement with the intensity of direct eye contact that she hoped reinforced her message.

Caroline was nodding and murmuring agreement.

"Well," Tara began slowly, "there is a time for trying out new paths and I have been quiet about this for long enough. I suppose I knew this day would come eventually. I am happy to tell my story now and to trust that you women will ensure that the consequences are not awkward for me and my family that are still in the North."

"I promise you that," said Caroline sincerely. "My hope is that your name need never be mentioned in what comes next. I just need to know if there are covert influences that were, and still are at work in DePRec. I know that something happened that frightened you away from an exemplary project that you had worked hard to establish. If my instincts are correct, that covert

303

threat may still be operating and may well have been an ingredient in Helen Breen's murder."

The food arrived at this point and they organised themselves with plates and coffee and settled their full focus on the conversation that now seemed so pivotal.

Tara dipped a chip in some mayonnaise and nibbled at it tentatively. Then she inhaled deeply and began to speak.

"I don't know how much you know, Caroline, about the establishment of DePRec so I'll sketch in a bit of detail as context for the main part of the story." She wound a strand of wiry hair around her finger and fixed her eyes beyond her two companions, as if looking into the past. "As you will be aware, in the early 90s Northern Ireland received large quantities of what was locally referred to as Peace Money. There were different strands of funding but the main thrust was that projects were to make a contribution to building the circumstances that would help the peace process take hold and become sustainable. There was wide scope and it became quite a skill developing and writing up lengthy funding applications to the various intermediary bodies charged with allocating the money. I discovered that I had the knack and I was suddenly very busy. I had done a Master's and PhD in Equality Studies in Dublin and I was working in the college as a junior lecturer at the time, trying to find my academic niche. My interest was in the broader social inequalities that people in the

North had in common that were often obscured by the sectarianism that saturated all aspects of life ... education, employment, politics, policing too as you'll be aware ... nothing was immune really."

Caroline nodded in agreement. This was all familiar to her.

"Anyway, influenced by my work in Equality Studies, I began to develop an approach to peace-building that was multidisciplinary and we accessed funding from different sources for diverse elements of the work. There was money for looking at women's issues and so we developed a course that looked at women's role in war and in peacekeeping around the globe. The participation of local women across the community really opened up new perspectives for everybody. There was funding for increasing sustainability of employment and we worked with trade union groups to develop modules that would strengthen solidarity across sectarian lines. That was where Ralph Wilson was a tower of strength, back in the day. Anyway we grew fairly rapidly and the beginning of DePRec was set in place. By the time the Good Friday Agreement was signed in '98 we had amassed considerable expertise and the College gave us backing as an autonomous centre of study. DePRec eventually outgrew its total dependency on recurrent funding applications to become a well-respected academic centre. We were still recipients of EU and US and even Irish Government funds and with that there was always a thin line to be walked to maintain academic freedom and satisfy the expectations of funders. We had to avoid being perceived as too orange or too green, more sympathetic to one side in the conflict than another."

She paused to bite into her sandwich and sip at her coffee.

"I'd say that was often a difficult diplomatic dance to perform," said Caroline, "given how many shades of opinion there are in Northern Ireland and how far removed one can be from the other. I assume that you were appointed as the Head of the Centre at some point in all that." She was impressed at how little self-promotion was involved in Tara Donnelly's account of what was an impressive achievement for a very young woman.

"Yes, I was. Over a ten-year period I became a Senior Lecturer and Head of Department. In my final year there, that was 2003, the Centre had sufficient income and enrolment to merit a professorship and I applied for that and was appointed."

"I suppose I have to ask now what happened to make you feel you had to leave all that behind?" Caroline posed the question with genuine interest.

There was no pressure in her inquiry and yet Alice watched a little anxiously as her friend embarked on this difficult part of her story.

"I was accustomed to attending open meetings in different communities. I saw it as part of keeping in touch with peace-building on the ground. Sometimes it would be a debate or discussion in Catholic west Belfast or Loyalist east Belfast or some rural area or another. Around the time of the Good Friday Agreement referendum there were a lot of such conversations taking place. In the aftermath of the passing of the agreement there was inevitably unrest and even riots in flash points especially where orange marches were contentious. The peace process wasn't the instant remedy that some people wanted and for others it went too far too quickly in terms of power-sharing. There was too much forgiveness for some and not enough punishment for others. That's the nature of conflict and its legacy, I know. Anyway, after one such evening meeting ... sorry, first of all I should say that often I didn't go alone to such gatherings. There was an ongoing issue of my personal safety and the name Tara Donnelly would have announced my cultural origins to anyone in Northern Ireland, where we learn to interpret such signals as part of our upbringing. So on a particular evening I was to go to a community meeting in East Belfast along with Ralph Wilson and he was unexpectedly called away just when we were meant to head off. He got a message to say his wife urgently needed him at home but when he got there it had been a misunderstanding and she was fine. I think now it was a ruse to get me into the area alone. I went ahead by myself and as I was leaving a guy approached me and offered me a lift. He was pretty unremarkable but I guess that's part of the job description. He was in his thirties, casually dressed and had a quite cultured accent. Not run-of-the-mill east Belfast by any means. Of course I declined but he mentioned my brother's name and was surprised and even a little hurt that I didn't remember him. He knew where I lived and said he was passing that way. He was convincing. I tell myself I was tired and happy to get away quickly from an area where I was less than comfortable. Anyway I went with him ... stupidly as it turned out."

Tara was visibly distressed reliving the memory but neither Alice nor Caroline interrupted.

"In the car he made it clear he knew a lot about my family and I was unnerved by some of the detail he had at his fingertips. Things that were family matters not known to others, especially people you didn't even recognise. He actually drove me to my door, which was a relief at the time but terrifying when I had time to think about it. When I went to leave the car he locked the door centrally and said he needed to talk to me. He said that DePRec was beneficiary of considerable government support and that it was time to pay back some of the trust that had been placed in us. Time to show a little loyalty to the Crown. We clearly had established relationships of trust with many groups and we were ideally placed to pass on important information that we picked up in the community to those charged with ensuring that nothing derailed the fragile peace process. He was persuasive and at that stage only mildly threatening. He said this was the way to protect our work and ensure continued backing for any new venture we might come up with. In fact he suggested that in-depth research with ex-prisoners and community activists would be of particular interest. He would ensure funding was available to us. There would be no censorship of anything we wrote as long as the information they required was passed on. Anyway, you get the picture. He said he would give me time to reflect and he would get back to me and he unlocked the car and watched as I went into my house. Of course I realised he was an agent of the state and that I was possibly being recruited as someone who would pass on strategic intelligence – internal specifics about opinions being voiced in places that they couldn't easily reach. Or, maybe he was making it clear that I was in the way and needed to be replaced by someone more malleable. Who knows? I spoke to absolutely no one about it and not long afterwards he appeared again when I had almost begun to think he had moved on to another more pressing project. This time he was more threatening. He said that it was payback time for DePRec and I needed to be grown up about my responsibilities. If I wasn't prepared to willingly do what he asked then he would have to find ways of persuading me. He mentioned a relative who would have been financially vulnerable at the time and whose family would have been devastated had he lost his job. He said he could make sure that my family suffered ill fortune and that I would rue the day that I tried to go against his wishes. Of course I protested but he was unfazed by that." She was halted briefly, reliving the helplessness of that moment, and then continued. "If I thought I could complain about him I was a fool, he said. He would never be exposed for reasons of operational strategy. He was untouchable. He used that charming phrase – 'shit or get off the pot' – and I knew I needed to get away as quickly as possible."

Alice and Caroline waited respectfully as Tara got to the end of her story.

"I handed in my notice and moved south where I was lucky to find another post before too long. I knew that to keep my family safe I needed to be of no further use or interest to this man or others like him. I have never set foot in Northern Ireland since that time and I can only assume that the State found another source of information who was more compliant than I could be." She sipped her now cold coffee and pushed the remains of her sandwich away from her across the plate. Then she looked up at her two companions and smiled. "It's a surprising relief to have said all that out loud! I think I'll have another cup of coffee and stop talking now."

Alice caught the waiter's eye and ordered three more coffees. She was watching Caroline Paton process what she had heard. Her expression was one of resolute determination.

"Thank you, Tara. You have given me more information than I expected and I think I know where it may take me next in solving this case. I have one last thing to ask you. Eleven years later, would you recognise this man now, if you saw a picture of him?"

"I still have bad dreams about him. He is still fresh in my mind so I'm sure I would."

"Good. I hope I will get back to you soon with some images. Maybe later this evening. And, again, let me say that you need not be named or involved in any way in the working out of this case. You have my word on that. Now let's have some hot coffee ... and maybe a little bit of cake." She raised an eyebrow playfully at the two women and called the waiter again to bring a selection of cakes.

Alice admired Paton's firm but gentle approach and was relieved that her promise to Tara had been well founded. She could see where this case was headed and it would take all Paton's wiles to bring it to a safe resolution.

They said goodbye to Tara in the car park and headed off in their different directions, knowing that there would be more contact in the next day or so.

Caroline asked Alice if she had driven in Ireland yet and she said she had a rental car during her stay in Wicklow at Christmas.

"Great. You drive and I'll get in touch with the chaps back at the Barracks." She tossed the keys to Alice and took her place in the passenger seat. "No point in letting any more grass grow under our feet now, is there?"

It was after four now and the landscape around the border looked more menacing than it had done in the winter sun. Alice had a sense of needing to get past Ravensdale as quickly as possible and was relieved when they were past the looming dark of the forest, back in the North and heading for home.

41

As he drove to the head of DePRec's home, Bill Burrows considered his earlier video call with the murder victim's brother, Frank Breen. As he had predicted, Frank had been more focused when he was receiving a call from the police station than from his mother's house and within her hearing. Burrows had questioned Frank Breen closely about his classmate Janet Baldwin and her close friends during her final few years at school. Frank had remembered the names of several men with whom the young Janet had been close and a woman that he associated with being her best friend. Without much difficulty Bill had tracked down June Carson, who still lived locally, and he had arranged to call with her later in the afternoon. When he had explained that he was looking into events back in their school days, she had promised to look out any old photos by the time he got there. He hoped to have that trail followed to its conclusion by the time they were in their evening meeting.

Burrows rang Jackson Bell's doorbell just after two o'clock and the man himself answered it almost immediately. The sergeant apologised for the unannounced intrusion and asked if he might have some of his time to clarify a few issues.

Bell showed him through to his study at the back of the house and offered refreshments. Numerous familiar images of murals from around the city were framed and hung on one wall of the room. The other walls were shelved and filled with books and a large desk faced the window into a small garden. There was no sign out there that any member of the Bell family had green fingers. Passing through the rest of the house, Burrows had been struck by how barren and comfortless it appeared. A few dismal framed biblical quotations were all that might count as décor. There were neither mirrors nor any of the usual trappings of home like a television or sound system or even family photographs. Bell's study was cozy by comparison.

"How is your investigation progressing, Detective Sergeant?" The question was hesitant and seemed posed almost casually rather than out of any real interest in the response.

Bell was less impressive away from his role as the person in charge in DePRec. He seemed deflated and vulnerable in a way that Burrows couldn't fathom.

"I'm glad you asked," said Burrows courteously. "I have a few further questions I'd like to ask you, Professor. We have made some progress in our inquiries and I have been wondering if by any chance you have thought of any outstanding issues that you have so far neglected to tell us and that might be relevant to Helen Breen's murder."

At this suggestion Bell looked taken aback but Bill continued calmly.

"These may be DePRec matters or issues to do with your relationship with the deceased and that might have some bearing on why she was killed." The detective extended an open palm towards the professor, inviting him to respond.

Bell was clearly accomplished at maintaining protracted silence but Burrows was not inclined to repeat or reframe the question. He waited. He had Breen's photograph of Bell in a local gay bar in his inside pocket and was happy to use it as a prompt if need be.

"If you are referring to staff gossip about my being in a sexual relationship with Dr Breen, then I can assure you that is all unfounded." Bell's nostrils flared and he pressed his lips together in exasperation. "It is difficult for some people to understand why one might admire and appreciate a colleague without having some carnally primed motivation. I assure you, Detective Sergeant, there was no such impetus between Dr Breen and myself. I have a wife and daughter whose stability is important to me, and I would protect them vigorously from any slight to my or their reputation."

As a family man Burrows identified with the urge to protect and he framed his next question cautiously. "Professor Bell, has anyone ever suggested to you that they might threaten to disturb the peace and stability of your family by disclosing something they would find unpalatable?"

Bell blanched visibly and hung his head.

His breathing became laboured and his hands were interlocked in front of him as if he had begun to pray.

"I ask you this, Professor, out of no desire to distress or harass you in any way. It may be that our discussion need never go any further than this room and the Murder Squad detectives. I make no promises but we are aware that the motive for this killing goes beyond workplace rivalries and we need to know what might have provoked someone to kill Helen Breen."

Again there was a long, silent pause. Burrows touched the photo in his inside pocket and decided to wait a few moments further. He met Bell's frightened gaze and wondered how such a clever man could have got himself into such a position in this day and age. OK, Northern Ireland was not the most liberal place in the world to be gay but there was equality legislation and substantial protection against discrimination. Bell's fear of losing his family was clearly an enormous factor in his closeted behaviour and Burrows empathised with the torturous dilemma in which he found himself.

"If I tell you, Detective Sergeant, I will need some promise of protection." He met Burrows' eyes as he made this suggestion.

Burrows balked at the idea. Time to toughen up, he thought.

"I understand that you may be wary of talking openly, Professor, but this is a murder inquiry. Your life choices are your own business but if they have violent consequences then they become a matter of police concern. My job is to discover who murdered Helen Breen and I suggest that if you have information pertaining to that matter that you tell me now and allow me to get on with my job." He was not as indignant as he sounded but knew it was time to push this man across his threshold of reticence.

"Of course you are right, Detective Sergeant. I am being small-minded. Forgive me." He inhaled deeply and looked directly at the detective. "For over ten years now, I have been the informant of an MI5 agent working out of Holywood Barracks."

Burrows felt a jolt as he heard this but he kept his expression calm and nodded slightly to urge Bell forwards with his revelation.

"I know him only as Alan, although I am sure that is not his real name. He persuaded me that gathering and passing on intelligence that would safeguard the fragile Northern Ireland peace would be a noble act. I was never totally convinced of that approach although as a Quaker peace has always been something I value."

Bell inspected his still tightly clasped hands. He looked up and met Burrows carefully controlled facial expression.

"In actual fact, the night before Helen Breen was killed he told me he no longer required my services. I had always been a reluctant participant and passed on as little data as possible to him. Anyway, he told me he had recruited a replacement that he hoped would be more compliant than I had been. I don't recall his exact words but it was something strange to do with old friends being more reliable than strangers. He reminded me of my ongoing duty of confidentiality unless I wished to experience unpleasant consequences."

Bell appeared somewhat relieved by this admission as if he had complied with Burrows' demand and could now be left in peace. For his part, Bill considered how to follow this unexpected revelation and uncover the piece of the picture that was still not forthcoming.

"How were you persuaded to take on this role, Professor Bell? As you say you were disinclined to do so." Bill already knew the answer but needed to track back to Helen Breen and her place in all of this. He thought of what Caroline would do in his place and moved forward one cautious step at a time. Again he watched as Bell struggled with exorcising his deeply buried demons.

"Well, what can I say? This man, Alan, was surprisingly well informed about many matters that one might have assumed to be private." He began his explanation with an air of wretchedness. "He constantly amazed ... or maybe more accurately alarmed me about his knowledge of the internal business of DePRec."

He hesitated momentarily and tears welled in his eyes. His shoulders rose and fell as he suppressed the sobs that rose from within his rigid body. He seemed shocked to find himself crying and wiped awkwardly at his streaming eyes with his ironed white handkerchief. Finally, after some minutes during which Burrows stayed perfectly still, he met the policeman's insistent gaze and realised there was no way back from his position.

"OK," he relented. "He had information about my private life that he knew I really would not wish to be publicly known ... in particular, I would not wish it to be known by my wife and family for whom it would be both painful and traumatising."

Bill waited quietly while Jackson Bell found the words to describe his personal shame.

"You see, Detective, as well as being a husband and a father, I am also a homosexual." He said this desolately as if it were his burden rather than any personal choice. "I have often mused that I am at once a reluctant family man, a reluctant gay man and I was also a very reluctant informant and betrayer of my academic ethics. Despite my pious exterior, DS Burrows,

319

I am a tarnished being with little inner peace." He stopped then and nodded slowly and repeatedly at the truth he had just uttered.

Burrows withdrew the compromising photograph of Bell that Helen Breen had stored and handed it to him. "Did Dr Breen know about your sexuality, Professor?"

Bell considered the image before him and looked blankly at Burrows.

"I don't understand. What is this? I have never seen this photograph." Bell appeared genuinely at a loss.

"When we visited her home in Hillsborough, the photo was found in Helen Breen's files. It was with other items featuring colleagues in compromising situations that we must assume she kept in case they became of use to her. We have to consider that someone may have killed her because she threatened to expose them in a manner that they found particularly objectionable."

"Well, I am deeply surprised by this." He waved the photograph dismissively and returned it to Burrows. "Helen Breen was the only person who knew of my propensities but it was not an issue for her. I was assured of her loyalty and in almost a decade that confidence never faltered. I can't imagine why she would have such a collection of items and I am not sure that I want to damage my memory of her by speculating about that. She was never anything to me but a most devoted colleague." Bell's face was crumpled and he looked like the antithesis of his normally controlled self.

At the sound of the front door closing Bell became even further agitated. "My wife and daughter have returned from Bible study." He went to the open door of the study and looked from Burrows along the entrance hall towards the incoming women.

The Detective Sergeant decided to grant Bell a reprieve for the moment and trust that these matters could be returned to if that became necessary. He rose to leave and Bell nodded in gratitude for the detective's discretion.

"Thank you for your help in these matters, Professor Bell," Burrows announced rather formally as he carefully replaced the photo in his inside jacket pocket. "We will be in touch next week to update you about our progress."

As Bell showed him out Bill caught a glimpse of mother and daughter standing in the kitchen unwrapping some dishes of food obviously destined for the evening meal. They were strangely old-fashioned in their sombre dress and both had thick waist-length plaited hair, the beauty of which almost stopped Burrows in his tracks.

42

By the time it reached six thirty on Saturday afternoon the three members of the Murder Squad team were well and truly ready to share their new findings with each other. Mountains had been crossed and they were weary and excited at the same time. Caroline had surpassed herself and ordered in pizzas for a Saturday treat. She had also evidently cleared out the staff canteen of all chocolate produce and an array of carbonated drinks. A copy of the still picture from the 80s porn video was affixed to the evidence board and each team member was looking protective about the pile of notes before them on the table. Burrows sat at the ready with an array of whiteboard markers.

"So I don't know about you guys but that felt like a long day," said Caroline. "Let's get on top of what we've got. If it's OK I'd like to start … just be sure to leave me some pizza!"

She began with her morning review of the outstanding forensic and CCTV analyses reports. Aside from a few fabric threads and human hairs that had transferred from the remains, there had been little to glean from the forensics on the freezer in Marine Biology where Helen Breen's body had lain throughout the Christmas holiday period. The maintenance staff and the staff member who investigated the problem with closing the freezer had sufficiently contaminated the rest of the scene to render it quite useless in terms of evidence. Inside, the wrappings on the head of the victim had been standard institutional issue and there were no prints or useful markings that might help identify those who had placed the remains there. All Helen Breen's clothing and hair samples retrieved from the garments had been bagged and stored for further crosschecking should a suspect be identified. She reminded them that images were available on the shared drive. The immediate area around the freezers was also included in the initial forensic sweep but revealed nothing other than evidence that a rigorous cleaning had taken place. Paton told them to bear in mind that what was significant was that the moving and positioning of the body was almost certainly the work of two people passing as cleaners. They were not remarkable in any way to the security guard, nor clearly visible on the CCTV footage. For now they would assume that the two replacement cleaners had done that job but they had not necessarily been the murderers. The almost meticulous erasure of the signs of killing in Breen's office was in contrast to the stubborn brutality of the murder. That appeared to be the single-minded work of one person according to the autopsy findings. These facts suggested a murderer who was supported by a follow-up team who covered the killer's tracks and delayed the discovery of the corpse for several weeks. She asked them to bear in mind the organisational structure that would be needed to implement such a murder strategy.

"Let's not forget as well," she continued, "that the cover-up extended way beyond the place of death and the subsequent relocation of the remains in a freezer in another building. Had it not been for the storm and the disruption that caused, Helen Breen might still be residing undiscovered in that freezer. All her electronic devices, laptops and mobile phones, both from work and home, were carefully removed and therefore unavailable for examination. The possibilities for digital forensics are limited given that we have, as yet, no hardware but that may yet change. We can hold on to the possibility of some remote access through the college system if we need to but I doubt there is much to be gained from that. This may be yet another distraction on the part of the killer to keep us looking in the wrong direction." She paused. "Another point. Breen apparently carried a large handbag that was also absent from the scene. Similarly, the swiping of the victim's passkey at nine thirty-six suggests that someone other than Breen herself did this and the key was then taken and disposed of along with her other belongings. The messages sent to Jackson Bell and Liam Doyle were from Helen Breen's college email account but they were not sent by Breen, who was already dead. The timing suggests that this was not the work of the cleaners who were still in the Marine Biology Centre at this point. We might deduce that it was the murderer who had removed the devices from the office when they left, who then sent these messages later the same evening ... unless of course there is yet another actor involved in the scene. Again there is a rapid shift from enraged murderer to calculating and technically savvy strategist." Paton furrowed her brow and clamped her lips so that they turned downwards. "It is becoming increasingly difficult to keep up with the number of potential players in this drama."

There was a protracted silence as they all reviewed this suggestion. Then Paton continued.

"So, holding all that in mind and moving onwards ... forensics from Hillsborough confirms that Doyle was there, made himself a cup of tea and left the dishes in the sink. No attempt there to conceal his presence. Again we know from CCTV that he collected her car as requested in the email and drove it to Hillsborough where he left it expecting her to return later. His mobile phone records show all those attempted calls and no

325

responses. His prints were also on the car as would be expected. Doyle's presence in Hillsborough enabled the removal of any devices that might provide links to the killer... or possibly was intended as a red herring to implicate Doyle and send us off on a wild goose chase. Probably both of the above. The search of Doyle's house did not reveal any devices other than his own laptop and phone that confirms his account of things as being entirely accurate. Are we agreed Doyle is no longer a suspect?"

She looked around for any further comments on Doyle but they were all agreed.

"Next there is the CCTV of the evening of the murder and in particular the time leading up to the killing ... and the swiping out of Helen Breen's card at nine thirty-six. There is considerable traffic in the area around the end of evening classes at nine twenty and the subsequent twenty minutes when things gradually calm down. There is no sign of Bell or Wilson, which supports their claims that they were not in the college that evening. CCTV also backs up Professor Janet Hartnett's account of herself. She clearly approaches the swipe machine at nine-thirty as is recorded. She then has a conversation with a number of students and after that it becomes unclear what happened as there are too many people milling about to track her. Might she have had Breen's card and waited for the remaining six minutes to swipe it out, ostensibly after she herself would be perceived to have left? The security guard does not remember noticing anything one way or the other as he was dealing with numerous enquiries about lost property and such like and totally distracted. So, Hartnett remains in the picture?"

Burrows and McVeigh both strongly agreed.

"We will both add to this theory later," Burrows said hurriedly so as not to interrupt Paton's flow of thought.

"Good. So now I want to give an account of my meeting this afternoon with Tara Donnelly, the founder of DePRec. This was useful and, thanks to a steer from Alice Fox, suggests that because of the nature of its political work, DePRec has been very much of interest to the Security Services over the years since its foundation."

She recounted Tara Donnelly's account of the attempt by Security Services to recruit her, the threats to her family and her own safety and her subsequent hasty departure from DePRec. As Caroline spoke it became clear from the expressions of both men that she was striking harmonious chords with their own findings. Her report was nonetheless unrushed and she finished by saying that she planned to place an inquiry with MI5 to ascertain if they had any current business in DePRec. She wanted to take the team's advice first so as not to risk alerting a potential suspect that they were closing in.

Burrows reflected that Paton looked even more stern and determined than usual and he knew this to mean that she had a sense they needed to tread very carefully. She reached for a slice of pizza and a can and sat back to listen to what her colleagues might add to her revelation.

Burrows took the floor.

"I think I can usefully add to that, Boss." He checked with Ian that he was happy to hold off for the moment and consulted his notes. "I will begin with the outstanding detail in relation to Wilson, Doyle and Bell. Doyle, you have pretty much covered, ma'am. He was more of a victim of Helen Breen than an assailant. Despite a difficult start in life he has made something of himself and she saw his fragility and exploited it. I think we are all agreed that he is off our suspect list. Wilson too is mostly bluster and enjoys a good rant about the ills of capitalism and its proponents. He is more dangerous to himself than to anyone else as his blood pressure must rocket when he goes off on one. Ian followed up with Angela Wilson, his estranged wife and they did have a long Skype call on the evening of Breen's murder. She can verify he was in his home and her Skype account has details of the time and duration of the call. She also said he can be very argumentative and annoying but is basically harmless. Thanks to Ian for that feedback." He sipped his can of orange and sifted his notes. "I had an interesting follow-up with Professor Bell this afternoon. It actually takes on a whole added significance in the light of the Tara Donnelly experience."

Burrows related how he sought to ascertain if Bell had a motive for killing Breen because she was holding him to moral ransom because of his sexuality. The emergence of Security Services in pressurising Bell's role as an informant had surprised him but made sense now. Bell had assumed the mantle rejected by Tara Donnelly and, as recently as the night before Breen's murder, had been relieved of his position as a preferable replacement had been found. Burrows reported that Bell had repeated the agent's words about his replacement being something about the reliability of old friends.

"So the new DePRec informant is someone already known to our handler ..." mused Paton. "This is all getting very murky indeed. OK, what else have we got?"

Burrows continued. "I called Frank Breen this morning and talked about the school days when he and Janet Baldwin, as she then was, were in the same class. He wasn't part of the rugby set but both his sister and Baldwin were. He repeated that he didn't think Helen and Janet were close but they did mix in the same set although Helen was younger and less integrated. She wouldn't have been involved in the same party set that Janet Baldwin was quite central to. In sixth form they had partied quite hard he recalled but it was around the time of his father's sudden death and that overshadowed a lot of his memories of those days. I sent him a copy of the photo and he had not seen it before. He recalled there had been a flurry of scandal involving Baldwin in their final year but he was outside that circle and it was not really of interest to him. Frank had some old school journals that he had looked out and remembered the names of a few young men and one young woman in particular that Baldwin was close to. He sent copies of a few class photos, which included the people he thought Baldwin socialised with. I tracked down the woman, June Carson, and called to see her after my visit to Professor Bell."

Bill took a gulp of his drink and a bite of pizza while Ian enquired about the names of the young men he had mentioned.

"Let's see …" Burrows consulted his notes. "Here we are. Frank said that he thought that Janet was close to two guys both of whom played for the first rugby team. One was Nigel Power and the other was Samuel Kennedy." He raised an eyebrow inquisitively at Ian. "Does that tally with anything you've got?"

"Yes, sir. I will let you finish and then I think I will be able to join a few dots."

They simultaneously felt the satisfaction of a set of disparate pieces drawing more closely together and refocused their attention to the steady unfolding of evidence.

"June Carson had not remained in touch with Baldwin after college when their lives had separated once and for all," said Burrows. "She did not know that Baldwin, now Hartnett, was back in Belfast although she had heard on the grapevine that her old friend's marriage had broken up. Not much remains private in this small place." He had a number of photos in his hand now and directed them to copies he had made for them. "Anyway, as promised, June Carson had gathered up some old school photos and she talked me through some of the connections. There is an overlap with the pictures that Frank Breen sent. I asked Carson about Helen Breen and she grimaced and said she was an unpleasant, precocious young girl whose company she had mostly avoided – but that Helen had tagged along with their crowd occasionally and been difficult to dodge completely. Apparently she could turn the charm on when it suited and had a certain influence in the group even though they were older than she was. You'll see both Power and Kennedy feature in a number of these pictures. Kennedy was Janet's boyfriend for a portion of their final year at school and June had been seeing his friend Nigel. It wasn't a serious affair and they had split up before the end of the school term. She described it as fizzling out when cramming for exams took over from other priorities. I showed June the still photo of Baldwin and the two guys and she appeared genuinely shocked. I asked if she recognised either of the men and, although I thought she hesitated, she said it was impossible to say given the poor quality of the image. I asked if she knew where either Power or Kennedy was now and she said that she knew nothing about Nigel Power. He had been

331

a high-flyer and had gone to an Oxford College from school and they had lost touch. Kennedy had gone on to play rugby for Ulster but had been brain-damaged as a result of a tragic sports accident and required full-time residential care after that."

Burrows sat back and shuffled his pile of papers.

DI Paton tapped the notebook in front of her. "Let's take a short break, guys, and Bill, if you can capture some of this latest evidence on the board that will be very useful. I want to place a call to the Super before he heads to the golf club for his Saturday night out. I need him to do some diplomatic telephone calls for us and there is no time like the present."

She headed off towards her office with the promise of a prompt return. While Burrows fixed pictures to the board, wrote names and connected arrows, Ian readied himself for his input with steadfast concentration.

Within a matter of minutes Paton returned, took her seat at the table and reached for more pizza. "Right, Ian. Where did you get to with Janet Hartnett and the story behind the picture? We are all ears."

"I'll start with a brief bio. Janet Baldwin did Social Policy at Queens and then moved to Bristol University where she did a Master's and a PhD. I'm wondering if she and Kennedy were involved when she was at Queens and if she was still here when he had his brain injury."

"Interesting," interjected Burrows. "During the autopsy Cynthia did say that the perp might have some understanding of brain injuries. Hartnett's ex and her son both experienced head injuries."

Paton and Ian both registered this connection and McVeigh continued.

"She met Dr Robert Hartnett who was a lecturer in Bristol University and they married in 1997. While she was doing her doctorate, she got a part-time job in City of Bath College teaching Social Care and specialising in care of the elderly. She and Hartnett had one son called Rory who was seriously brain-damaged at birth and has required special schooling and considerable additional care throughout his life. They were unable to have any more children. She got a fulltime post in Bath, was eventually promoted to senior lecturer and then in 2008 moved, as principal, to a London College specialising in professional and academic qualifications for those working in care and therapeutic professions. At this point Robert Hartnett remained in Bristol and their marriage did not survive the commuting and care demands. She moved to Belfast City College in September 2013 as Head of Faculty of Human Sciences, which as we know includes DePRec. I have unearthed details of her publications and numerous committee memberships but I don't think we need to go into those now." He switched to a separate file and extracted some pages. "I had some luck too with William Baldwin, the father. He's a man in his mid-seventies who owned a busy hardware shop on the Newtownards Road in East

Belfast. It was sold when he retired some ten years ago and he and his wife Norma moved to the bungalow in Crawfordsburn where they now live with Janet and her son Rory. He is a Mason and a member of the Orange Order and in the 80s was an open supporter of the Ulster Defence Association (UDA). That would not have been unusual for a business owner in that area where failure to back the local unit, even tacitly, would not have been good for trade. In later years Baldwin cleaned up his image somewhat and became involved in Belfast Rotary Club and he plays golf in Holywood Golf Club. Your recollection of his involvement in some dubious fundraising activities back in the day were correct, ma'am."

Paton smiled unassumingly and motioned to McVeigh to keep going.

"In the mid to late eighties there was a considerable push on raising funds in paramilitary organisations – for arms, in support of families of political prisoners and for rent, printing costs and administration of community-based offices. There were door-to-door collections, fundraising events, profiteering drinking and social clubs linked to various groups and of course donations from wealthy sympathisers. These ventures were mostly but not entirely above board. There was also a darker side with attempts to capitalise on an emerging drug trade and a market for pornographic merchandise. Most of that was distributed overseas for obvious reasons. Northern Ireland is too small to keep the lid on the identity of even amateur porn stars, if material were circulated locally. In 1988 there was a case under investigation where some entrepreneurial chaps had decided to get into operating gambling schools, drug-running and even some moviemaking. A file was opened and your DI Rogers was keen to pursue the matter but pressure was brought to bear and the file was closed, allegedly for a lack of evidence. I managed to get a copy of that file and I understand why Rogers was peeved. There is quite a lot of detail in there, including mention of Baldwin's somewhat threatening intercession about the community unrest that might result in bringing charges. He wasn't the only one who advised against continuing. Some internal weight within the force was applied and things ground to a halt. There is nothing in the file to suggest that Baldwin had any family interest in the case so we have to assume he kept that connection to himself."

"Are we surprised by that at all?" Paton remarked meaningfully.

"However … there are parts of the evidence file that are redacted including some of the names of those interviewed during the inquiry. These include the initials of an N.P. and an J.B. that might well be Nigel Power and Janet Baldwin. I didn't manage to locate a copy of the video but judging by the age of Breen's photo it hasn't seen the light of day since it was made. If there was a copy it may well have surfaced in the rugby circle that Breen was part of … If need be I can try and follow that up tomorrow."

Paton made hand signals to suggest slowing the pace of things. "Let's see where we are. I think we may be looking at a Sunday morning stroll along the beach in Crawfordsburn." She smiled at the two men with exaggerated enthusiasm. "Helen Breen had held on to an image that was potentially damaging to the reputation of Professor Hartnett and at least one of the men in the image. We have an ongoing Security Services connection to DePRec that seems to have involved gathering information by means other than that passed on by Professor Bell. He was surprised by the handler's knowledge of internal departmental matters. We need to think that if someone has been using digital and other surveillance here they may well be ahead of us and know we are closing in." She made a scribbled note on the paper in front of her. "The reference to old friends and Bell's replacement with a new contact suggests a history between the special agent and a newly arrived college staff member. In many ways now Professor Janet Hartnett becomes more and more interesting."

"We have discounted her up until now as she had no obvious motive," said Paton. "Now we can say that the potential to be discredited when she had just created a new life for herself and her son here might have made her desperate. Her opportunity was also doubtful because she was off the premises too quickly to cover up her tracks after the killing. We have CCTV footage of her clocking out at nine-thirty, or thereabouts, and her family would undoubtedly confirm her arrival at home at the usual time. But what if she had an accomplice? What if there was someone else who also wanted to get Helen Breen out of their hair? If Hartnett was played and encouraged by our friendly agent, she could have killed Breen and left the building as usual with a promise that the tidy up would be in the hands of the professionals."

Her colleagues watched as she closed her lips tightly and assumed her most resolute expression.

Burrows joined in the speculation. "If we are dealing with a member of Security Services personnel who has a personal axe to grind then some aspects of the case become a lot more explicable. There has been a fair amount of strategising and manipulation that you might not get with an ordinary violent assault. Access to cleaning services would also be all part of that service, I imagine."

"One thing springs to mind in all that," McVeigh reflected. "Whoever committed the murder is likely to have been quite messed up afterwards. Was it 'red and grey matter' the autopsy said? There will have been some personal cleaning up to be done too before the person could face into the public space again."

"Or," Paton retorted, "perhaps it was enough to

clean superficially and put on a winter coat that would cover any mess long enough to get the person away from the scene. Let's look closely at the CCTV footage of Hartnett leaving the college on that Thursday evening. What was she wearing? What was she carrying? Might she have had Helen Breen's bag with her?" Paton was thinking fast and the focus of the chase was narrowing rapidly. Caution was paramount at this stage so as not to mess things up. "We need to be careful about our next moves here. Bill, get the photos of the young Nigel Power to Professor Bell and Tara Donnelly and see if he's a match for our agent Alan. Get some stills of Hartnett leaving the building that Thursday and let's see if she had any additional baggage and what she was wearing. I'd say that wouldn't have been a job she sent out to the dry cleaners. Ian, make a call at home to the retired school principal and see if he remembers what became of Nigel Power. Which Oxford College did he go to and where did he go after that? I wouldn't mind guessing he was recruited from there to the Security Services and found his way back to home turf. He won't be a happy chappy if he finds we're digging into his filming past!"

She paused and tapped the table with her left hand while scrolling through her phone with the other.

"I'll make a few calls to caution those that Alan may have issue with for helping our investigation, in case he decides to go visiting. I don't think he's a very pleasant character and obviously used to blurring the lines of demarcation around what is legitimate information-gathering and what is playing big-boy spy games." Her brow furrowed. "Alice Fox, for example, may well be on his radar. I need to let her know that she needs to be very cautious of strange men. I've asked the Super to clear a path for us into Holywood Barracks where our spook will undoubtedly be based. There was a time when spying and gathering anti-terrorism information was placed ahead of solving a crime, in terms of priority. Placed ahead of safeguarding life itself." Paton paused to consider the shocking reality of what she had said. "That is no longer the case and there will be no protection offered to a member of the Security Services that has choreographed and colluded in a murder. Not on my watch." She studied the table in front of her for several moments and then met the watchful gaze of her colleagues.

They all knew how fragile these new policing values were in practice. Many of the old guard had been reemployed after accepting generous early retirement packages and their influence hadn't altogether gone away.

"I'm afraid I'm going to have to renege on the early night, team, but I think I will be able to make it up to you sooner rather than later."

There was no complaint as Burrows and McVeigh savoured these last stages of the hunt as much as Paton did.

"Bill, check if the warrant I asked you to apply for, when I phoned earlier, has arrived. If not get the desk sergeant onto hassling for it pronto. We'll take an hour or so to get organised in terms of the ID on Power and Hartnett's outfit and baggage when leaving the building that night. I'll need colour copies of those images for the search team. I will take a driver and three uniforms and go and bring in Hartnett. I'll leave three guys behind to search the Baldwin place. We may even find some vintage memorabilia in Daddy's attic. Bill, call in a discreet armed unit and you and Ian head to Holywood and see if Agent Alan would like to come in for a chat. We'll talk to Mr Baldwin too but that will keep. Let's deal with the murder first. I am happy for him to stew until tomorrow and take care of his poor unsuspecting grandson. Back here for nine o'clock and ready to roll."

43

When Caroline Paton dropped her off after the trip across the border, Alice felt unusually drained of energy. Aside from work and family she had become used to a fairly solitary life and her recent level of activity had been quite hectic. On Botanic Avenue she stopped to collect the makings of an evening meal, including a good bottle of wine from the off-license near her house.

She was concerned about Tara and phoned her as soon as she got home to check she was still feeling positive about sharing her history. They talked for a while about the Helen Breen case and then their common academic interests until Alice was sure her friend was feeling no ill effects from her disclosure. She promised to phone Tara later that week and update her on the investigation. Perhaps some good would even come of all this. She was tempted to call Mairéad Walsh too but thought it best to leave it until Monday and catch up with her in work.

It was before nine when Alice decided that what she needed was a run and got out her head torch and checked the batteries. She knew the route well from early morning runs in all weathers and could navigate the less well-lighted parts of the terrain with ease. The rain that had been ever-present through the day was easing off now. The exercise would help settle her mind and stop her speculating about what was happening in the Grosvenor Road Barracks. Had they closed in on the killer? She was sure she would find out soon enough. She changed into her running gear, did some stretches and headed for the river. The initial terrain was urban and quite populated. She passed the university sport's centre and the riverbank Lyric Theatre and then on along through a residential enclave towards the beginning of the towpath. The various boat clubs were closed up and in darkness but the nearby bar and tennis club were brightly lit and busy with early evening drinkers making no effort to control their volume.

Once onto the towpath she switched on her head torch and settled into her easy running pace. At the outset there were a few straggling walkers but the path was mostly clear. She ran, rather than jogged, enjoying the speed and the way her body coordinated to produce a comfortable, rhythmic pace.

Relaxing into the motion, she was relishing feeling

the stresses of the day dissipate when her phone vibrated in her jacket pocket. It was probably someone from home hoping to catch her for a chat. There would be a message and she would return the call when she got back. She vaguely considered that it might be Caroline Paton but was too invested in her exercise now to consider stopping.

The sense of running into the tunnel of darkness ahead was one that Alice found both symbolic and exhilarating. She enjoyed the idea that her headlight just gave her enough visibility into the path in front of her to allow her not to stumble over the immediate unknown. She was absolutely obliged to stay in the moment. Around her, the night sounds changed from urban to rural. The river flowed calmly and quietly producing only the faintest lapping sounds as it met the bank or some overhanging boughs. An occasional night bird called through the darkness. The earlier eeriness of Ravensdale Forest revisited her fleetingly and she shook her head slightly to dislodge the notion, creating a dramatic rush of shadows with her headgear. A flutter of fear threatened her sense of calm but was gone in an instant.

Further ahead she heard the traffic of the motorway where it crossed the towpath and she slowed slightly. Occasionally after rain there was a mucky pool of water gathered where the path crossed beneath the low bridge and it was best not to get wet feet. The passing overhead traffic produced successive waves of moving bright lights and the accompanying sound of rubber on the damp road surface.

Ahead, under the dimly lit concrete subway a fleeting movement caught her eye and a figure stepped into her path, clearly intent on blocking her way. His outline was distorted by the shifting shadows and loomed larger than life across the path before her.

Alice stopped, breathing fast but fully alert to what was happening. She gauged the distance to the man, his height, weight and level of fitness. He was similar in height to her and more strongly built but Tae Kwon Do was about agility and focus more than brute strength.

She kept her headlight fixed on his eyes, watchful for a movement that would signify some more active intent. She knew about patience and could wait for him to blink. If she was right and this was Tara Donnelly's spook then she was sure he would be armed. His hands were in his pockets, which was not a good sign so she mentally prepared for the appearance of a weapon. Again she slowed her breathing and waited. In her head she was poised to block any move he made but she could tell by his composure that he wasn't going to make this easy. He was evidently enjoying himself.

"Well, well, well, Dr Fox! I'd have thought you would have had enough excitement for one day. Out gallivanting with the murder squad and then having lunch with the lovely Tara. I was going to call on you at home but then I saw you heading out for your run and decided to meet up al fresco instead."

His voice was strangely soft and sonorous, his accent more BBC than Belfast. After he spoke his top lip contorted upwards towards the left in a silent snarl and his dark eyes widened as he continued. His control began to slip into anger and Alice knew that would eventually lead him to make a crucial error. Her concentration was unwavering as he began to raise his voice.

"I have just about had it with smart-assed bitches messing with my business. First there was Helen Breen sticking her nose into affairs that didn't concern her and threatening to use the follies of youth against respectable citizens like Professor Hartnett and myself. The nerve of her when you consider how she got her own kicks! And now there's you mixing with bad company in West Belfast and pointing DI Paton in directions she might never have figured out for herself. You have made me very angry, Alice Fox. Very angry indeed."

Alice merely raised her eyebrows and said nothing.

With a leer, he produced a number of cable ties from his left pocket and waved them tauntingly. "It would be such a shame if you were to fall and hurt yourself out here away from anybody. Who knows when you'd be found?"

He moved towards her and then the flash of hard metal caught her eye as he pulled the gun from his righthand pocket. She responded with such speed and agility that he barely had time to change his facial expression from smug to horrified. All in a split second, Alice crouched to create momentum and with full force kicked his weapon arm sharply backwards. The pistol flew in a high arc and splashed quietly into the river. As he struggled to regain his lost balance, she followed through with a double-front kick that made high contact with his jaw and a secondary lower flick that connected directly with his groin. His face was frozen in an expression of pain and disbelief but Alice had one move left to complete his demise. Before he could even begin to collapse, she fell to the ground on her left hip and with a lightning extension of her right leg, delivered a sharp blow to the man's knee. Then he crumpled. The initial high kick had produced a cracking sound from his jaw and Alice was sure he wouldn't be talking so freely in the near future. She effortlessly stood up to her full height, still feeling calm and watchful.

"*Fucking bitch* ..." He slavered as he discovered the full extent of the damage to his jaw. From his position on the ground, he moved his hand awkwardly towards his inside pocket but he was too slow and Alice wasted no time in jumping with her full weight on his splayed fingers. There was a cracking sound followed by some more growled expletives.

Alice gathered up the plastic cable ties that had fallen beside him. A rusted metal ring was set into the original towpath wall and she quickly attached each clammy hand of the now groaning body securely to the ring.

"I guess it's you who'll be hanging around hoping to be found before the chill sets in, dick!"

She checked his pockets and removed his second handgun, mobile phone and car keys. There was a pathway to the right of the motorway bridge that she reckoned led to the road where he must have parked in order to intercept her.

On her way to the car Alice took out her phone and dialled Caroline Paton's number. The detective answered almost immediately.

"Did you get my message then?" Caroline said.

"I did not," said Alice, "but if you were calling to warn me about a nasty guy who might be out to get me, I've just met him and I didn't like him one little bit!"

Caroline was on her way to Crawfordsburn to collect Janet Hartnett. Alice gave her location and Caroline said she would redirect Burrows and McVeigh to go and collect her and her 'assailant'.

Alice laughed loudly at that, but Caroline had already hung up.

44

What began as a complicated operation for DI Caroline Paton became surprisingly simple. On their arrival at her Crawfordsburn home, Professor Janet Hartnett met Caroline and her support team with cool disdain. They were finishing their evening meal, she explained at the door and Saturday evening was not a convenient time to talk. Perhaps they would like to make an appointment for Monday during office hours?

Caroline Paton maintained her dignity and explained that this was more than a casual visit and suggested that their business might be better completed inside the house rather than publicly on the doorstep. Her message hit home and they were admitted without further fuss.

Hartnett was sitting at the kitchen table with her son and her parents, all of whom were visibly surprised by the entry of DI Paton and four uniformed police officers.

Mr Baldwin stood immediately and declared his outrage at the interruption to their evening. He announced pompously that it was his intention to phone the Detective Superintendent immediately and stop this invasion of privacy.

For a brief moment Caroline regretted that the language of human rights could be deployed so casually by people these days but pulled back and responded courteously.

"I think that would be ill-judged, Mr Baldwin. I have here a search warrant requested earlier today by Detective Superintendent Graham McCluskey and authorised by the duty magistrate. I am not sure that your opinion on the matter would be well received by DS McCluskey on his Saturday evening off." She fixed him with her most chilling stare. "Professor Hartnett, I will need you to accompany me to the station for questioning in relation to the killing of Dr. Helen Breen. My colleagues will remain here to search these premises. Mr and Mrs Baldwin, I would like to confirm that you will take responsibility for the care of your grandson so that he is not unduly discommoded by the presence of my officers."

They nodded halfheartedly, obviously shocked by the sudden turn of events and the upheaval in their solid middle-class existence. Mrs Baldwin's bottom lip was quivering and she looked appealingly towards her husband for some way to stop the slide further into this nightmare. For his part, Mr Baldwin appeared frozen and helpless, all bluster gone now as he looked towards his grandson who was making deep indentations on the tablecloth with his fork.

Janet Hartnett tried hard to maintain her cool exterior but she was clearly shaken and made it apparent to her family that she thought it best to comply with the request to go with Paton and her driver. The three remaining officers set about their search while the family remained seated at the kitchen table. The uniformed officers had been briefed to gather all electronic devices as well as any old papers or video material that might be in an attic or garage. In particular they were to collect Professor Hartnett's red carry-on luggage and her black woollen coat with the hood, both of which were identified on the CCTV footage the night that Helen Breen was killed.

Paton could see that Mr Baldwin was convulsed with rage and his wife would undoubtedly bear the brunt of any care work there was to be done that evening. He would be even less pleased when she questioned him the next day about his knowledge of the image of his daughter that Helen Breen had kept hidden all those years.

Driving back to the city, Burrows called to say that they too were on their way back to the station. He was bringing Alice Fox so that she could make a statement and had called the on-duty doctor to check if Power required immediate hospital treatment for a suspected broken jaw and a groin and knee injury.

Earlier in the evening, both Bell and Tara Donnelly had recognised Power from the image sent to them and Paton was confident that Hartnett would make a full confession and incriminate him as a prime accessory to murder. She made sure during the phone call to mention Nigel Power by name and observed the impact on Hartnett through the rear-view mirror. Behind the fragile composure it was obvious that she realised that the game was up.

Burrows and McVeigh had found Nigel Powers attached to the metal ring under the motorway bridge, alternately moaning and swearing profusely. Earlier reports from MI5 had made it clear that he was not operating officially in any matter to do with the death of Helen Breen. She may well have been a threat to the stability of his newly recruited source, but this no longer allowed him a licence to kill, or support the concealment of a murder. There would be no intercession on his behalf from Security Services in this matter.

Nigel Power, alias Agent Alan, had more or less given himself up in the wake of his encounter with Alice Fox. After an initial show of bravado, when he heard that he would receive no protection from his employer he became suddenly docile. His superiors had confirmed that he was known in the Service as a loose cannon who had developed bad habits when the imperative to get intelligence had been more urgent. Now that the pressures of information-gathering had diminished in Northern Ireland, he was under less rigorous scrutiny and had evidently gone rogue. Attention in global intelligence-gathering had moved to Islamic fundamentalists and cyber criminality and Northern Ireland and its small numbers of dissidents was much lower down the agenda. Unfortunately, this had left him scope to indulge his nostalgia for intrigue and sadistic power games. Burrows had a mixed response to this information. He wondered how Power's skills could have become so discredited when they were evidently essential to his role in previous times. However, he recognised that this time the bias was falling in their favour and so accepted it quietly.

The night was not as long as it might have been. The search team had returned with numerous items for forensic scrutiny found in Hartnett's wardrobe. They would check hair and skin samples taken from Hartnett against material found on Breen's clothing. There would be a match. Other items belonging to Breen had been located in a plastic bag at the bottom of an old laundry basket in the back of Hartnett's garden shed. There too they found the red suitcase and black winter coat, both of which would reveal evidence of the punishment meted out to Helen Breen. For there to have been such an elaborate clean-up after the murder, in Professor Hartnett's home there had been no such attention to the detail.

On Sunday morning when they had visited Holywood Barracks, Breen's home laptop and mobile phone had been found in the storeroom off Nigel Power's office. His copious digital and paper files in relation to DePRec would provide interesting reading and a white van with several sets of number plates was also thought to be of interest.

When the very demure Janet Hartnett eventually cracked, the level of vitriol against Helen Breen had surprised even Caroline Paton. Stored up over decades, Hartnett had unleashed her resentment of Breen's more privileged social standing. She fumed about Breen's superior attitude to the Baldwin modest family business beside Helen's own beloved father's impressive refrigeration empire.

When asked during questioning why Breen had been placed in a freezer Hartnett had shamelessly stated, "I thought she would feel at home there."

Hartnett claimed that Breen's subtle manipulation of people back in their schooldays had come flooding back when the younger woman greeted her like a long-lost friend in the corridor outside the departmental office. Once reignited, Hartnett's fury had gradually escalated. She had played along with Helen Breen but that hadn't stopped Breen recalling the near-scandal that had blighted young Janet Baldwin's final year at school. Not known to many and mostly long forgotten, the suggestion that this woman would use it against her for her own advancement was a step too far.

For his own motives, Nigel Power had been appalled that Breen's threat would have implicated him. This rage was more to do with her audacity than any concern about his involvement in pornography. He had encouraged Hartnett to kill Helen Breen, painting an elaborate picture of what might result for her if Breen's photographic evidence had got into the wrong hands. He had promised to use his many skills and contacts to cover her tracks as they would both be more secure without Breen in the picture.

When the two had been charged, signed full and complete statements and been committed to cells for the night, Caroline Paton and her team had met to debrief. Satisfaction dispelled their exhaustion for the moment but they knew that wouldn't last and rest must come soon on the priority list.

And there was a bonus prize! Amongst the treasures found in the Baldwin-Hartnett home had been enough material to implicate Mr Baldwin in a historic criminal case. His own daughter had not been the only underage victim of his skullduggery and a whole collection of pornographic images and films would make interesting evidence for the crime squad to examine. DI Caroline Paton would interview him first about any role he may have had in aiding and abetting his daughter's recent crime and this time there would be no support from any brotherhood and no cover-up. Mr Baldwin had finally met his match in DI Caroline Paton.

Alice had been driven home by DC McVeigh and assured by Caroline that her contribution had been crucial in solving this case. They established their intention to pick up on the promised leisurely meal as soon as it was possible.

45

In Mairéad Walsh's office on Monday morning there was a small gathering of individuals who had heard the early-morning news announcement that Helen Breen's murderer and accomplice had been arrested and charged. The two accused would be held in custody while the case against them was being prepared. Given the gravity of the charges there would be no bail available to either of them. The PSNI would hold a press conference later that morning and DI Caroline Paton would confirm that the police murder squad were satisfied that they had solved the case, as promised, in a timely manner.

The Belfast City College President had made a brief statement emphasising the quality of his staff and their commitment to ensuring a safe learning environment for all third level students. There were two significant vacancies on the staff now that would need to be addressed when an appropriate amount of time had elapsed. Jackson Bell would address the DePRec staff at coffee break that morning and encourage them to get back to normal working routines as soon as possible. They would plan a memorial for their colleague whenever the family had been allowed the time to arrange her funeral. Her brother and family would take the opportunity to visit from Australia and Agatha Breen would have some joy in the wake of her bereavement.

True to form, Alice Fox said nothing about her contribution to the resolution of Helen Breen's killing and as soon as possible she quietly slipped away from the noisy chatter. She settled herself at her desk to come to grips with the 'to do' list that she had been evading for the past week.

Tomorrow, she had a table booked in the Welcome Restaurant when she and Caroline Paton would enjoy an undemanding evening in the company of newfound friends. The prospect filled Alice with satisfaction on a number of counts.

As she turned again towards her academic pursuits, her attention was captivated by the sunlit wintery vista of Belfast Lough outside her office window. She sighed deeply. She had made the right decision to take this year away from all that was familiar to her. The impact on her view of life was certainly a positive one and the remainder of her time in Ireland was suddenly looking very interesting indeed. Alice Fox felt well and truly ready for whatever new exploits might come her way.

Acknowledgements

I talked about writing this Murder Mystery for a long time before actually getting around to doing it. Now I find myself embarked on writing three of them and I am delighted by the prospect. Of course, we never really do anything alone and lots of people have encouraged and supported me in this new métier. I am thankful to you all, too numerous to mention, for the words of interest and encouragement.

Niamh and Jackie listened to early chapters and carried me forward with their enthusiastic response. Those who read full versions of what became lovingly known as MITA merit special gratitude: Margaret Ward, Susan Miner, Michelle Page, Trina Barr, Dominique Faure and John Brady all gave a critical response to an early version. Michelle Page became my authority on all things to do with police procedures and her past as a

Lowell PD detective has been an invaluable source of good pickings. Maureen Lyons and Nessa Finnegan helped me sustain belief in the possibility of publication and the Zoom dramatisation of MITA early in the Covid pandemic gave us all some laughs. Thank you to Leah, Nessa, Jerome, Bojana and Ann for that. Brian, Jessica, Chloë and Anaïs regularly listened with interest to accounts of my writing life and never gave the impression that I was fooling myself. Thank you for your belief.

John Brady, DJ Colbert and Ursula Barry were invaluable when things started to get serious and there was talk of needing agents and contracts and other such daunting things. Joining the Irish Writers' Union demystified a lot of technical elements of publishing and also provided a sense of solidarity, which is important for me.

Thanks to Elaine Mullen, Paula Campbell from Poolbeg became an early and a fairly constant prop throughout the production of this book, much of which has taken place during the period of lockdown. She pointed me in the right direction and I was more surprised than anybody else when I arrived there. Gaye Shortland, Poolbeg's editor, was what I dreamed of all along: a meticulous, insightful, critical reader who liked my book and knew how to make it better. She has been kind and uncompromising in equal measure and has my full appreciation and respect in exchange for her labours.

Above all, for sharing the fun, the panic, the drudgery and the unbridled joy of it all, I thank Ann Hegarty whose loving kindness knows very few limits ... and I have tried very hard to find them. She has embraced the idea of social justice fiction since I decided to have a go at writing it and I would not have persisted so happily without her.

Made in the USA
Coppell, TX
23 August 2021

61041885R00203